Hermann Geiger

Lydia

A tale of the second century

Hermann Geiger

Lydia
A tale of the second century

ISBN/EAN: 9783337072254

Printed in Europe, USA, Canada, Australia, Japan

Cover: Foto ©Andreas Hilbeck / pixelio.de

More available books at **www.hansebooks.com**

LYDIA:

A

TALE OF THE SECOND CENTURY,

TRANSLATED FROM THE GERMAN

OF

HERRMAN GEIGER OF MUNICH.

PHILADELPHIA:

EUGENE CUMMISKEY, PUBLISHER,
1037 CHESTNUT STREET,
1867.

INTRODUCTION.

How beautiful to behold the silent dawn of morning, lighting up the solitary summits of the Glætchers! Height after height begins to wear the first beams of the rising sun. While the bases of these mighty mountains are hidden from the view by a thick veil of blue mist, naught appears but their lofty heads peeping, as it were, from amongst the clouds. A similar spectacle discloses itself to the eye of faith, when it casts a glance into the golden morning of Christianity, and discovers those gigantic heads surrounded by the brilliancy of the sun of Justice. An invigorating air wafts across from them to us, upon our remote point of view; we are astonished at the characters, firm as a rock, which raised them above their contemporaries, and imagine we hear the blood gushing from their hearts, and falling into the stream of the general martyrdom. This stream flowed on for three hundred years, and formed the boundaries between the heathen and the Christian world. Such a look as this did the writer of these pages cast into that golden age.

But as the succession of these great men stretches out like a lengthened chain of precious gems, he drew for his purpose a more confined perspective, and chose that period in which the Emperor Marcus Aurelius wielded the sceptre. This period embraces about twenty years,—from A. D. 161 to 180: the most renowned heroes of the Faith, which occur in this time, are St. Polycarp of Smyrna, the Philosopher Justin of Rome, and the Apostle of the south of Gaul, Bishop Pothinus.

The martyrologies that mention these men, are, above all others that have come under our notice, the most to be relied on. The untiring Irenæus is a connecting link between the Eastern and Western Churches. Pope Soter in Rome, Dionysius of Corinth, and the learned Athenagoras, who, from a follower of the Grecian philosophy, became a disciple of Christ, lived also in the time of Marcus Aurelius. But in order to bring these professors of the Faith, who with respect to place are so widely separated from each other, into the same compass, it requires the personality of one whose trials were contemporary with the above-mentioned men, like the veil of mist that obscures the depths of the valley, and scatters itself round the foot of the mountain. This person is Lydia, an Eastern slave. Some difficulty occurred at the question, in which of the numerous cities of the then kingdom of the world the connecting points of the tale should lie.

Rome, the chief city of the immeasurable empire, would have been, above all others, the one most suited, and it dares not be forgotten. But the seat of refinement and the asylum of worldly wisdom were to be found, at that time, neither in Rome nor in Italy, but in that once great city of Greece, Athens.

In the time of the Anthonys, the imperial court at Rome so highly appreciated the Hellenish refinement, that the best teachers were called from Greece to instruct the heirs to the throne, and the higher schools. Everything that laid claim to refinement was from Greece, just as with us the French language has become the mother-tongue of high life. Marcus Aurelius was himself a disciple of the Grecian school of philosophy, and wrote his "Maxims" in Greek. Herodes, Atticus, Demonax, Athenagoras, Aristides, Lucien, Pausanias, and other illustrious writers, we find in Athens at this time. For the propagation of Christianity, Greece was looked upon with as much importance as Italy: in the latter, politics had their seat, in the former, spiritual power; and for this reason, the princes of the apostles chose both these countries for their missionary labors. The courageous Peter ventured to remain in the imperial city, but the learned Paul journeyed to Greece. Therefore is Athens chosen as the scene of the incidents.

The Hellenish worship may excite some interest, as it

explains itself in a heathen sense. There is a great chasm between Roman and Grecian paganism, and incomparably nobler were the religious views of the new Platonic schools than the coarse faith of the Romans. The researches of the Greek sages were not fruitless; various as were their systems, they were at least all united in the same opinion, that the perception which the people of the earth then had of the Divinity, was unworthy of it. In addition to this, the Grecian Mysteries, which could be traced as far back as to the primitive history of the people, preserved their ancient faith; and perhaps after this, it was the Eleusian mysteries that saved those remnants of past knowledge which may be looked upon with justice as a divine revelation. But apart from those most important mysteries, into which almost all those who had any pretensions to refinement were initiated, there flowed in the principal Greek towns another source, which assisted in altering the ideas of inferior paganism, and in showing in purity the image of the Divinity. There were not only communities of Jews at that time in Delos, Kos, Milet, and other islands, but their religion was practised in the great Corinth also; and St. Paul found a synagogue even in Athens.* Who would therefore doubt, that just the most renowned Grecian thinkers and teachers of the people have not drawn from this source?

* Acts of the Apostles, xvii. 17.

All this philosophy then, this Judaism, and those mysteries, had worked together, in cutting off, piece by piece, this Anaconda of paganism, which bound up the Roman world, until that "Sun-clad Woman" stepped forth from the house of David, and for ever crushed the serpent's head.

The most remarkable events of Marcus Aurelius' time have not been passed over, particularly the war against the people of the Danube, which for each descendant of the ancient Germans is of no small importance, and is circumstantially described; whereby much of their ancient manners and customs, according to Tacitus, have been made known to us.

It is now some years since Lydia began to tread the insecure path of publicity. In her wanderings she has been nowhere received with coldness; in many places greeted most warmly, and in all, treated with that consideration due to her sex.

Unhappy, persecuted Poland gladly availed herself of her consoling presence, and looked upon her as a suffering sister in the Faith. The maid, the wife, the mother, and the widow, have been alike instructed by her good example. The desolate and afflicted have found in her all they could desire; for while her generous hand dispensed a temporal blessing, it was ever accompanied by a word of consolation and advice.

PREFACE

TO THE AMERICAN EDITION.

⸺◦⸺

In this age of frivolous romance or indistinct piety, it is refreshing to fall upon a work filled with sound principles and pleasurable development as the present volume.

Lydia, in her historico-religious character, is of the class and family of Fabiola and Calista; and though a younger, is not an unworthy or unseemly sister.

A volume so interesting and instructive as that now presented to the American reader, is peculiarly beneficial: for it must be admitted, though numerous and influential as may be the members of the Catholic Church, that there still exists a prejudice and pressure from without that in no small degree prevents the vigor and growth of sound Christian principles. The temporal prosperity of the country, and the concomitant desire of appearing well before the people, have introduced a spirit of extravagance and forgetfulness by no means favorable to religion.

The blamelessness of the lives, and the acknowledged virtues of the early Christians, proved insufficient to protect them against the strong prejudice of a jealous and unbelieving majority: and in the nineteenth, as in the second century of the Church, do we find, in too many instances, a lack of that firmness and moral courage which we so admire, but do not always practise.

It would sound strangely, perhaps, to compare the unjust prejudices of the Grecian pagan of the second century with the misrepresentations of the nineteenth in our own midst; but this however may be understood, that now, as then, it requires the patience and charity of Lydia to conquer the pride and worldly-mindedness of Metella.

In the hope, then, of strengthening the faith, whilst it sustains the hope of the children of the Church, in their daily conflict with the outward world, this volume is placed in the hands of the American reader,—a reprint of the London edition of the present year.

DECEMBER, 1866.

CONTENTS

CONTENTS.

LYDIA.

CHAPTER I.

THE YOUTHFUL CAPTIVE.

A. D. 165.

THE confused cries and clamors of a throng-
ing multitude fill the slave market of
ancient Smyrna. In one part an overseer screams himself hoarse upon the supe-
rior qualities of his merchandise, whilst another of his caste beats poor children most
unmercifully, and the sobs and whinings of
these unhappy ones mingle with the imprecations of
their castigator.

Each one set up for sale, has a placard suspended
from his neck, on which all his qualities are written.
On many of these can be seen the words, "Calligraphos"
or "Pedagogos," because the wearer possesses the necessary acquirements for either a Tutor or a Teacher. The
upper end of the market is occupied chiefly by Africans,

from burning Lybia, with dark skin and woolly hair; deplorable creatures! their ears pierced, and their feet chalked, a sign that they have crossed the sea. Close to these, cooped up in laths and cords, are young negresses, from the interior of Ethiopia, black as ebony. They seat themselves on a checkered carpet, crouching closely and anxiously together. Bread, fruit, and wine are placed before them, but few partake thereof, as they were told that those good things are merely given them for a time, to make them robust, that they may afford the gormandizing Romans a dainty meal. At the lower end, the eye falls upon entire herds of white slaves, from every known country under the sun. Amongst these are the emaciated Isaurians, formerly pirates in the Mediterranean, looking most piteously. In striking contrast stands the athletic Cappadocian, proud of his race and stature; frivolous and faithless, it is true, but, as his placard jestingly remarks, as the bearer of a litter, most useful, and as well beloved as the horses of his country. In the midst of this multitude of slaves, of Greeks richly apparelled, and of Romans eager for purchase, might be seen passing on, a modestly attired female, of noble bearing, but whose dress, that of a widow, bespeaks her of the middle class. Her scrutinizing gaze lingers long upon the youthful forms of the captive Christians, — but she finds not whom she seeks, and wanders on by the nearest way to the public prisons. "Shall I rejoice, or shall I complain," sighed the afflicted one, "that I found her not amongst them, or whether, after six months, is she still in prison, or have they reserved her for the coming festival?" "Merciful God!

suffer not my child to be torn to pieces by wild beasts, amidst the jeers and scoffs of an applauding multitude!" Agonized with such thoughts, Charitana reached the gates of the prison, knocked with trembling hand, and craved admittance. She informed the jailer, that she was in search of a daughter, named Seraphica, who, immediately after the execution of Polycarp, had been cast into prison; and that for several months she had heard nothing of her fate.

"Seraphica!—the daughter of a purple-dye merchant?" growled the jailer,—"and one of the Christian Religion, and but seventeen years old? Yes, you can see her in a few days: She will then celebrate her wedding on the feast of Mercury, with a young and beautiful panther; the most cheerful Ethiopian that can be found."

Pale as marble and trembling with horror, Charitana stood before the savage jailer, from whose scornful lips she had just heard the probable fate of her only child.

"I see you have some fruit," continued he; "I'll place it before her at the feast already mentioned."

"Unfeeling man, you mock me! Has icy death never torn from you a beloved child? Have you never stood by the death-bed of one dear to you? If not, you can never understand what I now suffer. Oh! I conjure you to grant me this solitary consolation!—Allow me to speak to Seraphica before she leaves the prison for the festival!" "Where is your purse?" asked the jailer. "If it be well filled, matters can be favorably managed." "No, heartless man, gold and silver have but sparingly fallen to my lot, but the laws of Rome, which grant to the condemned a feast before death, are not so severe as to refuse a mother a last interview with her beloved child.—Were I to offer you the little money I possess, you would not be contented.—But I remember now, I have a treasure—a great treasure—one I have inherited, and which can be divided between you and me, without decreasing. I can give you as much of it as your heart desires, as soon as you grant my petition."

"Extraordinary promise," replied he. "What is the value of that treasure?"

"Of more value than this terrestrial orb, even were it of Diamond." The jailer's countenance brightened up. "In any case a great exaggeration," said he to himself.—"Still it might be as valuable as a diamond."—Then turning round, he seized upon his keys, and gave Charitana a sign to follow.

They passed through long and vaulted corridors, where nothing broke the silence that reigned around, save the hollow echoes of their footsteps. At length they stood before a low and narrow door—unlocked—the bolts withdrawn—and Charitana is in the presence of her daughter.

O happy moment!—a sweeter in this place of sorrows none had ever known! But silence! Yonder sits the youthful captive—not suspecting who is near. Her right arm is chained—the left supports her head, and she is in a deep slumber. "Ah perhaps," murmured Charitana in a low voice, "thou already knowest what awaits thee in a few days! Perhaps fearful visions are even now passing before thy weary eyes!—Yet, no, those features speak not of fear; that countenance is as a

mirror reflecting interior peace and holy resignation."—
In her fettered hand, she loosely holds a girdle; upon
which she had evidently been ruminating; and so had
sunk to sleep.—She drops the hand, and the girdle falls
from her listless fingers. She moves—smiles—and
holds converse with herself.—"Yes,—yes, never-to-be-
forgotten Polycarp!—Not on parchment, but on far
nobler material have I written all thy words!—Polycarp! shall we meet again? Soon?—O it will be some
time yet! *Until then let us have hope ever before us, and
never lose the pledge of our righteousness.'"* *

Charitana having placed the fruit upon the ground,
stood immovable before her dreaming child. But as
soon as she heard the words "O it will be some time
yet," she could no longer refrain from shedding a flood
of tears.

At length, in a subdued voice, she pronounced her
daughter's name, "Seraphica! do you know who is
here?"

The young girl answered dreamingly and slowly, as
though she felt obliged to reflect on every word.—
"Here?—Here are peace and solitude."

"Seraphica, thy mother!"—"Mother? No, she has
fled!" and sighing heavily, she dashes a tear from her
pale cheek, and casts her half closed eyes on the girdle
at her feet. Suddenly she perceives a form before her,
she shudders—and quick as lightning raises herself
from the ground, and exclaiming, "God of all goodness!" casts herself into her mother's arms. "Do I
dream, or art thou really she, or art thou an angel who

---

* These were the words of St. Polycarp to the Philippians.

·visitest me?   Wondrous!—through closed doors in this gloomy dungeon!"

"Yes, dearest child, it is thy mother! Life without · thee seemed more painful than death itself. Six anxious months have I wandered through the mountains, where I found true and loving hearts; one alone was wanting —and that was thine. But now I will not leave thee until I know thy fate.

"Since that dreadful day, thou hast been ever present to my mind. When I heard that thou wast seen in the Amphitheatre, oh what anguish did I not endure! Hour after hour passed on. My worst fears were verified: I heard that thou wast taken prisoner." "Yes, mother," replied Seraphica, "though most unworthy, I have been chosen to suffer imprisonment and chains for the sake of my Redeemer. It was a dreadful day, yet one replete with blessings.

"O hadst thou seen our venerable and saintly Polycarp!—Couldst thou but have gazed on those features of a hundred years, glowing with charity, peace, and simplicity!

"Many feared that his great age would have rendered him unable to reach the place of martyrdom, with that heroic fortitude expected from one who had led a life so holy. But how groundless was that fear! O mother, hadst thou but seen that saint in death!"

"Still, my child, I had the happiness to meet our holy Bishop in the suburbs of the city, a short time before.

"He was driving in the chariot of Herodus, and Niccetas, his father, sat near him. Both were trying to induce him to call the Emperor the Most High God, and to offer incense before his statue. But finding their entreaties vain, with savage fury they dashed the venerable old man from the chariot, and his face, coming in violent contact with the pavement, was deeply wounded. He arose covered with blood, but proceeded on his way as joyous, as if he had suffered nothing. This was the last time I beheld him.

"The sanctity of his life is ever present to my mind. I think I hear him still, relating the conversation he had had with St. John and others, who had seen our Lord, and all they had told him of His doctrine and miracles."

"But, dearest mother, thou wast not witness of his last hours, of his farewell discourse. — Thou didst not see him as he passed the bodies of young Germanicus and his companions, who were the first that suffered, and stood before Quadratus, who, in a voice of thunder, said to him, 'Swear by the fortune of the Emperor, despise Christ, and I promise thee thy freedom! Swear!' At this command the spectators pressed forward, in breathless expectation of his answer. Polycarp replied with a slow and solemn voice:

"'Already six and eighty years have I served my Lord, and He has never yet done injury to me, but on the contrary, He is always heaping favors on me. How can I curse my King—Him who has redeemed me? But knowest thou not of the future judgment—and of that unquenchable fire, lighted by eternal justice, to torture the wicked?' The people burned with the desire of seeing the judicatory inquiry at an end.

"They had already looked on blood, and drunk from

it a new desire for murder. At this moment a voice
was heard from one of the principal seats of the Amphitheatre, 'Let wood be conveyed hither!' This was
echoed by a thousand voices. 'Wood! Let wood be
brought hither!' In a few moments a huge pile was
erected. Quadratus gave the signal; and Polycarp,
turning to his faithful followers, bestowed on them his
last Benediction, unloosed his sandals, removed his
girdle, and with a firm step ascended the pile; a living
testimony of the words of St. Paul:

"'Who then shall separate us from the love of Christ?
Shall tribulation, or distress, or famine, or nakedness, or
danger, or persecution, or the sword?' As it is written:
'For thy sake we are put to death all the day long: we
are accounted as sheep for the slaughter.' 'But in all
things we overcome, because of Him that hath loved us.
For I am sure that neither death, nor life, nor angels, nor
principalities, nor powers, neither things present, nor
things to come; nor might, nor height, nor depth, nor
any other creature, shall be able to separate us from the
love of God, which is in Jesus Christ our Lord.'

"As the executioner was in the act of binding him to
the stake, he said in a low voice: 'This precaution is
unnecessary. He who gives me strength to bear these
flames, will also give me strength to bear them
patiently.'

"He then commenced his dying prayer: 'Almighty
God, Father of Thy dearly beloved Son, Thou God of
angels and the Powers, Thou God of all creatures! I
thank Thee, that I have the happiness to partake of the
Chalice of Thy anointed One. Accept me into the num-

ber of Thy martyrs, receive me as an agreeable offering. I praise Thee for all things, and glorify and magnify Thee through the High Priest, Jesus Christ, to whom with Thee and the Holy Ghost, be all honor now and in eternity."

"While many of the faithful, who were present," continued Seraphica, "were offering up their prayers with him in silence, there arose suddenly a clear, bright flame on high, which caused a deathlike stillness in the multitude, and behold the miracle! The roaring element arched around the saint, like a mighty sail swelling with the wind. A deep sound of horror echoed through the crowd, as they perceived this visible and miraculous interposition of the God of the Christians.

"When Quadratus saw that Polycarp was untouched by the fire, he made a sign to one of the executioners. All waited anxiously for the fresh commands, and in an instant one of the executioners, appointed by the Proconsul, sprang upon the pile, like a tiger upon his prey, and plunged a dagger in the old man's breast. Polycarp stood motionless, but as his breathing became quicker, the blood flowed profusely from his wound into the flames beneath. He sank at length upon his knees, closed his eyes, rendered his mighty soul to Him who gave it, and his body to the flames."

Here Seraphica was silent; the strongest emotion for some minutes overpowered her. She leaned her head upon her mother's shoulder, and her raven hair fell upon her pale face, like a veil of mourning. "Let us be comforted," sobbed forth Charitana, "Polycarp has won the crown of life. He was an unwearied champion, and now

3

his eternal sabbath has begun.   He fought the good
fight, and went to receive his reward on the very day
on which the Eastern Church commemorates the death
of our Redeemer."

Charitana, thinking it possible, that in a few days
more Seraphica would follow in the footsteps of the holy
Bishop, continued: "The life of every good Christian is
a martyrdom, which ends but in death."   Seraphica,
whose mind was wholly occupied with the last hours of
the holy Polycarp, heard but little: her mother's words
died on her ear, and she continued uninterruptedly:
"The sanguinary deed was scarcely completed, when the
people cried aloud: 'Long live the Proconsul and Roman
justice!'   The multitude applauded, but we Christians
wept in silence.

"His sacred relics were scattered to the winds by the
excited people.   We still lingered on, and felt as though
Polycarp, phœnix-like, had risen from his holy ashes, and
overshadowed his orphan children with his protecting
wings.   The sandals, staff, and girdle of the saint, lay
untouched before us.   We hastened to secure these precious mementos.   Some had already possessed themselves of the sandals and staff, whilst I, endeavoring to
seize the girdle, felt in the same moment a hand upon
my shoulder, and a rough voice spoke aloud: 'Behold,
this is one of the poisonous plants that spring up from
such seed!'—and in the twinkling of an eye, the girdle
was twisted round my arm;—I was bound, led across
the Arena, and cast into one of the dark cells of the Amphitheatre.   This then, dearest mother, is the girdle of
which I speak; and these are the spots of his holy

blood." Charitana took the sacred relic and pressed it to her lips. Tears fell from her eyes, but they were not so much for Polycarp, as for her noble-minded daughter, who seemed to suspect nothing of the probable fate that in a few days awaited her. "Well, Seraphica," said the mother, on returning the girdle, "when shall we meet again?" "When our Heavenly Father wills it!" she answered, and resumed her former discourse: "As I was being led from the Amphitheatre to prison, one of our friends, Irenaus, the priest, who was Polycarp's beloved disciple, met me. He recognized me, drew closer, and admonished me in Latin as follows: 'Hold firmly the doctrines of your Saviour, which the Holy Ghost hath imprinted in thy heart.'—Yes, I will preserve it—yes, to my last breath." "When shall we meet again?" repeated Charitana; "which of us shall be first called hence—thou or I?"

Seraphica perceived the anguish with which the question was accompanied, and seizing her mother's hand, replied: "We shall die in that very hour that God wills, and not when man conjectures. On my account cease to be anxious. *'I shall not die yet.'* I have besought our Lord not yet to call me to my eternal home. I wish to suffer, but not to die; I burn with the desire of showing to the world, in the mirror of a pure life, the doctrines of our Redeemer, and to relate to many of the unbelievers, what the Son of God has done for man: and not till I have fulfilled that mission, shall I be called hence. It may be long till then! God has heard my prayer, and my Guardian Angel has revealed it to me." Suddenly loud knocks were heard at the door. — The jailer commands Charitana to depart, and does not even give her time to take leave of her beloved child.

Seraphica was again alone; she reflected on the words: "Which of us shall first be taken hence?" but the answer gave her no anxiety. Casting her eyes on the lovely fruit which her mother had brought, she took a pomegranate, and on dividing it, she discovered in the centre some pieces of gold: they were evidently secreted there for Seraphica, that she might therewith soften the heart of her savage jailer. She tasted the fruit, but could not eat, for she was unable to swallow.

The jailer detained Charitana at the door of the prison. "Well, it seems you have forgotten the promise you made before I allowed you to enter. Did you not speak of a magnificent diamond, that you were to give me? — Come, where is the precious stone?"

"You are right," replied Charitana, "I promised you a gift of more value than this terrestrial globe, were it composed of diamonds. This treasure is the mystery of Faith, and those who possess it, become a free people,— yes, become kings and princes. I will impart to thee those mysteries."

"How, fool? Will you take upon you the part of Apollo, who once stuck upon the Phrygian king a pair of long ears? You want to make a Midas of me! — No — no; you must be the cheated one, not I. Do you hear the noises coming from the slave market? those are the cries of the Christians undergoing the lash. Thou, . fool, art also a Christian, and one of the worst. I overheard distinctly your conversation in the dungeon, and this very evening I shall hear the gold and silver I shall receive for your detection, jingling in my pocket." He then thrust the unhappy mother into a cell, and closed the door with such violence, that the noise echoed like thunder along the corridors.

3 *

CHAPTER II.

THE EARTHQUAKE.

FTER the conquest of Asia Minor by the Romans, Smyrna, one of her most celebrated cities, was obliged to pay her share of the yearly tribute imposed on the province, in wool, carpets, mohair, tapestry, nutgalls, and above all, gold-dust from the rivers Hermos and Paktolos, and whatever luxuries the extravagant Romans could desire, in Asiatic perfumes and cosmetics, which were brought to the harbor, and shipped for Rome, as were also slaves in great numbers.

Notwithstanding this heavy tax upon the people, trade flourished, and the population became so numerous, that the shady gardens and capacious quays, which surrounded the lovely bay, could scarcely accommodate the various classes of the inhabitants, who thronged there, for their evening promenade, to enjoy the cool sea-breezes.

Here also might be seen the Roman Proconsul, Statius Quadratus, attended by his body-guard. It was to him the merit was due, that the tribute flowed in so freely.

Quadratus turned aside from the crowd, and walked towards the shore, when he met Asmenes, a priest of Isis, who had been educated in Egypt, for the service of that goddess. He bowed to the Proconsul, who said to him, "Well, Egyptian naturalist, tell me whence comes this oppressive heat, at this unusual season of the year?"

"A difficult question," replied Asmenes; "although in the calends of November, we have a heat which seldom occurs in the height of summer. I did suppose the evening would have become cool, but it seems just as if the heat increases in the same degree as the sun recedes. I wonder whether the Christians, who fare but badly in the market, have not used some mysterious means against the sun!"

"What do you mean?" said Quadratus.

"It is said," replied Asmenes, "that the Thessalonians are masters in necromancy, and that there are more soothsayers and magicians amongst them than amongst any other people. But for my own part, I think that the greatest are to be found amongst the Christians. It is beyond doubt, that at the death of their great Prophet, the sun withdrew his light for three hours; and it is also related that in bygone times, the sun stood still in the heavens for three days. It was only this spring, when Polycarp was before your tribunal, a mysterious voice spoke to him, which was distinctly heard by all present.* But thanks, a thousand thanks to you, noble Proconsul, who have granted our petitions, and well rid Smyrna of

* As Polycarp entered the Amphitheatre, a voice was heard from Heaven, "Take courage, Polycarp!"

that sorry scoundrel.— Ha! look at them bound in the ship yonder! O may Isis grant thee for this, health, happiness, and prosperity!" Both advanced a little farther up the walk, which led to the shore. Several caravans returning from Arabia, and laden with its treasures, passed them by on their way to the city, there to deliver them on the coming market-day, and to reload with other wares, to sell again in their own country.

Quadratus was a man of mean education, and very superstitious; he continued to dwell upon the witchcraft, which, according to the priest of Isis, lay in the hands of the Christians; and as the heat increased, his anxiety became the more intense. At last, he stood still, and looking towards the West, said, "Do you see that strange appearance?" convulsively seizing the priest's arm. "Look at that unusual red, covering the heavens! It cannot possibly be the reflection of the setting sun, which appears yonder on Argos. What are the gods about to send us?" Asmenes looked in silence on the spectacle. Deeper still became the glowing red, the higher it rose in the heavens, till it ended in a deep violet hue.

On the extreme verge of the horizon, a pale yellow gleam extended along the North, West, and South, until it approached the East, where it was scarcely visible; and little bluish vapors rose from the sea, which became larger as they ascended. The temperature then changed into that of a rough, sharp harvest season; small clouds danced, spectre-like, here and there, upon the surface of the water, and rising in the air passed over the city, and spread themselves on the neighboring hills.

"Do I deceive myself," said the Proconsul, "or are we actually in a thick fog? I feel fearfully cold too. Let us hasten home: I fear the worst, either pestilence, or war, or a general devastation." "It is the departure of the Christians," said Asmenes; "they are preparing all this for us; I have expected nothing less than that their departure would be connected with some such display. Thus, when in old times they fled out of Egypt from king Pharaoh, they did similar things, and even divided the Red Sea, so that they passed through as if on dry land; while Pharaoh and his whole army found death in attempting to follow them. And it is very possible, that their departure now will also be accompanied with bad consequences."

With this apprehension, they separated, the priest to his dwelling, and the Proconsul to the palace, for consolation from Herod, the Irenarch.

A number of dark Smyrnians were passing along the streets, some seeking the open air, others the harbor; for the oldest inhabitants understood the signs, and remembered that they were always followed by a greater or lesser convulsion of the earth.

Quadratus, accompanied by his body-guard, then hastened home. His palace formed a wing of the citadel, which was so elevated, that one could scarcely fear any danger. He durst not trust himself in the open air, for he dreaded the unusual excitement called forth amongst the greater portion of the inhabitants, by his cruel persecution of the Christians. No sooner had he arrived at the citadel, than he ran anxiously through all the apartments, and looked out at the starry heavens, first

C

through one window, and then through another. He, who has so often proudly rocked himself in his Sella, and laughed as he looked on, while the combatants in the Arena are torn to pieces by lions, or the condemned Christians cast to wild beasts, has now become a trembling coward, as soon as he sees his own life in jeopardy.

Herod showed more courage. He preferred to watch the operations of nature. When all was silent and motionless, he mounted his steed, and rode with some friends to a beautiful valley outside the city, which to the present day is called the "Valley of Paradise."

Midnight was approaching; the heavens were beautifully clear, and a solemn stillness reigned around. All listened with breathless attention, yet no sound could be heard of that hollow, subterraneous rumbling which usually precedes a convulsion of the earth. Even one amongst the party, who laid his ear close to the ground, could not discover anything to cause alarm.

Herod suddenly thought that he heard, not far distant, something he could not define. His friends were divided in their opinions, till it was soon discovered to be the reiterated barks of a watch-dog, on the roof of an adjacent villa. The barking echoed along the valley, and became gradually stronger and quicker, till it broke out into a loud, tremulous howl, which was soon taken up by several other dogs in the neighborhood. "A remarkable omen," said Herod, as he shook his head thoughtfully. On a sudden, the horses, with manes erect, pawed the ground, reared, plunged, and dashed with their riders, foaming, on.

Close to the city, the greater part of the inhabitants, weary of watching, and exhausted with anxiety, returned to their dwellings. While some wondered that the appearances were so much dreaded, others were inquiring if the same signs had ever been observed before, without having been followed by evil consequences. The more cautious took balls of stone or metal, and suspended them by threads or long hairs from the ceiling of their rooms, in order to detect the first motion, and save themselves by immediate flight. Watches were placed on nearly all the houses; but the silence was unbroken save, from time to time, by a footfall, or the anxious whisperings of human voices. Although the guards were so numerous, still they were insufficient to protect the property of the inhabitants from plunder. Thieves were lurking in all directions, hoping to profit by the general consternation.

Asmenes, the priest of Isis, on his return home, discovered that a great robbery had been committed in his absence. Occupied with the things that were then passing, he had forgotten to lock up his effects carefully, and behold! he found himself robbed of his new golden *Sistom*, or "Isis-rattle." Complaining to his goddess, that she did not protect her own property, and burning with rage, he armed himself with a sharp knife, and ran down to the vestibule, thinking probably, that a second attempt would be made on his house. He waited there a long time. The cheerfulness wherewith a little company of captive Christians were wending their way through Hercules Street, towards the sea, formed a striking contrast to his fury. The slave-masters, fearing the worst, wished, for greater security, to put them aboard the ships, and send them out to sea when the signs became sufficiently alarming.

The procession approached an arch, with two torch-bearers in advance. The captives were entoning one of the beautiful canticles of their persecuted Church, as they passed along. Asmenes stole behind a pillar, and as the words, "Laudate Dominum omnes gentes," fell upon his ear, he muttered to himself, "These are the blasphemers, the robbers, the cannibals, who are bringing so much misery on Smyrna! Now they approach! Nemesis will deliver them up to my vengeance:—an agreeable sacrifice to the Shade of Hades!" Seizing his knife, he darted forward, exclaiming, "Thieves! give me back my Sistrum—my golden Sistrum!"—and—crash!—a terrific rumbling like thunder, rolls beneath. —The earth, no longer able to restrain the pent-up element, bursts asunder at the very feet of the heathen priest,—he totters—falls, and in an instant finds his grave. The fiery element just liberated, rushes with ungovernable fury along the streets.—Another shock:—house after house heaves;—towers totter;—castles are rent asunder, and street after street are heaps of ruins.

But what of the wretched inhabitants? They run to and fro in wild despair: they call on the gods to help them :—"Help! help! ye gods, or we are lost!" Some, in frantic haste, hurrying to the shipping; whilst others seek refuge in the mountains, or in the adjacent fields. The darkness increases the horrors of the awful scene.

The upper part of the city remained still undisturbed. The massive edifices and principal temples had as yet withstood the fury of the element. Many of the people fled on the wings of terror to the temples of their gods; particularly to the great sanctuary of Homer, which was soon densely crowded. The confusion reached its height; flight was impossible, on account of the innumerable piles of smoking ruins, that everywhere impeded the steps of the unhappy fugitives. Men, women, and children of every class, whom terror had deprived of their senses, might be seen, here and there lying among their fallen dwellings. The dead were carried into the open places by hundreds, still greater was the number of wounded, bruised, and maimed: and heart-rending were the agonizing shrieks of those who were lying half buried beneath the scorching ruins, unable to afford themselves the slightest assistance.

The increasing darkness suggested the necessity of seeking the aid of torches; and he who was fortunate enough to pick up one, hoped by its means to find his way out of the city. But the endless heaps of rubbish, the rising exhalations, and the clouds of dust, rendered escape impossible. Even where a free passage was left, the red flickering light of the torches served only to make the "darkness visible." In several parts of the city, the fire burst forth again with redoubled fury, and destroyed, with incredible rapidity, everything within its reach. Some maintained that it proceeded from the earth, whilst others thought it was caused by the fires of the forges and of the dwelling-houses buried beneath the ruins. Each one had something terrific to relate, and many were of opinion that the end of all things was at hand, and that the world was about to be destroyed

4

by fire.   Suddenly cries were heard from the quarter
where stood the palace and citadel: a fresh chasm in the
earth was issuing forth another destructive fire.

Statius Quadratus hoped to save himself by taking
refuge on the highest terrace of the citadel.   But he
hoped in vain; for whilst on bended knees he was imploring the protection of the gods, a roaring flame issued
from the foundations, and forced its way through the
palace till it reached the terrace where he was.   Terrified at the sight, he drew back so far, that he had no
other choice but to cast himself down from the height,
or become a victim to the devouring fire.   "Ten thousand sesterces to him who helps me!"   But the flames
have already claimed their victim.   A scream, a faint
moan, and Statius Quadratus has finished his wicked
career.

Up to this time, by the fall of such masses of dwellings, no less than the tenth part of the inhabitants lost
their lives.   Those who had sought refuge in the Temple of Homer, were nearly all crushed to death by the
falling of the roof and pillars; but what appeared most
strange was, that the bronze statue of the poet himself
was split from head to foot.   More fortunate was the lot
of those who, like the Christians, sought in the first
instance to save themselves by sea.   The unusual calmness of the waters formed a striking contrast with the
destruction and devastation which raged on the shore.

Two hours after the tremendous shocks on land, the
sea began to heave and swell at the mouths of the
Hermos.   Although the tide was then at the ebb, it
rose, with the greatest rapidity, far above the highest

flood-mark. On a sudden, a volcanic force beneath raised the foaming waters mountain-high, and bearing the richly laden vessels on their convulsed bosom, swept them as if triumphantly across the stone pier, and cast them into the city. Then gaining a height of more than eighty feet, they passed over the highest buildings, still standing, and in their course quenched the volumes of flames which were issuing from all parts of the city. As if the sea were charged to complete the work of desolation, its waters receded slowly, leaving the shattered vessels mingled with the smoking ruins; * and in its return, bore back in thousands, the dead bodies of the inhabitants. In such horrors the night passed on.

At last, impenetrable darkness gave place to the morning-dawn. The earth was at rest, and the sea had resumed its wonted calm. The survivors, although they had lost all, looked upon themselves as enviable mortals. Strangers embraced each other, as though they had been dear friends meeting after a long separation.—It was a sad mingling of joy and sorrow. On one side could be seen fathers and mothers weeping over the dead bodies of their children; on the other, children inconsolable for the loss of their beloved parents. The morning sun rose in splendor, and the sparkling waters danced in his beams, as if rejoicing to meet again.

What form is moving yonder on the heights? pale and slender, robed in white, enriched with the golden hues of the rising sun; bearing a broken chain on one arm, and a girdle on the other. It seems as though it

* One large-sized vessel was found in the centre of the ruined Theatre.

were the guardian spirit of this once great city, mourning over its fall. Slowly and thoughtfully she passes on, till she reaches the still smoking ruins of the citadel. She pauses, and casting down .her soft dark eyes, surveys the desolation that lies before her. The spectacle surprises her, but her mien betrays neither fear nor horror. Her expression is that of silent resignation to the will of Him who makes the earth his footstool. She was roused from her reverie by a voice exclaiming, "Seraphica here! The captive at liberty! The victim of death standing over the tombs of her persecutors!"

Seraphica answered with a gentle gravity, "Yes, Irenaus," for it was he, "the captive is free. After one had opened the door of my prison to announce my approaching death, another, mightier than he, rent its strong walls asunder, and I was liberated. I now stand gazing on a city whose splendor has vanished from the earth. Even whilst I am now speaking, I see several buildings falling into ruins.—Irenaus, is not that my mother's dwelling? Oh, what of her, revered master? Is she amongst the living or the dead?"

"You could scarcely wonder," replied Irenaus, "if she had shared the fate of so many. But no, Seraphica, she is saved, but saved by slavery. She and some of her companions in the faith, were, last night, shipped for Rome. But delay not to save yourself; your chains show that you are a captive."

An hour later, Seraphica was seen standing on the deck of the only safe vessel to be found in the harbor. She was on her way for Greece. One look—as the vessel receded from the shore, and it was the last, upon the ruins of a city where she had spent her few and momentous years.

She could discern her mother's half-destroyed dwelling on the projection of a hill; but the palm-trees and little garden had disappeared. And behold! while she was still gazing, the walls gave way, the roof fell in, and nothing remained of her once beloved home.

4 *

CHAPTER III.

METELLA.

E will now conduct our readers to charming Attica, so often celebrated in the poet's song,—to the land of great generals and lawgivers, to the cradle of philosophy, to the seat of the Muses, and to the place of refuge for the Faith.

The fame of Athens had, at this time, out-grown itself, and began to tend towards her ruin. But even then she was in possession of all the intellectual acquirements of past ages, and enjoyed the results of the thoughts, actions, and labors of her forefathers. For this reason, it is the ripest and most beautiful period in her history. As the sun increases in beauty, whilst sinking in the West, so did Athens when verging on her downfall.

The Emperor, Adrian, loved Athens more than any other city in his vast dominions; and all the magnificent edifices and new regular streets on the other side of Adrian's Arch, extending wide, and forming, as it were, a second city,—were the work of this great Emperor. After this vast addition, Athens could accommodate

180,000 inhabitants. Adrian's Arch which thus connected the old city with the new, and which to this day is in good preservation, proclaims the later history of Greece in that degree of development in which the Roman life was bound up with that of the ancient Greek, and which had blended both nationalities into one.

Outside the old city, to the north-east, was a pyramidical mountain, called Lycabett; at the present time it is overgrown with thorns and brushwood. As tradition runs, Pallas, the tutelar goddess of Athens, was at one time fully occupied in ordering materials for building the Acropolis, which was dedicated to her. She was carrying even the Lycabett in her arms, when a crow fluttered round, and announced to her the birth of Erichthonius. Seized with terror, she let the mountain fall, close by Athens, where it now stands.

At the foot of this mountain, from the summit of which the traveller has a charming view of Athens towards the citadel, and of the blue sea, were the palaces of the Greek and Roman nobles, who had settled there; and one which occupied the first place amongst them, was that of a Greek matron, named Metella. It stood not far from the principal entrance to the famous aqueduct, built by Adrian, and a little higher than the magnificent royal citadel outside Athens, which strangers still admire.

Like all the edifices of Adrian's time, Metella's palace was of Roman architecture: still the better taste of the Grecian was not wanting in the lightness and elegance with which the design was carried out. Inserted on the front of the vestibule, was a marble slab, on which might be read the name of the owner. Over the door of the principal entrance stood a brazen statue, representing Hope, with the inscription, "Dum spiro spero," "As long as I breathe I shall hope."

Guarding the porch or entrance-hall, was a slave, beautifully attired. He bore handsomely wrought fetters, which he rattled from time to time, thereby to give himself the appearance of a doorkeeper. His walk, and the ease with which he swung his chain, proved that pride knows how to govern all classes of society, down to an ignorant doorkeeper.

Metella tarries on the Pergula, a name given to a pavilion on the roof, and which is supported by gilt pillars. The lady, in all her natural elegance, reclines on a couch; and near her stands a marble table, on which lies an unfolded book-roll. It is the work of a Roman poet, her darling Virgil, whose eclogues she is reading. She raises herself, and taking her pen, writes down one of the most beautiful passages, on the re-perusal of which, her eye, and the movement of her head, show plainly, that the depth of some of the poet's words are not clear to her. But some of the verses please her so much, that she reads them aloud.

"Sicilian Muse, begin a loftier strain!
Tho' lonely shrubs and trees that shade the plain
Delight not all. . . . .
    The last great age, foretold by sacred rhymes,
Renews its finish'd course; Saturnian times
Roll round again, and mighty years, begun
From their first orb, in radiant circles run.
The base degenerate iron offspring ends;
A golden progeny from heav'n descends: . . . .

The lovely boy, with his auspicious face,
Shall Pollio's consulship and triumph grace;
Majestic months set out with him to their appointed race.
The father banish'd virtue shall restore,
And crimes shall threat the guilty world no more.
The son shall lead the life of gods, and be
By gods and heroes seen, and gods and heroes see.
The jarring nations he in peace shall bind,
And with perpetual virtues rule mankind.

. . . .

Mature in years, to ready honors move,
O of celestial seed! O foster-son of Jove!
See lab'ring Nature calls thee to sustain
The nodding frame of Heav'n, and earth, and main;
See, to their base restor'd, earth, seas, and air,
And joyful ages from behind, in crowding ranks appear,
To sing thy praise, would heav'n my breath prolong,
Infusing spirits worthy such a song;
Not Thracian Orpheus should transcend my lays,
Nor Linus crown'd with never-fading bays;
Though each his heav'nly parent should inspire;
The Muse instruct the voice, and Phœbus tune the lyre." *

"Virgil, thou speakest beautifully," says Metella, "but I cannot understand thee. Nearly fifty Olympiads have passed since thy death, and I know nothing of that child of the gods, who is to expiate guilt, and to redeem the world. There are a people in Asia, who believe that a god had lived amongst them, but he came to an evil end.

"When will the human mind find truth upon earth? It will ever stand before an enigma, and never solve it, for that enigma is itself."

She takes up a book, in Greek, an old work on history,

* Dryden's *Virgil.*

which relates the misfortunes of Cyrus, king of Persia.
She has scarcely read a few pages, when she seeks another chapter; nor does that content her. "Always the
same," murmured she, "Cyrus broke up and advanced:
here he commenced; Cyrus liked this, and wished that
you also might partake of the enjoyment."

"No Xenophon," she exclaims, "thou art ever bread
without salt, tasteless and unpalatable."—

She seizes the scrolls and casts them down on the polished Mosaic floor, so that they roll against the marble
balustrades of the balcony.

"O time! O time!" she continues, "how unjust thou
art sometimes with the works of the human mind!
How often dost thou break to pieces in thy iron mortar
the best and most beautiful, and scatterest it to the winds,
scarcely leaving a remnant for us, whilst thou carefully preservest in thy sanctuary the insipid and weari-
some works, presenting them anew from one generation
to another!

"But what want we with a book in this city!

"Athens lies open at my feet,—a book of which
Cecrops, seventeen hundred years ago, wrote the title-
page, and Theseus, the first chapter,—a work, each
leaf of which tells of wisdom, of power, and of character. O let me read in thy pages, thou great, thou
lovely city!"—

"ATHENS, THOU FEAREST THE GODS, and carriest the
traces of thy piety written on thy marble forehead—on
that Acropolis rich in temples.

"Countless statues hide the sanctuary of Pallas from
my view. Through gratitude to the gods, under whom

Ægides fought and conquered, our forefathers erected the Parthenon,* and its founder, the immortal Pericles, speaks from every column an earnest assurance to future ages, that a nation is never so strong, nor so powerful abroad, as when its religion is strictly observed at home.

"Behold, in the centre of the Parthenon, the colossal of the Athenian Promachos. Her gigantic form, towers above terrace, dome, and cupola; and her brazen, plumed helmet and shining spear announce to the distant lonely fisherman of Sunium, that thou, lovely Athens! art under the protection of Pallas.†

"ATHENS, THOU ART JUST! and whoever doubts this, let him look at the Areopagus on yonder hill, in whose hall of justice the Archons, during the solemn silence of night, assembled in council, to pass judgment on the crimes committed against religion and the state.

"ATHENS, THOU ART BRAVE! and if a barbarian knew nothing of thy fame, that statue of Apollo yonder, would break the silence, and relate to him how the youths leaped and wrestled there, and how they are to this day a subject of astonishment to the Romans.

"ATHENS, THOU ART THE SEAT OF SCIENCE, AND OF WISDOM! Thy Theatre, thy Lyceum, thy Sculpture-Halls, thy Academies, thy Colonnades proclaim it.

* The Parthenon suffered the greatest devastation, in 1687, when the Venetians, at the taking of Athens, threw a bomb-shell into the powder-magazine of the Acropolis, by which the roof of the temple was blown into the air. Still at the present day, a forest of magnificent columns stands: a splendid edifice over which 2300 years have passed without entirely destroying it.

† Promachos and Pallas are other names for Minerva. This famous statue was still standing in the fourth century, after the departure of Alaric.

" Truly all thy monuments are leaves in this wondrous book, which thy sons have written, to declare to future ages, of what greatness of mind mortals are capable."

Whilst Metella was in this excitement, the sun had moved nearer to the olive-groves that lay between Athens and the sea, casting a rosy hue upon the thousand statues of the Acropolis, as if they were blushing at the praises Metella had just bestowed upon them.

At this moment, Metella's blooming son and future heir entered the pavilion. He saluted his mother and informed her, that her slave-master, Bogus, had just returned from Smyrna; but that he had brought nothing she had ordered, except an Asiatic slave. He added that Bogus had related wonderful things of Smyrna, which was almost entirely destroyed by an earthquake.

Metella, full of thought and astonishment, rose from her couch, and leaving the pavilion, sought Bogus, for further news of Smyrna's fate; with whom we shall now leave her, till we relate some features of her life.

Metella was by birth a Greek, and before her marriage, bore the name of Chrysophora. She was acquainted from her youth with all the works of the ancient writers. Her father was Atticus, who was born at Marathon, one hundred and four years after the birth of Christ, and was one of the greatest men of Greece, — a famous orator, a Roman consul, then tutor to Marcus Aurelius, and at last Prefect of Greece. Although this celebrated man was such a favorite at the court of Rome, and could boast of the personal friendship of the two Antonys, he still remained thoroughly Greek, and prided himself on his noble birth, which he traced as

far back as Miltiades, who conquered tie Persians on
the plains of Marathon.

Like a true Greek, he strove to keep up the renowned
sports of his country. The spectators assembled for the
Olympic games were often parched for want of water,
and he caused an aqueduct to be built for their convenience, at Olympia, by which he won the applause of
all Greece. In beautifying Athens, Atticus gained great
merit, but little thanks: the famous Odeon at the entrance of the Acropolis, the ruins of which are still
standing, have immortalized his name. He had also
the merit of erecting an hospital, and of beautifying the
Stadium,* which accommodated 20,000 people.

In Adrian's time, there lived in Athens an estated
Roman, named Metellus, a man of noble descent, who
could trace his origin to that Metellus who in the year
147 B. C. gave the death-blow to the freedom of Greece.
He had reached a middle age, and retired into private
life, where he first found time to think of marriage.
Whilst in Rome, he had told Atticus, the then consul,
of his desire to espouse his daughter, Chrysophora.
She was an only child, for her brother died young, and
her mother, Regilla, soon followed him. The negotia-
tions in this business were attended with obstacles which
could not be removed by the suitor. The young and
rich heiress, according to her father's desire, was to give
the preference to a son of Greece, to which choice she
evinced but little inclination, and Atticus was obliged
to take the petition of the suitor into consideration. In
addition to this, both Metellus and Chrysophora had

* Stadium, where the bull-fights were held.

5   D

attained that age recommended by Aristotle for a prudent marriage.*

Chrysophora had been seldom in Athens, while her father, whom she always accompanied, was generally in active service. Metellus having for some time sojourned chiefly in Greece, had not seen her since her childhood.

The circumstance of the betrothed, not knowing each other, although they were shortly to be united, is frequently to be met with amongst the ancients.†

As soon as the aged Atticus had signed the contract for his daughter's marriage, Metellus journeyed at once to Peloponnesus, where Atticus so frequently resided towards the close of his life, to go through the ceremony of the betrothal. It was early in the morning when he reached Elis, the longed-for house; and he impatiently entreated his future father-in-law to let him have a sight of his bride. Atticus excused her, as she was still occupied with her toilet. In fact, she had just ended her morning dream, as she was aroused by her slave, who announced to her the unexpected arrival. Chrysophora wishing to appear in full holiday charms, ordered her slaves to bring forth her costliest robes, and to seek from her caskets the richest pearls. While one was occupied in preparing the rouge, another was powdering richly with gold dust, according to the fashion of the times, her raven hair, until it had attained a reddish hue. A slave passed even Atticus without a token of

* Aristotle says, Vol. vii. 18, that the woman should marry at 18, and the man at 37.

† "We are allowed to try a stone jug before we purchase it, but the wife cannot be seen, lest she might not please, before she is taken home." Theophrast oy. Ḥyeronym. Jovim i. 48.

respect, so great was her haste in carrying to her mistress, sandals embroidered with the finest pearls,—a
sign that the toilet duties would soon terminate. But
as the blooming girl desired to please still more by her
natural charms than by her ornaments, she left on the
renowned cosmetic of bread and milk, with which she
covered her face every night before retiring to rest,
until her toilet was completed, contrary to the usual
custom. Atticus concluded, when he saw the slave
carrying his daughter's sandals, that the important task
was finished. He then thought of complying with the
earnest entreaties of Metellus, and led him to his daughter's chamber.

Conceive her terror, when she heard loud steps upon
the stairs! A slave hurried to the door, to stop the entrance of the guest; but he, driven on by exhausted patience to see his long chosen one, forced the slave aside,
and stood before the horror-stricken Chrysophora. The
terrified slaves, instead of gathering round their mistress to screen her from his view, concealed themselves
in the remotest corners of the room. There stood the
vain Chrysophora—gorgeously attired, with the fatal
paste hanging in fragments from her lovely countenance,
showing here and there a strange contrast between the
delicacy of her complexion and the gray hue of the
cracked and dried-up cosmetic, which stubbornly ad-
hered to the right cheek, to the forehead, and round the
left eye.

Her heaving bosom betrayed the passion that raged
within. Her eyes, or rather eye, for the left was half
concealed behind its casement of dried bread and milk,

flashed with rage. At length her tongue found utterance, and her wounded pride sought consolation in declaring, that she would recall her promise, and break the contract.

We see that even in this hour of dire humiliation, her woman's tact did not wholly desert her. She feared that this discovery would lessen the esteem of Metellus, and furnish a plea for breaking the contract. So she took care, in the midst of her confusion, to threaten the dismissal of her lover, when she thought he was likely to dismiss her, and it required all the flowery eloquence of an Atticus to make clear to her the folly of her resolution.

Metellus' cool deliberating character took advantage of the confusion. He enjoyed a privilege which any Roman would have envied, that of seeing his bride before marriage, and seeing her too in an unguarded moment. Her majestic form was his beau-ideal of perfection, and the *visible* portions of her charming countenance exceeded his most sanguine expectations; so that, making every allowance for the little ebullition of temper he had just witnessed, he concluded that he had the greatest reasons to congratulate himself on the choice he had made. Having now fully satisfied his curiosity, he *put on* an embarrassed air, and making an humble apology for the intrusion, left his affianced lady to finish her toilet, and to distribute due castigations amongst her trembling slaves.

After this dilemma, the ceremony of the betrothal was completed by Metellus placing a ring on the third finger of his future bride's left hand; for the ancients believed that a nerve passed from that finger to the heart.

A day in the coming June was decided on for the nuptials, as that month was regarded as the most fortunate of all the year.

The haughty bride attired herself on that day, commensurate with her youth and rank, and the solemnity of the occasion. She wore, according to the custom of the Greeks, a long white robe that fell in rich folds, confined at the waist with a woollen girdle. Her feet were provided with sandals brought from Morocco. Her hair, parted into six long curls, was beautifully interwoven with wreaths of flowers; and her entire dress was completed by a rose-tinted veil, which fell gracefully over her majestic form.

The marriage ceremony was performed in her father's house, at Elis.

Sacrifices were offered to the goddess Hera, and the gall of the victims was thrown away, as a sign that all bitterness was to be banished from this union.

The marriage was confirmed in the presence of several witnesses, after which the guests partook of the wedding-feast. There was one sad heart amongt them—that of the aged Atticus. To the left of the table where he sat, was a cover for one, which remained untouched during the feast: it was that of his departed son, whose place at table, although he had been many years dead, remained unoccupied. There is so much that is touching in this trait of Atticus' character, that even the historian Lucius, who loved to dip his arrows into the sour dregs of Attica Sarcasm, here would have refrained from it. A

5 *

custom was still observed amongst the Romans, which descended from the ancients, who, as it is known, robbed the Sabines of their daughters. Therefore, in imitation of this, the bride was taken off during the feast. In some cities this custom is still practised. Young girls accompanied the bride to her chariot, one of whom carried a distaff, to remind her that spinning and household affairs are the proper portion of a matron.

The festivities commenced the following day, at the house of Metellus, in Athens. The bride herself received presents from her friends, and began to enter on her duties as mistress of the house. The old Hellenic principle was also to be observed by her: that it was for the man to speak and have authority, while the woman's duty was, to devote herself to her husband and children, and to superintend the domestic arrangements.

The bride now took the name of Chrysophora Attica Metella, or, for brevity, Metella. But with her name she did not lose her desire for knowledge, which she had sought after from her childhood. She knew how to unite it, in a fitting manner, with the duties of her state.

Time spared Metella's youthful charms but for a few years. Her beauty faded, and various misfortunes told her but too soon, that man's life is ephemeral, and that he cannot with certainty count on the morrow. Still her desire to please was nearly as ardent as before; but she sought to gratify it in another form. As she could no longer boast of her personal advantages, she endeavored, by the depth of her knowledge and by greatness of mind, to attract admiration; and as riches came to her assistance, she soon had numerous friends, who enjoyed the luxuries of her table, and bestowed in return, what to her was more agreeable, their unqualified eulogies. There was scarcely a lady in Athens so much renowned for learning. She not only read the works of all the poets and philosophers of Greece, but also studied them under the careful guidance of the best masters, and above all of her renowned father. Later on, many troubles crossed her path: first, she lost her beloved parent, who had passed the remnant of his days partly in Kephisia, where he possessed a magnificent estate, and partly in his birthplace, Marathon. Her husband quickly followed.

Lucius, a very talented and excellent youth, was the only fruit of this marriage. He had attained his fifteenth year, when he was called on, according to custom, to perform the most melancholy of all filial duties, — to hold, with averted face, the funeral torch, and set fire to the pile on which his father's remains were to be consumed. His mother deeply felt the loss of her husband, for although he had little taste for learning, still it never disturbed the harmony that existed between them. Scarcely a week passed that the faithful wife did not go to the "Sacred Street," or "Cemetery," to adorn a tomb, on which was an inscription beginning with the words, "Pause, O Traveller!"—and which covered the urn that contained the ashes of her lamented husband.

These bitter blows of fortune proved fruitful towards the development of her soul. From this time, her former longing to shine in learned conversations and disputes,

considerably lessened; and a strong desire awoke within
her to ornament her future life through noble works of
virtue, which somehow seemed to her brighter and higher
in value than learning. This great desire had only lately
inspired her soul. We find here in Metella three devel-
opments of character; and who does not often discover
these changes through life? — First there was the love
of exterior natural gifts; then followed the love of the
endowments of the mind; and lastly came love of the
adornment of the soul.

Now let us glance at the newly arrived travellers.
We have been informed that there was a young Asiatic
slave, just come from Smyrna. It is no other than Seraphica. In the consternation that reigned in the harbor
of her native city, it was not difficult for the merchant
of the vessel in which she sought refuge, to claim her as
his own property; and as he had large dealings with
Metella, he made a present of the young stranger to his
rich customer.

Metella had scarcely looked on Seraphica's youthful
and attractive form, than she gave an approving nod
to the slave-master, and asked him her birthplace. As
she was born in Lydia, she was to be called in future
after her province, — "Lydia." The last that Seraphica
held as her own, was her Christian name, and that too
must vanish. She stood a stranger among strangers, far
from her native land, from her kindred, and from her
companions in the faith; — she who now commands her
is a heathen. Nothing more then remained for her, than
a look towards the blue heavens — common to all, and

to place her trust in Him whose throne is beyond the stars. "For His sake she had given up all, and therefore her trust in Him was boundless. For He who could speak naught but truth, gave her the holy assurance, that she should receive a hundred-fold in this life, and life everlasting." (*Matthew* xix.)

CHAPTER IV.

THE TIROCINIUM.

N the magnificent square near Adrian's Stoa, the people of Athens might be seen crowding about a porphyry pillar, on which hung a decree, beginning with the words "Bonum Factum." Those who stood near the placard could scarcely be induced to leave it; whilst others did their utmost to copy the contents, and those at a distance, though they stood on tiptoe, still could not see to read more than the two words, "Bonum Factum,"—"A good deed." At last, some who stood nearest to the pillar turned round to those at a distance, and called out, "War is publicly proclaimed against the barbarians!"

Almost at the same instant, a herald passed through the square, and in a voice of thunder announced the Emperor's declaration of war against the people of the Danube; and that both Emperors—Marcus Aurelius, and Lucius Verus—were to head the armies in person. Scarcely had the herald ceased to speak, when the people expressed their unqualified approbation by loud and continued applause.

Amongst those who were thirsting for war, was the youthful Lucius, who still wore the long *Toga Prœtexta*, striped with purple. With glowing cheeks, he hastened to some companions of his own age, to relate the news, and to consult on what part they were to take in the matter.

At this time, Metella was completely ignorant of what was passing in the city. She was at home, and for pastime, according to the singular custom of noble ladies of that day, had a tame serpent coiled round her neck, and was feeding it with crumbs of bread, whilst with her foot she beat time to distant music.

At this moment her copyist approached with a sheet of news he had just finished, and laid it on her richly chased silver table. While she was reading it, Lucius rushed in with flying Toga:—"Mother! mother! have you heard the great news? War against the Marcomanni, and the two Emperors are themselves to be in action, and to accompany the army to Aquileia. And all the youths capable of wielding a sword are called on to make preparation."

"Quietly, my son," replied Metella; "you storm as if you were Mars himself. Do you not know that the Sages never repeated anything so often to youth, as. 'Not so fiery!' You have left your Toga behind you: pick it up."

"O how stupid!" replied Lucius: "but no wonder! I have lost my head as well as my Toga; but the loss of the latter is a favorable omen." He lifted up the Toga, and again approached his mother. "This is exactly what I would beg, that you will allow me to doff altogether

this Toga of the boy, and to put on that of the man."
And looking big with importance, he drew himself up
to his full height, and, with head erect, marched up and
down the room, followed by the eyes of his mother,
who, with maternal pride, thought there was only one
Lucius in the world. He stopped suddenly before her;
"Dear mother," said he, "I should like to be a soldier,
and join the campaign; young Quintus, the Proconsul's
son, is not older than I am, and he has just told me that
he has leave to go."

"Quintus' father has other children; but should—
Metella lose her darling Lucius," she said, placing her
hand upon his head, "she has no one on earth to love.
Say, my dear child, can you cause me such anguish?"

Lucius, a little daunted, answered in a subdued tone,
"Ah, mother, must then all be killed who go to the war?

"Perhaps," said he, taking courage from her silence,
"I may never meet with such a chance again in my
whole life, as to go to war with an Emperor—two Emperors:—think only,—two Emperors, mother!" Lucius saw that he was gaining ground, and continued,
"Do you remember how as a school-boy, instead of writing on my tablet the names of great men, I used to draw
little soldiers. Don't you see then that the military pro-
pensity was born with me?" Metella shook her head
with a sorrowful smile.

"Dear mother, you do not expect me to become a
Stoic, an Academic, a Peripatetic, or even an Epicurean?
—No! by the sacred oak of Dodona," shaking his head
jocosely, and with a hearty laugh, "I have no vocation
for any of these! I think I see myself reflecting on

the works of nature: staring at the heavens, with mouth half open, and head thrown back at the risk of injuring my spine, and measuring distances between the stars!— No!—no such tame occupation for me: that I will leave with pleasure to the philosophers and astronomers. I never see the tombs of the heroes at Kerameikos without envying their immortal fame. For the future, I shall be like Themistocles, who could not sleep at night for thinking of the fame of Miltiades. My grandfather, Atticus, often related how he was descended from the great Miltiades; and you, dear mother, have assured me of the same a hundred times. Do you remember what my father said to me on his deathbed: 'When thou becomest a man, be faithful to the Emperor till death'?"

"O yes! but he quickly added,—'and obey your mother.'"

"But, mother, you know the campaign will not start this Autumn—not till the coming Spring. By that time, you will be able to reconcile yourself with your son gaining a few leaves from the laurels of his immortal ancestor Miltiades. But if I am to join in the Spring, I must certainly get my white Toga now, and go through the exercises, the whole Winter, in the field of Mars. Therefore, dear—dear mother, the Toga Virilis! I beseech you to say, yes! Yes, mother, the man's Toga! Think only—I'm seventeen!"

"Patience, patience, my son; you shall have your man's Toga at the proper time."

"But *now*, dear mother,—not when the others are gone?"

6

"No, no."

"Therefore, may I go to the wars?—may I, dear mother?"

"Well, then, if you believe that this will secure your happiness, my dear son let it be so. Go, and may the gods protect you!"—

At these words, the afflicted mother tenderly embraced her son, saying, "Remain always my child, as long as I remain thy mother, and I trust thou wilt ever be a good one, and well-pleasing to the gods."

The joy of Lucius knew no bounds. He saw himself in spirit a Freeman of Athens, and one of its bravest warriors; and could scarcely await the day on which he was to stand before the Proconsul, and receive from his hand the manly Toga.

"Mother," said he, "don't you think that in eight days it will be time to change the Toga? Until then I'll conduct myself right well."

Metella laughed at this acknowledgment, and ordered a calendar to be brought, that she might see what festival was to be expected in Autumn. She found that the festival of the siege of Troy would be celebrated on the 15th of October. "That is for a *second* Achilles just the very day," added the mother, jestingly. "On that day you shall become a recruit."

"On the 15th of October," exclaimed Lucius, "that will be an important day! True, there are several weeks till then, but the 15th of October will be a magnificent day!—That *will* be a day of rejoicing!" So said the fiery youth. "Now I must hasten to Quintus.—Farewell, my own dear mother, farewell;" and in a moment he was out of sight.

Metella studied how she could make this festival, called Tirocinium, sufficiently important, that it would leave an indelible impression on the mind of her son; and she resolved on asking the Proconsul to make his address of exhortation for the occasion most impressive and affecting. She next remembered—all the friends she would have to invite, not one of whom she dared to forget.

The Tirocinium of the ancients was a festival which made a deep impression on every youth. It was intended to celebrate the transition from youth to manhood. In a solemn public address they were exhorted to fulfil the duties of thoroughly good citizens. The great deeds of their ancestors were set before them; and if their forefathers were not renowned, they were reminded of the virtues of their nation. When it happened that some citizen was brought to justice on account of a misdemeanor, the judge took care to remind him forcibly of the resolutions and promises he had made at his Tirocinium.

We shall now see how the young Lucius celebrated this feast. A number of the noblest youths of Athens were summoned to appear before the Proconsul. All Metella's friends and relations were already assembled in the palace, but the lady of the house and her son, for whom the feast was given, were not yet visible, for they were still in the *Lararium* or temple of the household gods; where Lucius might be seen standing with outstretched arms, in fervent supplication imploring a blessing on his future life. During a solemn prayer dictated to him by the priest, he vowed to the gods to treasure virtue above all things, and to hate vice. Then full of awe, he touched the knees of the statue, turned himself round to the right, and remained again standing before the divinity. His mother prayed by his side in silence. She wrote down on a waxen tablet, a promise to the divinity, that, if her son lived to return from the wars, she would offer to the gods the spring produce of all the herds on her estates. Her prayer ended, the wine-offerings commenced.—The fire burned on the small marble altar; the youth seized a golden cup, and filling it with wine from the sacrificial vessel, cast a portion into the flames; the remainder he poured at the feet of the divinity. He then placed a cake upon the altar, and whilst it was burning, he strewed the choicest incense from Arabia on the flames, which diffused a delightful perfume through the whole sanctuary.

The mother then advanced towards her son, and took from his neck the golden amulet, placed there by his father at his birth, and which was meant to keep him in constant remembrance of filial obedience, and to serve as a preventive against danger and certain diseases. Metella placed it as an offering at the feet of the divinity. Lucius, still dressed in his Prætexta, with a cheerful countenance, left the Temple, and joined his friends, who were anxiously awaiting him. After having received congratulations on all sides, and covered with a thousand blessings, he was numerously attended on his way to the Proconsul.

At this period the Athenians no longer held their usual assemblies, as at the time of the Republic, outside on the Pnyxhill, rich in historical memories, and which

was celebrated by the renowned orators, but in the theatre of Dionysius,* where many youths were now assembled awaiting the Proconsul, to receive the *Toga Virilis.*
At last he appeared and seated himself, when one youth
after another, accompanied by his friends, advanced
towards him, laid down his Prætexta, and received from
his hands the Toga Virilis, which was of white, bordered
with purple.

The Proconsul exhorted each one separately on the
signification of doffing the Toga. "The purple stripes
of the boy's Toga," said he to them, "have always reminded you, during your boyhood, that you were to lead
such a life, that, when you became men, you might
deserve to wear the purple-bordered Toga, as a sign of
higher service in the state. You must also never forget
. that you are the descendants of those renowned Greeks
who delivered their native country from the hands of
the Persians." After the duties of a citizen had been
impressed on the minds of the youths by a most eloquent
address, they were then surrounded by their friends, who
vied with each other in offering them their congratulations. Lucius with his friends ascended the heights of
the Acropolis, there to recommend himself to the protection of Pallas. The Cella of the Temple was open,
and they devoutly approached the Prostyhon, the so-
called Sanctorum, the vaulted roof of which was painted
blue, and studded with stars; this was a portion of the

* To this day, the high and beautifully finished orators' stone, upon which
men like Demosthenes stood, as well as a great number of Amphitheatrical
stone seats, are yet to be seen on the Pnyxhill. The Forum in Rome scarcely
affords more interest than this place of assembly of the people of Athens.

6 *   E

temple set apart for the most solemn rites of their worship.   Here stood in all her imposing splendor, and elevated to a considerable height, the ancient and renowned
statue of Pallas, covered with immeasurable quantities
of gold and ivory.   The devoutly inclined prayed before
her with great fervor, while the less devout feasted their
eyes on the magnificent statue, the masterpiece of the
celebrated Phidias, and then on the elaborately chased
golden lamp that hung before the goddess.*

Lucius, on his way home, looked every now and then
with particular complacency on his *Toga Virilis*, and
smiled upon his friends for approbation, who gravely
assured him, that he had already quite the appearance
of a citizen, which he was too modest to acknowledge,
but did really think so.

"A beautiful feast," said he to them, as he descended
the superb marble steps of the Temple; "but there is
one thing I felt keenly as I invoked the goddess, pro-
tectress of Greece.   The Greek youths must submit to
be invested by a Roman magistrate, fight under the nobles of Rome, and accept an Emperor who looks upon
Greece as a province, and calls her Acacia.

"It was otherwise in former times!   O that it were
still so!   If my grandfather were now living, he would
speak to-day, at table, of nothing but the Field Generals
of ancient Hellene.   How would my mother rejoice, if

---

* Pausanius, the disciple of Herodus Atticus, in his description of Greece,
I. 20, says: "Kallimachus completed a golden lamp for the goddess, which
contained sufficient oil for a year, although the lamp burned day and night.
The wick was made of Spanish flax, which has the quality of not being consumed by fire.   Over the lamp arose a bronze palm which reached the vaulted
ceiling, attracted the smoke upwards and then dispersed it."

she were to see the ancient Hellenes arise! That was the reason, without doubt, that she looked so sorrowful to-day, when we parted with her previous to our entering the Theatre of Dionysius."

But these serious thoughts quickly vanished, for Metella met and welcomed them cheerfully; and after a repeated exhortation to the son of her heart, she ordered the attendants to announce that the feast was prepared. The guests presented Lucius with many rich gifts, after which they sat down to table, where nothing failed in either delicacies or amusements. There were jesters, jugglers, and musicians, each contributing his mite to the general hilarity. Here might be seen the difference between Grecian and Roman enjoyment. The Greeks found the noise and jesting incompatible with the customs of their nation; whilst the Romans, poorer in their intellect than in their sensual appetite, found in this amusement, and in feasting, the highest entertainment. Many of them would have been perfectly contented, to use Lucian's words, to eat undisturbed a sucking-pig and sweet cakes, and in place of learned conversation, sink their heads, heavy with wine, upon the cup they were holding.

From this time forward Lucius attached himself to distinguished men, who were well versed in the art of war, and who exerted themselves in training their client as a first-rate soldier. He performed his military exercises every day in the field of Mars, full of burning desire to face the enemy, and to tread in the renowned footsteps of the great Miltiades.

CHAPTER V.

THE HAIR BODKIN.

OME months had now passed since Lydia had entered Metella's service as a poor slave. Slavery was to her as a wilderness, that stretched its parched surface under the scorching rays of the sun, far beyond where the eye can reach. But as once, in olden times, the pious Ruth wandered alone over the stubble-fields of Booz, gleaning after the harvest, so Lydia wanders over her wilderness, carefully endeavoring to garner up the fruits of good works. The character of Metella was just one that gave her sufficient opportunity to practise self-denial; for those who appear so amiable and courteous to guests and friends, are often severe and cruel tyrants towards their dependants. We shall soon be acquainted with Metella's private character.

Lucius had just been called to the field of Mars, to take part in a greater display than usual of military tactics. In passing by his mother, he greets her affectionately, and begs of her to witness the field exercises from a neighboring building. He had scarcely left the house, when an invitation arrived from the Proconsul, inviting Metella to join some guests who were to meet the generals at his house, after the exercises of the day.

Metella called a domestic, and as no one heard her, she *whistled** for a slave outside to enter. She then gave orders to have fitting attire prepared for her, and to arrange her best jewels; for the Proconsul, according to Lucian, was a man that paid great attention to exterior ornaments.

With flying steps, Arpis, the head-mistress of Metella's personal attendants, hastened to her lady's dressing-room, and brought forth a white tunic of the finest Milesian wool. The first had short sleeves, which merely covered the upper part of the arm, and were slit up the middle and fastened with golden clasps, according to the old Doric style. The neck and skirt of the shorter tunic were trimmed with a stripe of double-dyed Sidonian purple, — a distinction allowed only to matrons of noble birth. That part of the under-tunic which appeared below the knee, fell to the ground in ample folds, and was terminated by a rich fringe. Arpis was at great pains in providing her lady's dress; and with wonderful dexterity she raised it on a stand, and fastening the white girdle round the waist, saw that the tunic hung over the cincture in graceful folds.

A second slave exerted herself in arranging the head-dress, and fastening the diadem, under which the hair was to fall in light ringlets on the temples. A magnificent bodkin of chased gold, surmounted with a figure

* A custom in those days. Origen greatly disapproved of it for Christians.

of Iris in carved ivory, completed the head-dress; but it was not added till the toilet was completed. The bodkin was a much admired piece of workmanship of an ancient sculptor: the figure measured four inches, and was finished in all its parts with the choicest and most elaborate carving; it could be screwed off, and replaced by another, according to fancy. With a reverential awe she placed the precious bodkin on the toilet-table. She had good reason for doing it with all possible care; for on one of the gold chains called *Cathedra*, which ran round the upper part of the dressing-chair, was a whip of plaited wire, which, when occasion required, was quickly brought into action. It was just as though Juvenal had Metella in his eye, when he wrote on the Cruelty of Matrons to their Slaves.

> "Poor Psecas decks her head,* herself in tears,
>   And her own locks all dangling round her ears,
>   Her neck uncovered, and her shoulders bare;
>   Not saved from vengeance by her utmost care.
>   'Why is this lock,' the mistress storms, 'too high?'
>   Poor girl she rues the crime; one hair's awry!
>   What's Psecas' fault? is she to feel your blows,
>   If 't is your will to quarrel with your nose?"
>   — JUVENAL, *Sat. VI.*

Lydia brought the shoes, and then arranged some of the folds of her mistress' dress. Metella, according to the fashion of the day, used paints, and ordered an oval mirror to be placed before her, so that she might improve and soften off with a hair-pencil, what her maid had begun in rougeing as well as in the shading

* (Her mistress' R. P.)

of her eyebrows. It suddenly occurred to her that she
had a still deeper black, which could be used with a
greater effect; and as there was not much time to be
lost, she called Lydia hastily to bring it. The order
was scarcely given, when the unhappy slave, in turning
suddenly round to fulfil the command, knocked against
the toilet-table, and the bodkin rolled, fell, and lay on
the floor in pieces. The unfortunate slave had not time
to utter a word, before her mistress, inflamed with anger, sprung from her chair, and in a state of frenzy,
pounced, like a beast of prey, on the terrified Lydia,
and stuck her long pointed nails into her arm. She
then with abusive words seized the whip, and swinging
the metal knots in the air to give her blows greater
force, struck the poor slave lying at her feet most unmercifully, till she was covered with blood. Her groans
excited no pity, and she was carried insensible from the
apartment. The lady continued to storm, and even the
slaves who were present could not find sufficient words
to express the full extent of the offence. But to appease their infuriated mistress, they out-vied each other
in bestowing a volume of praises on the magnificence
of her attire, and the gracefulness of her slender form.
Such flattery never failed to pacify her.

The toilet finished, nothing more remained to be done
but to throw around her the light white mantle, which
hung in graceful folds over her left arm, and reached
the ground,

All this time, six powerful Syrian slaves were waiting
for her in the vestibule, with a long and easy sedan.

The ancients found it more agreeable to have themselves carried in a litter on men's shoulders, than to be drawn by horses through clouds of dust. In addition to this, the streets of all the cities in the south were so narrow, that carriages were nearly useless. Those narrow streets were, notwithstanding, most advantageous, as they afforded a cool shelter from the sun nearly the entire day.

Metella's sedan was made of finely polished citron wood, on the upper part of which were two poles drawn through, for the convenience of the bearers. The interior, lined with costly stuff, was sufficiently large for reclining, and was provided with rich cushions and a footstool.

The lady descended from her toilet to the sedan, and on her way through the vestibule, her roguish parrot in his ivory cage greeted her with his well-conned speech of flattery.

A boy placed a footstool before the sedan, while the waiting-maids, arranged in a double row, with their arms crossed on their breasts, bowed her off, with all reverence and with no small pleasure. Metella folded her highly perfumed mantle round her, motioned for her little Maltese dog to be brought to her, which she half covered with her mantle, remarking with a smile that her little favorite has a cold, and sneezes often. Metella petted her little darling, and tantalized him with her golden bracelet. She reclined in the sedan, so that she could remain unseen by those whom she wished to avoid saluting.

The lady has taken her departure, and it is now time to inquire after poor Lydia. She was in her little room, resting on a cushion. Ophne, her assistant in the shoe department, hastened to wash the wounds of her maltreated friend, and to give her all the comfort in her power. She expressed the greatest pity, and assured her, that she had herself often been made to feel the effects of the whip. She then began to relate Metella's cruelty in former times, and seemed to find a consolation in doing so. Lydia listened for a few minutes, and interrupted her, saying, "This time, dear sister, our good lady had cause to be displeased. Think only of my awkwardness whereby this disaster happened, and then of the loss she has sustained. We must be just, Ophne, and keep in mind the good qualities of our mistress. Think of the discipline and order she observes in her house; the many blessings she bestows on the poor; and the religious duties she performs so conscientiously every day." Ophne was astounded at hearing such words from Lydia, and at such a moment. "Those are praises," said she, "that we never bestow on our mistress, unless in her presence. When she is absent, we relate to each other her bad qualities. But I have remarked that you never flatter her; on the contrary, what you say sounds more like blame. But one thing you must acknowledge sincerely: is it not true that you feel rather stormy within, whenever you think of her cruelty, and that you will never forgive it." "In a certain sense, dear Ophne, you are right. I have never to forgive anything, because I never feel myself offended." Ophne reflected for a moment, and repeated the words to herself, "I have nothing to forgive, because I never feel myself offended." She could not understand how a

7

poor ill-treated servant, who dares have no other revenge than that of the heart, could resign that also. She was far from suspecting that the man who bears patiently, in faith and hope, suffers also with a holy love. But she resolved that she would, while on her way to the currier's shop, where she was just going, reflect on the sentiments she had heard. Turning to her fellow-slave, she gave her a hearty kiss on the cheek, and said, "You gentle lamb, give me some remedies that will help me to conquer my anger: I should wish to be like you exactly in this respect."

"For a Christian there are many remedies: first, the clear knowledge of one's own imperfections; secondly, meditation on the sufferings of our Redeemer; and thirdly, forbearance and indulgence towards the errors of our neighbor."

"No, my dear, I do not want remedies for a Christian, but for a heathen such as I am."

"I heard once," replied Lydia, with a smile, "that a certain philosopher, who was much given to anger, determined on carrying about him a mirror, so that when anger darkened and distorted his features, he might behold in it their ugliness, and thereby conclude upon the far greater deformity of the interior.

"One word more, Ophne; does not the currier to whom you are now going, sell sheets of parchment? Pray be kind enough to bring me a few."

'What has a sandal-maid to do with parchment," said Ophne, "and where shall I get the money to purchase it?"

"What I want with the parchment, dear child, I cannot tell you, but in any case I can give you the money for it. I have a few pieces of gold which my mother gave me when I was a captive in Smyrna, probably thinking that thereby I might be able to purchase a little civility from the jailer. I did not avail myself of it, but kept the money secreted in my dress, and brought it with me to Athens." Lydia placed it in Ophne's hand.

"But you must tell me," said Ophne, "what you are going to do with the parchment. If you don't, I assure you I'll come back empty-handed. I always looked upon you as my dearest companion in misery, and to a prudent friend you may say anything."

"Well then," said Lydia, "if it must be so, I'll tell you.

"Our mistress asked me lately, when I told her that I was a Christian, if I could not procure for her the famous defence written by the Christian philosopher Justin, and delivered to the Emperor Antoninus Pius. I have in the mean time, through the kindness of our Bishop Quadratus, received the writing. And now I should like to copy it, and surprise Metella with it on her approaching birthday. She does not know that I am a calligraphist, and her joy will perhaps be the greater when she finds the roll in her library. And now, child, you know all; go and bring me the parchment." Ophne stood before her fellow-slave as if transfixed by enchantment. With a gentle pressure of the hand, she gave her to understand, on leaving the room, how clearly she had seen into the depths of her heart.

But a sweet feeling of heavenly enjoyment, such as the

good alone experience when they have performed a generous deed, flowed through Lydia's soul. It appeared to her as though a divine voice whispered to her, "This time thou hast acted well, for when I was fastened to the cross, I prayed for my executioners; I commanded my disciples to love their enemies, to do good to them that hated them, and to pray for those who persecuted and calumniated them."

Lydia had often heard this very exhortation from the lips of her holy bishop, St. Polycarp, who wrote the same in a letter to the Philippians:—"We cannot rise with Christ if we do not avoid rendering evil for evil; on the contrary, we must show mercy. that God may show mercy unto us."

Ophne has returned and brought the parchment with her. Lydia commences to arrange the sheets, draws the line for writing, takes the instrument in her practised hand, and copies the address, "Sent to the Emperor Adrian." She hoped to be able to bring in Justin's defence on a few rolls, and was lost in admiration, as she proceeded, at the beauty of thought, and the clearness, with which the mysteries of the Christian doctrine were explained. She rejoiced at the favorable impression which the writing was likely to produce on the mind of her mistress. She found herself unable to write more than the superscription, as her hand trembled violently at every letter, and in addition the night was far advanced.

Laying down her iron style,* her mind reverted to the actions of the day just at an end. Now and then

* The pen of that time.

she cast her eyes upon the simple cross which hung in her room, and was tastefully encircled with the girdle of St. Polycarp, with which her hands had been bound when she was taken captive in the Amphitheatre of Smyrna. She knelt down before the sign of her crucified Redeemer; for she had much to say to Him ere she completed the duties of the day. With what delight did she fulfil the mandate of our Lord: to pray for those through whom she had become one merit the richer! "Accept, O God! the little affliction of this day, as if my dear mistress had suffered it for the love of Thee. If my patience were agreeable to Thee, do not ascribe this little merit to me, but to her. And should she ever deserve thy anger, then, O Lord! punish not her but me. I offer up myself for her. One grace grant unto her, O Lord!—the grace of knowing and loving Thee, our Lord and Saviour, Jesus Christ."

While she was thus praying, she did not perceive that a hand had drawn aside the curtain which concealed the door of her room,—a few minutes, and it was again closed softly, unheard by Lydia, and Metella passed noiselessly along the corridor.

During the entire time of the military exercises, and the evening entertainment, Metella was greatly discontented with herself. The remembrance of her cruelty towards her poor slave pressed heavily on her soul; and it appeared impossible for her to retire to rest without finding some excuse to say a friendly word to the ill-treated one

But as she found Lydia on her knees, pouring out her griefs to her God, she was seized with a holy awe, and

7 *

departed without uttering a sound. She withdrew into her private sanctuary, there to be reconciled to her offended deity for her conduct; and lighting some frankincense, she strewed it at the feet of the statue, and intermingled the action with penitential prayers. She pressed her forehead glowing with shame to the feet of the statue; but the cold goddess seemed to recede from her: the sculptured form had neither heart nor consolation for the oppressed suppliant. The poor heathen, with a heart full of contrition, resolved on performing an especial act expressing the deepest compunction,— such an act which we never meet with in succeeding centuries, and which had something in it most humiliating. She bent her head and spat three times into her bosom. Then she arose, and retired to her chamber.*

This was a penance amongst the heathens, which had its foundation in the idea of showing themselves before the divinity in the deepest degradation, after having committed a wicked deed. In the Christian religion we have some such custom in the striking of the breast three times, to express thereby, that as the heart is the seat of our injustice, so it deserves to be punished.

* See upon this, Bottinger's "Sabina," A. M. O.

CHAPTER VI.

THE SACRIFICES IN THE TEMPLE OF JUPITER.

HE warlike exercises already mentioned, were carried on throughout the entire winter; and Lucius applied himself to the duties of his vocation with such zeal, that he had already gained the reputation of being a well-disciplined soldier.

The Spring of the year 167, in which the imperial troops from the north of the Adriatic were to meet on the Alps, had commenced. Orders were issued from Aquileia, near to where the two emperors had passed their winter, that the people should use all the means in their power to invoke the favor of the gods. The greatest importance was attached to this campaign. It had to carry the banner of the Romans to the eastern banks of the Danube, and to announce the fame of their victorious arms to the surrounding barbarians as far down as the land of the Jazygan, now called Hungary, and the woody shores of the Theiss. The enemy was known to them; and the renown of Ariovist, the general of the Marcomanni, and of Armin's victory, were

well remembered by them; and could they have forgotten the bravery of the Germans, they had a memento
of it, in the annual procession of the Capitoline geese,
which by their cackling once saved Rome from a nightly
attack of those barbarians. Countless sacrifices bled on
the altars of Aquileia, as well as at Athens. All the
purifications customary since the time of Numa, were
performed. There was also a Lektisternium of seven
days celebrated, which consisted of meats being offered
to the gods on small tables, before which the statues
were left lying, but those of the goddesses were placed
sitting.* To the east of the Acropolis, not far from
Adrian's Arch, where, to this day, sixteen gigantic pillars of Corinthian architecture stand, was the magnificent temple of Jupiter Olympus. This edifice was supported by a forest of pillars, one hundred and twenty in
number, and was two thousand three hundred feet in
circumference. It was Adrian who completed this ancient building. A countless number of statues ornamented the whole, but the one which held the first place,
was the famous colossal statue of Jupiter Olympus, in
gold and ivory, finished by Phidias. In addition to
this, was the stupendous memorial to the Emperor
Adrian, which had just been erected by the grateful
city. This colossal structure could be looked upon as
one of the seven wonders of the world, although not
counted as one, and the ruins, to this day, make an
astonishing impression on the traveller; which can only
be exceeded by viewing the remnant of the Acropolis,—
a city of gods reduced to fragments!—

---

* Stolberg's History d. R. I. viii. 8, 73.

A clear morning smiled from the heavens; the sun had scarcely appeared above the horizon, when the men of Athens fit to bear arms assembled together in their coats of mail and brazen helmets, glittering in the morning sun. Lucius was also ready, and whispered mysteriously in his mother's ear, that the Augurs complained, the day previous, that the sacred chickens would not feed, and that at the last augury, neither a raven nor a crow had appeared. ".Obstinate ravens," added he, "at other times they will croak all the day long."

"Therefore we must pray the more for the assistance of the gods," replied Metella, who was just having a parsley wreath twined through her hair. "An unfavorable augury," said she, "is a serious matter, for thereby people lose courage. Have you not heard what the oracle at Delphi has proclaimed?"

"Oh, the oracle," said Lucius, "that knows no longer whether Crœsus is boiling a lamb or a tortoise.* The golden treasures of Delphi would be more acceptable to us now than its leathern oracles, and a Pythaulus is more thought of in those days than a Pythius."†

Metella now began to reflect seriously on the approaching war, on the unfavorable account of the Augurs, the

---

* A jest on the famous words of the Oracle in the time of Crœsus, who sent, a messenger to Delphi to ask what he was doing at home at that moment. The Oracle gave a correct answer: " That the king was standing before a caldron boiling a lamb and a tortoise."

† There were at this time, according to Pausanius, ten books, great treasures, in Delphi: Pythaulus the combatant with the Dragon. (Phyton was called Pythaulus.) The Oracle gave its last answer about the year of our Lord 366, to Julian the Apostate: " Say to your king that Phœbus has no longer a shelter."

F

probable fate of her only child, and on the sad farewell that awaited her in a few days. While she was buried in these melancholy thoughts, Duranus, the boy whose business it was to strike the hours on the Clepsydra, slipped between the rich Indian curtains hanging before the entrance of her apartment, and announced the hour to her, so that she might hold herself in readiness to at-tend the sacrifice.

What a magnificent and exhilarating sight it was, to see the thousands crossing the plains outside Athens, on their way to the Temple! The vivid flashes from the steel helmets and naked swords; the shields, glittering in the rising sun; the helmet-plumes, floating gracefully on the breeze; and above the heads of the warriors could be seen in thousands, halberts, lances, and standards, — and banners of golden-winged eagles, waving and flutter-ing in the morning air. The legions arriving at the Temple, ranged themselves in order before the altars erected outside, which were richly decorated with wreaths and flowers. A herald stepped forward, and with a stentorian voice commanded profound silence. After the cry "Javele linguss," the priest of Jupiter, robed in a purple mantle, appeared before the entrance of the sanctuary, and the sacrifice began, which, this time, was to be all the more solemn, as Jupiter had not inhaled the vapor of sacrifice from Olympia for a long time. The incense was already burning on a hundred altars, and the smoke ascended from countless thuribles. Then the priest, with a loud voice, and raising his hands to heaven, addressed a prayer to Jupiter, imploring the defeat of the enemy, and the triumph of the imperial arms. He

promised that a portion of the booty, if the Romans conquered, should be appropriated to father Jupiter and his
Temple. Those who stood near the altars, touched them
in sign of consent; others embraced the statues of the
gods, multitudes of which were to be found amongst the
pillars of the temple; whilst many made a circle several
times round, keeping their fingers on their lips in sign
of their devotion.

When this was at an end, a number of magnificently
attired servants, whose duty it was to attend to the sacrifice, walked in procession up through the centre, which
was lined on each side by the warriors. Amongst them
was Popis, with tucked-up garments, who led a white
gilt-horned bull, which was without blemish, and was so
gorgeously decorated with precious stuffs and rich ribbons, that he could hardly be seen. Whilst the animal
was standing opposite the magnificent statue, which represented Jupiter grasping the thunderbolt, and seated on
a throne of ivory, incense was again thrown up and cast
upon the fires which burned on the altars. The smoke
was so dense that the pillars became invisible, and the
rich vestments of those who officiated shone through the
clouds of incense like sparkling gossamer. The priest
of Jupiter advanced, sprinkled the animal with lustral
water, scattered meal mixed with salt upon his head, then
took some finely powdered incense, and threw it on the
forehead of the bull, between the gilded horns. He then
tasted the wine, and gave some of it to the other priests,
who were standing round him dressed in white robes.
After the bull had partaken of a libation of this wine,
some of the hairs above his forehead were plucked out
and cast into the flames.

During this ceremony, Popis stood with his well-sharpened knife, awaiting the commands of the high-priest. On each side of the bull stood the firm-handed assistants of Popis, who partly had to lay hold of the animal at the moment of killing, and partly to catch the blood in the sacred vessels, and to pour it on the altars. Popis then asked the high-priest, "Shall I do it?" who answered, "Do it." At this command, he plunged, with a powerful hand, the sharp knife into the neck of the animal, and during the bellowing, the warm blood of the victim was caught in vessels and sprinkled on the altars.

As soon as the beast had bled to death, the office of Augurs commenced. They began to examine the entrails, and took out the heart and liver; but they examined the latter with the greatest exactness, as being the seat of numerous signs.* With a serious mien, they divided it into two parts, and repeatedly complained that this time it failed entirely in a certain fleshy protuberance. But the heart of the animal, and well-arranged entrails, gave more hope for a happy termination of the war.

The future was ascertained in this manner, and those parts of the victim which belonged to the gods were sprinkled with flower, wine, and incense, and placed upon the flickering embers. Upon this, the people approached and laid down their gifts, which were also burnt in honor of the gods; amongst these offerings were the most costly gold and silver ornaments.

But as this day's sacrifice was too important for only

---

* More advanced Physiology can give a reason why the liver was looked upon as the seat of mysterious signs or omens.

one bull to serve, so the heathens sent Jupiter a countless number of heifers, the principal of which were to be offered to the gods, others for the priests, and the remainder for the people, who sat down round the temple waiting for the feast, with the music of pipes, cornets, and flutes. The feast at an end, prayers were said aloud, the wine was handed round, and then the people were dismissed with the words, "You are allowed to depart in peace." We have now in a few lines placed before our reader a pagan sacrifice; and we leave it to him to judge of the religious element of the action.

Only one remark we wish to add upon the fundamental thought of the action. Sacrifice is the centre, not only of the Christian, but also of the Mosaic, and even of Pagan worship. He who makes the offering acknowledges that he is unworthy of the gifts of the divinity, and that he has forfeited them by sin. Therefore he places on the altars the most beautiful substitute of the gifts of the deity. fruits, animals, and treasures, in humble acknowledgment that he is unworthy of such blessings. The anger of God, according to the ancient faith, was to be entirely appeased only by a sacrifice of life, and hence came human sacrifices;— the blood of man was looked on as the bearer of life, and poured upon the altar. Later on, the blood of animals was offered instead of human blood; therefore the offerings of animals, according to the ideas of the ancients, and also of the Israelites, were a substitute for human offerings.

The religious ceremony we have just described in the Temple was intended to conciliate Jupiter, father of the gods, with mankind, and thereby to make them worthy

8

of his assistance in the coming war. For the same reason, we see the people of Athens, day after day, making their offerings, at one time in the citadel of Pallas, at another in the massively built temple of Mars,* and in numerous other temples of the city.

At length the day dawned in which the soldiers were to take shipping in the harbor of Piraus. It was the day of separation from family, friends, and country. Fathers reminded their sons of the old saying of the Spartan, "Either to return with, or on the shield."

With blessings Lucius extricated himself from the tender embraces of a mother who loved no one on earth more ardently than the fiery youth who now, for the first time, took the field. He knew how to comfort his mother, by placing before her the glorious future, and the high honors which the present war would secure. We shall soon see how he found, that youthful enthusiasm resembles a glittering soap-bubble which only too soon sinks into a drop of muddy water.

---

* The beautiful Doric temple on the west side of Athens is considered to be one of the best preserved ruins of antiquity, and is usually called the Temple of Theseus. Doctor Rosse mentions that this temple was dedicated to the god of war.

CHAPTER VII.

CHARACTERISTIC SKETCHES OF THE SLAVES, AND THEIR MODE OF LIFE.

HEN Lucius departed, his mother gave way to excessive grief. She now felt, for the first time, how tenderly she loved her son. While we leave her in solitude, retired from the world, with an ear for nothing else but the language of a mother's afflicted heart, we will take our gentle readers through the domestic portion of this lady's immense establishment, and give them a little idea of the characters and mode of life of its principal inmates.

To commence then:—In those buildings surrounding the court-yard were an unusual number of cooks, all of whom were well experienced in preparing delicacies. They spared no pains, this very day, in serving up favorite dishes for their afflicted mistress; yet they had not the satisfaction of seeing her enjoy them. The duty of carrying them to table devolved upon youths of the finest form, purchased from the distant north, with their much admired blue eyes and flaxen hair. Next was a capacious hall, the occupants of which remind us of our industrious factory-people. Maids were sitting behind a long row of looms, weaving stuffs, partly for their mistress, and partly for the numerous domestics of the house. In the garden were a still greater number of slaves, some planting vegetables, others weeding flower-beds, and looking after the fruit-trees. But in Metella's olive-gardens, vineyards, and in her country-houses, both at Kephissia and Eleusis, one could only form a perfect idea of the number and occupations of her dependants.

After this general survey, we will now place some of the above-mentioned beings individually before the reader. We will first introduce him to our favorite, who is just now standing in penance in the corner of the front impluvium, the fair-haired Duranus, whose duty it is to stand near the Clepsydra, or water-clock. When he perceived that strangers were coming, he hung down his head in confusion upon the little board suspended from his neck, upon which was written the fault he had been guilty of. As it had gone well with him for some weeks, he took down the whip that usually hung on the balusters, and mischievously secreted it in one of the arbors of the garden. At length his conduct required it, and it was nowhere to be found, till the severe Bogus discovered it, and deeply impressed it on the shoulders of the youth. In addition to this, a log was fastened to his foot, and he had been already standing half the day in a corner of the colonnade. Although he then looked downcast, still his usual aspect was cheerful. He bore a strong resemblance to the playful squirrel, which is happiest when climbing trees.

His gentle disposition often expressed itself in the soft plaintive tones he drew from his Tibia.*

When mischievously inclined, he would take his tambourine and drum upon it with all his might, till Bogus gave him a *sensible* hint that it was time to strike the hour on the Clepsydra.

This Bogus was a rough, hard-hearted man. He had spent some years in the army, of which he was not a little proud, as could easily be seen by the care with which he kept up his military deportment. He is Metella's slave-master, and carries a staff in his hand as the sign of his office, and has the superintendence and power of punishing the slaves. A cap firmly pressed down on his head, and tightened round his full, bloated face, gives one to understand that he is no longer a slave. Formerly he was one, having been taken prisoner of war, with other soldiers, and made to pass under the yoke in the market-place of Athens. He was sold as a slave to Metellus, from whom he had afterwards received his freedom. A scourge would have suited him better than a staff, for nothing gave him greater pleasure than to tie a slave up to a pillar, and fasten a heavy weight to his feet, in order that he might have him in a straight immovable position, to receive an uncertain number of lashes. His cruel disposition resembled Caligula's. This Emperor one day ordered several youths of the best families of Rome to be lashed, and then put to the torture, and this merely for pastime. His severity to his inferiors was only equalled by his cringing servility and uncomfortable politeness to his superiors.

* A musical instrument of that day.

8 *

A similar situation to that which Bogus had once enjoyed with Metellus, his deceased master, an old female slave, nearly sixty years of age, named Selina, enjoyed with his mistress. She was an African by birth, and had passed more than half her life with her present mistress. She had known Metella as a child, and was purchased by Atticus in the slave-market of Rome, to nurse his little Chrysophora. Her dark-brown African countenance formed a humorous contrast with the fair, delicate complexion of her youthful charge; and Atticus never thought that his little daughter looked lovelier than when she was reclining in the arms of her ugly nurse. Selina, therefore, knew the whole life of her mistress, and had so great an affection for her, that she preferred living as a slave with her, than to accept the freedom proffered her. But this affection was almost her only good quality, for in consequence of her evil dispositions, which increased with her years, she made herself perfectly insupportable to her fellow-slaves, and was so uncharitable, that she could not have a servant near her, to whom she did not speak in confidence against every other person in the house. In spite of this, it was to her a matter of the first importance, that she should bear a high character in the eyes of all. On the other hand, she was such a hypocrite, that she poured forth her flatteries not only on her mistress, but on the very meanest of the slaves. This cringing character is a quality in the Africans. Though so old, she daily used a number of superstitious means to preserve her dark beauty; and being ashamed of her short woolly hair, she concealed it with a handsomely folded turban. As she had been so long in service, she was able to put by a considerable sum, for she received monthly wages in six measures of corn and five florins in money. With her savings she had her own peculiar way of speculating, and resembled the Indian ant, which, it is said, collects gold out of the earth. She bought, from time to time, a cheap slave, made some profit by his labors, and then disposed of him at a great gain. Her last purchase was a first-rate gold embroiderer, who cost her but forty florins. She knew so well how to save her money, that she never, without absolute necessity, parted with a farthing. Nevertheless all this hoarding could secure her, in this life, no further distinction from her fellow-slaves, and none after death, save the solitary privilege of having her body consumed on the pile. But in order that our gentle readers may not imagine that all Metella's slaves were like the gray-bearded Bogus or the swarthy Selina, we will now say a few words of the gentle Ophne, of whom we have already spoken, and of Thrax, the dwarf.

Ophne, during the few years she had spent in the service of Metella, had passed through a series of difficulties. At first, she was employed in the lowest manual labor, then she was raised to the dignity of dusting her lady's sandals. Her next step in advancement was, that she learned to work in leather, so that she could finish off sandals to the perfect satisfaction of her mistress. With extraordinary facility, she could imitate the pattern of everything she saw, in the way of needlework, and complete it equal to the original; and one had only to give her a sign, and she brought exactly what was required.

It was irresistibly droll to see her, when chosen to accompany Metella on a walk. Fearing that her numerous friends would not observe her in company with her mistress, she bustled along, fanning her most attentively, then nodding to her friends, first to the right, then to the left, so that her perpetual motion would lead one to suppose that quicksilver ran through her veins.

Thrax, the dwarf, stood in direct opposition to the lively Ophne. At the age of five, he was purchased by a Greek slave-merchant, and his being extremely small for his years proved his greatest misfortune. His diminutive size suggested to his master the idea of training him for a dwarf. For this purpose, he was put in a dwarf-case, as Phinius expresses it, that, by constant pressing and a sparing diet of fruit, he might not exceed the required height—three feet. After having been trained, he was offered for sale in the public market-place of Athens, where the good Metella purchased him at a high price, but much more through pity than for a household fool. Thrax not being a dwarf by nature, had not their usual qualities of wit and sarcasm, but was, on the contrary, a gentle, harmless little fellow. A smile played round his lips, which kept up a medium between laughing and crying. In the goodness of his heart, he willingly allowed each one to make merry at his expense; but at the same time, although he answered in a friendly manner the questions put to him, one could see by the tears starting in his eyes, that his feelings had not been stinted with his growth. Metella, as well as her son, had always treated him with great kindness, and any one who required his departure had only to say something of the absent Lucius, whom he tenderly loved, and he would instantly disappear and hide either in a corner of the garden, or somewhere in the house, to give vent to his feelings.

It was useless to talk of freedom, either during the ancient Republic, or during the time that Rome was an empire; but when we know that this freedom was built upon the servitude of two-thirds of the population, we begin to change our opinion. To give an instance: Athens, in the time of the Governor Demetrius Phalereus, 300 B.C., had about 21,000 freemen, 10,000 half-freemen, and 400,000 slaves. Therefore there was a glaring disparity between freemen and slaves. The following is another historical example, which casts a blemish on the highly-lauded freedom of ancient Rome. It was a law, that, when a master was murdered in his own house by one of his slaves, and that the murderer could not be discovered, all the slaves of the house had to die. The rich Podanius Secundus of Rome was thus murdered by one of his slaves, and four hundred were, according to law, put to death. The people objected to its being carried out, and sought to save the unhappy creatures; but the Emperor Nero, to whom the shedding of human blood was a pastime, had the way, by which the condemned were to be led to death, lined with soldiers; and the cruel sentence was fully enforced. A record is still extant from which we may infer how great the number of slaves was which one master could possess. This law strictly forbade that a master, in his last testament, should grant freedom to more than one hundred of his slaves, if he had twenty thousand! "He is a poor man," cries Seneca, "who can find pleasure in a service of slaves more numerous than the army of a warlike nation, and in private edifices the circumference of which exceeds great cities, and when he compares what he already possesses with what he still desires to have, he is in comparison a beggar."

With so immense a number of the oppressed, we need not be surprised when the Roman history informs us, that from time to time they rebelled. For example, the insurrection of the slave Eunus and his sixty thousand followers, and later on that of Spartacus, who met the Romans in the field with forty thousand. They were conquered, and put to death by the sword, or crucified by thousands.

Some hundred years later, we hear the rattling chains fall from the hands of the slave; but who, many will ask, helped them to war and to freedom,—Eunus, or Spartacus, or One who stands higher than all Roman Emperors—God?

CHAPTER VIII.

JUSTIN'S APOLOGIA.

IT was Metella's birthday, and all vied with each other in presenting marks of affection to their good mistress. Graceful garlands were twined tastefully round the colonnades leading to the palace. The most beautiful fruits and flowers that field and garden produced, were brought in ornamental baskets, and placed in rich profusion. Some were occupied in strewing leaves and flowers, while others were mixing perfumed artificials, procured from the Egyptian florist, with the green garlands.

The newest and best works were exhibited; garments, girdles, sandal-ties, and fans,—all of which were received by the lady with great condescension and acknowledgment of the industry displayed.

But a present, that she found the evening before in her book-case, surprised her more than all the rest. It was a roll of parchment, on which the following inscription was beautifully written:—

"To the Emperor Titus Ælius Adrianus Antoninus Pius Augustus Cæsar; and to Verissimus his son, the

philosopher; and to Lucius the philosopher, son of
Cæsar by nature, of Pius by adoption, a lover of learning; also to the Sacred Senate, and the whole Roman
People: in behalf of those who, of all nations, are now
unjustly hated and aspersed,—I, Justin, son of Priscus,
grandson of Bacchius, of Flavia Neapolis, in Syria of
Palestine, one of their number, present this volume and
address."

When Metella read this long title, she immediately
guessed from whom the present came. But she was still
more astonished to find that it was written by Lydia
herself. Her Christian slave had already made a deep
impression on her mind, since the time she discovered
her on her knees before her cross, in her little room,
praying for one who had just treated her so cruelly.
She then formed a high opinion of her exalted virtue,
and this opinion was not lessened when she received
this last proof of her noble revenge.

"If the Christians thus reward injuries done them,"
said she to herself, "they cannot possibly be guilty of
those crimes which are attributed to them."

Metella then ordered the writer to be called into her
presence, and assured her that she admired more the
motive whence the gift proceeded, than the gift itself.

"This writing," said she, "I have long wished for,
but never could procure it till now. We must read it
together in a quiet hour; I value Justin so much, because he had the courage to proclaim his convictions.
Although Plato stands higher in my estimation than all
the other philosophers, still there is one thing in which
he is blameworthy, and that is, that, notwithstanding

his belief in the great Creator of the world, he sought in a speech delivered to the Athenians, to inculcate the popular belief in the plurality of gods, fearing that like Socrates he might lose his life.*

"Would you like to know the doctrine we hold? Perhaps it approaches nearer to yours than you suspect. We believe that Jupiter is the Beginning and the End, and that all things proceed from him.† Our school accepts also that Jupiter has subordinate gods, like messengers, who execute his commands. We therefore are widely separated from the doctrines of the lower classes, and from the flighty Romans. Their folly cannot stand.

"The poets have no right to make new gods, to embellish the history of their lives, and to force them on the people as truths. Homer and Hesiod ought to have been branded as impostors and sent into exile. Each one after, according to them, invented new gods, so that now we have trouble enough to remember even their names. There is no such thing as a god with goat's-feet."

After a short pause, she said, "With respect to this, do you know that very important oracle of the dead Pan?"

"Certainly," replied Lydia.

What do you know about it?"

"In the reign of the Emperor Tiberius Epitherses, the father of the orator Aurelian, together with many others, tound himself on board a merchant's ship, in the vicinity

* Justin calls this a punishable denial of Plato's better convictions. Virgil *f.* " Exhortations to the Greeks."

† Doctrine of Orphiger.

of the islands called the Echinades. The sun had gone down, when, not far from the island of Paxos, a voice was suddenly heard which called to Thamus the helmsman, who was an Egyptian, and whose name was scarcely known on board. A general astonishment seized all present, and the helmsman remained silent to the first and second call; the third time he answered, whereupon the voice swept loudly along the surface of the waters, and said, 'When you arrive at Palodes, announce that the great Pan is dead.'

"Not far from Palodes, Thamus turning his face towards the land, called out from the far end of the ship, 'Great Pan is dead!' Scarcely had he uttered these words, when a general lamentation issued from a multitude of voices on shore.* It is remarkable," added Lydia, "that this extraordinary circumstance took place just at the time of Christ's death."

Metella listened to her slave with pleasure. After a few words of praise, she said, "It would be more in conformity with your attainments, if for the future you attend to my *head* rather than my *feet*. I have therefore resolved, from this day forward, to make you my reader." This advancement filled Lydia with anxiety, being convinced that every preference excites envy, and that this would excite discontent. She therefore determined, from that moment, to be more obliging and friendly than ever towards her fellow-slaves, well knowing that an obliging manner blunts the arrows of envy.

"I know also," continued Metella, "that I have to make reparation in some way for my unkindness towards

* Plutarch upon the fall of the Oracle.

you a little time back. But to show you that I am not insensible to fine traits of character, accept this silver mirror as your own property, and dispose of it as you please." Lydia was too sensitive not to feel repugnance at receiving payment for the trifling pleasure she had afforded her mistress in the parchment-roll. But to refuse the valuable present would offend Metella, therefore she accepted it with humble thanks, and gave her mistress to understand that she knew how to value the gift.

Selina witnessed this interview from an adjoining apartment, and could scarcely refrain, when she saw Lydia leave the room with her present, from recalling her late awkwardness again to the mind of her mistress, and from adding her *charitable* remarks.

The next day, Lydia entered upon her new office, and commenced by reading the *Apologia.*

"Is it not true," said Metella, "that the philosopher, Justin, was a follower of Epicurus?"

"Justin," replied Lydia, "is a philosopher, and if I do not err, he wears, at the present moment in Rome, his philosopher's cloak, and gives instruction in the Christian doctrine. He is a native of Neapolis in Samaria, and formerly gave himself to the study of Plato; but as it did not content him, he became a convert to the Christian religion. As such, he wrote his Apologia for the Christians, to the Emperor Antoninus Pius and the Senate."

"We'll now read. But first of all, impart to me Justin's Christian ideas of God."

She commenced:*

* What follow are but fragments of St. Justin's renowned *Apologia.*

"We acknowledge the true God, the Father of Justice and of all virtues, in whom there is no mixture of evil. We reverence and worship Him and His Son, who came down to instruct us, and also the Holy Spirit."

"This faith," interrupted Metella, "is, without doubt, very different from ours. But still more unlike, and it is said even immoral, are the customs of the disciples of Jesus Christ."

Lydia read, in answer, the following passage:

"Now let us relate in what manner we have dedicated ourselves to God, having been created anew by Christ. Those who promise to live according to the precepts of Jesus Christ, are taught to pray and to fast, and to entreat from God the remission of their past sins, we praying and fasting with them.

"Then they are conducted by us to a place where there is water, and are regenerated, being washed in that water, in the name of God the Father and Lord of the universe, and of our Saviour Jesus Christ, and of the Holy Ghost. We there pray earnestly for them in common; and salute one another with a kiss; after which, to him who presides over the brethren, bread is brought, and a cup of wine mixed with water. And he having taken them, sends up praise and glory to the Father of all things through the name of the Son, and of the Holy Spirit, and employs much time in offering up thanks for having been deemed worthy of these things by Him: when he hath ended the prayers and the thanksgiving, all the people present express their assent by saying Amen, which in the Hebrew tongue signifies, *so be it.* Then they who are called among us Deacons, give to each of those present a portion of the bread and wine mixed with water, over which the thanksgiving has been made, and carry away a portion to those who are absent. This food is called amongst us, Eucharist, of which no one is allowed to partake, but he who believes that what we teach is true, and has been washed in the laver (of baptism), which is for remission of sins and unto regeneration, and who lives as Christ has delivered.

"For we do not receive these things as common bread and common drink; but as both flesh and blood of that same incarnate Jesus."

"According to this," remarked Lydia, "we are taught, that, as soon as the thanksgiving is pronounced over the bread, it becomes the flesh and blood of Jesus Christ, and passes over into our flesh and blood, to nourish our souls."

"The Apostles," she read on, "in the memoirs composed by them, which are called Gospels, have written, that Jesus gave them this injunction: that, having taken bread and giving thanks, He said, *This do in remembrance of me; this is my body*, and that, in like manner, having taken the cup and given thanks, He said, *This is my blood.*

"We have also, on that day which is called after the sun, an assembly in one place, of all who dwell in the cities or country; and the memoirs of the Apostles, or the writings of the prophets, are read. Then when the reader has ceased, the president delivers a discourse, in which he reminds and exhorts to the imitation of these good things. We then all rise together and pray; and when we have ceased from prayer, bread is brought, and

9 *

wine and water: and the president, in like manner, offers up prayers and thanksgiving with his utmost power, and the people assent by saying Amen. Those who are able, give money, according to their means. The president takes charge of the collection, and distributes it to the orphans, the widows, the sick, to those in prison, and to strangers; in short, he is the guardian of the oppressed.

"This meeting is held on Sunday, because this is the day on which Jesus Christ, our Redeemer, rose from the dead.

"So far as this appears to you truthful and reasonable, so give it due esteem. If it appears to you only empty talk, despise it. But do not condemn harmless men to death as enemies. But we·tell you beforehand, that, as long as you persevere in injustice, you will not be able to escape the judgment of God. But we exclaim, let it be done as it pleaseth God."

The learned Grecian listened to the *Apologia* with attention. She knew well the impression it had made on the noble Antoninus Pius, and that the Emperor had sent out orders to Athens, Larissa, Thessalonica, and other great cities, forbidding them to persecute the Christians. As soon as the *Apologia* was finished, the young Christian was obliged to answer numerous questions put to her by her mistress. For example, she required information on the life and miracles of Jesus Christ, and on his family. Above all, she admired the Founder of Christianity, on account of the calmness and greatness of soul He exhibited in his agonizing death. "Formerly," added she, "such a death seemed more fitting for a malefactor than for a great man. But Plato, who has also described the Just One, has taught me, 'Virtuous till death, he will be looked upon as perverse and unjust, and as such, scourged, tormented, and fastened to a cross.'* Since I have made myself more familiar with this view of Plato, I am more reconciled with the sort of death that your God suffered." Though she had not the most distant idea of becoming a Christian, still the *Apologia,* which held the highest place amongst writings of that description, was a means by which she became more intimately acquainted with the Christian doctrine.

Lydia recommended her mistress to speak on the religion with the most learned men, and named for that purpose, the then Bishop of Athens, the pious Quadratus, whom the Church now reckons in the number of her saints. She offered to make the humble Bishop acquainted with this wish, but said, if she preferred a conversation with a Christian philosopher, Aristides was one, and he also had composed an *Apologia,* which, according to Eusebius, the writer of Church History, was to be found in the hands of many. There was also the renowned philosopher of Athens, Athenagoras, who had written a book on the resurrection of the dead.

Metella promised to think further on the matter, and for that day put an end to the conversation.

---

* Rousseau acknowledges, in his Emil, i. 4, " Plato paints here Jesus Christ feature for feature."

CHAPTER IX.

THE SILVER MIRROR.

T is well known that the ancients were strangers to the luxury of glass mirrors, for the Phœnicians, afterwards called Tyrians, who first discovered the art of making glass, kept it a secret among themselves; and it could only be purchased from them for its weight in gold. It is recorded that even so late as the time of Nero, it was so expensive, that this Emperor paid £50,000 for two small drinking-cups of transparent glass.

The mirrors of those days were made of burnished gold or silver, for the nobles, while the lower classes had to content themselves with highly polished baser metals, or by looking at their reflection in a vessel of water. Later on, as the love of splendor became the order of the day, mirrors were made as large as the human form, and were at last set in precious stones. A single mirror cost a lady more than a dowry, and the daughters of poor generals were provided with this commodity at the expense of the city.*

* Seneca's *Meditations on Nature*, 1st Book.

The mirror which Lydia had received as a present from her mistress, was of an oval form, and although it did not sparkle with precious stones, still it was one of great value. Looking in it one day, affected her with more than ordinary melancholy, for her own features recalled forcibly to her mind the calm but suffering countenance of her mother. Lost in thought, her imagination carried her to distant Rome, and placed her in a narrow cell, wrapt in the embraces of her captive parent. Returning to her sad reality, she exclaimed, "O could I but know whether slavery or a prison separates us! how gladly would this precious mirror be parted with for thy ransom." At this moment she was interrupted by the friendly Ophne, who entered with a large parcel of ribbons, which she had just purchased. "You look melancholy, dear Lydia," said she, "but I'll tell you something that will cheer you. The man from whom we purchase our leather, has a grown-up daughter, named Aspasia; she is as light in her character as she is handsome, and on this account she is known throughout Athens. Only think, Lydia, she inquired most particularly after you. She would like to know you, and, if agreeable, would bring you into much company. But remember, she belongs to those of light character, or, as others say, she is one of the noted persons of Athens; and if I had not a solemn dread of your morality, I could tell you much more about her." Lydia was silent, and the other continued, "I have heard of her for the last two years. Latterly she thinks of entering the married state, but she must first have a good sum; and as she cannot get this, she must go on in the old way." Lydia still pre-

served a dead silence, and Ophne receiving no encouragement, said, "Now I must go to my mistress and show
her these beautiful ribbons, and give her back the remainder of her money."*

An opportunity offers itself here to speak a few words
upon the moral state of Athens, at this time. Still it is
an ungracious task to call up mouldering bodies to the
light of day, and where would you come to an end?
Therefore let this alone be understood, that the Athenians, immediately after the Persian war, put up a painting of Venus, under which was represented a procession
of the Athenians, and below, the following inscription,
written by the poet Simonides: "These called on the
goddess Venus, and for the love of them she saved
Greece." Solon himself, the Stoic lawgiver, caused a
temple to be built to the shameless goddess; and in a
short time the whole of Greece was a scene of abomina-
tions. In Athens, honorable marriage no longer found
a sanctuary. Vice was thus raised into a religion, and
therein lay the worst and most horrible of all errors of
which the heart is capable.

From the time that our young Christian had received
information of Aspasia, she made a firm resolution not
to oppose the wished-for acquaintance. But how different were the motives which drew them together! The
one had the intention to destroy,—the other to save. A
few evenings' later, Lydia and Aspasia were actually
seen at the corner of a street, engaged in deep conversation. Lydia was not a severe judge of morals, for she

---

* At this period, silk was as expensive as glass, and the Emperor Aurelius
refused his Empress a robe of that material.

knew that the human heart, even if under the pestilence of temptation it has lost blossom after blossom, still receives an impulse from God to bud anew, and, like the barren fig-tree which stood by the wayside, was not to be cut down immediately. She quickly discovered the untainted and redeeming qualities of the erring girl, and joined the better she advised, to the good already there. Several times she expressed a wish to hasten as much as possible the marriage she had in view. Aspasia was touched with such rare kindness, and although she had no idea of becoming better, this language, which she heard for the first time, was to her heart as refreshing as the nightly dew to a scorched heath.

During this conversation, one of Metella's slaves passed by without their observing her, and she could scarcely believe her eyes when she saw the young Christian speaking with a votary of Aphrodite.—It was old Selina.

Her astonishment was still more increased on meeting the same party, some days later, close to the Charon gate.* Aspasia's position had so touched the heart of the zealous Lydia, that she turned over in her mind, day and night, how she could in any way assist the strayed sheep, and snatch her from the errors of her ways, or at least help to the sum necessary for her marriage. It occurred to her that the silver mirror was of more value than her pay for three years' servitude, and that at that moment she could not dispose of it better than for the salvation of an immortal soul. Then she thought of her absent mother, and of the possibility that the

* Charon, so called because it led to the place of execution.

mirror might release her from her chains.   But the trust
she placed in Divine Providence gave her confidence for
the future, and decided her on parting with her mirror
for the present emergency.` Religion also suggested to
her, that her love for an unhappy erring soul must not
be inferior to that which she bore for her own mother.
According to her resolution, the following evening she
carried her valuable mirror concealed under her cloak;
—one Eye alone witnessed the act, an Eye that knew
and appreciated her intention.   What a touching impression did not this present make!   How expressively,
and with what childlike simplicity, did not the donor
assure the receiver that the mirror was not stolen, and
how often did she entreat her to say nothing of the matter!   Aspasia had not wept for years till then.   She gave
the promise to have her present converted into money,
and to change her way of life immediately.   There was
now a sort of friendship cultivated between two souls
who, in word and work, were without doubt widely
different, but still resembled each other in tenderness of
feeling.

After this act, a heavenly cheerfulness played in
Lydia's eyes, and an interior happiness, the cause of
which she imparted to none.   In this silent enjoyment
of her heart, she performed the daily duties of her state,
at one time writing, and at another reading for her mistress; but while these occupations were going on, she
knew little of the judgment that was passing on her in
the house.

Selina had been long waiting for a favorable opportunity to impart to her mistress, in secret, an affair which,

as she said herself, not only threatened the reputation of
the domestics, but also that of their mistress. This opportunity at length presented itself.

"Not many days ago, noble lady," so began Selina, "I
was an eyewitness to a detestable affair. Your wisdom
will scarcely believe it possible, that one of your domestics has rewarded your goodness with the most shameful
ingratitude. Others have labored for nearly half a century to gain your favor, and have scarcely once received
a present, while that black-eyed Asiatic, who is scarcely
two years in your service, has the most valuable articles
from your gracious hand. Young Lydia is just what we
always suspected her to be:—she had the courage to
attach herself to a doctrine which not only permits vice,
but commands it. These broods of hungry Christians
assemble together in the holes of the rocks; they seat
themselves on the bones of their slaughtered children,
and devour their flesh. That the magpies sometimes
steal money, is well known, and I'll not inquire *what
money* purchased the sheets of parchment which were
written on, not long since, for a birthday gift. Her
secret depravity of life I have at last discovered, thanks
to the gods!—Not long since, I saw her with a certain
Aspasia, who is well known in Athens as the finest berry
on the Upas-tree of vice,—and later on, in the evening,
I met them again speaking confidentially with each other
in the open square. What she whispered in that girl's
ear, who is not ashamed to go through the market laughing and dressed in her suspicious-looking gay costume,
is easily to be guessed at. Night increases the suspicion;
and to this most suspicious person, by whom we shall all

10

lose our reputation, you make presents, and distinguish her above all your other slaves."

Metella at once perceived Selina's malice, and calmly replied, "Sophocles says, 'Silence is the ornament of woman.'—Where did you see Lydia?"

"At the end of the Hermos street, noble lady,—at that place near Stoa's pillars where stands Lucian's magnificent dwelling."

"Do you really believe," said Metella, "that Christians commit the worst crimes, like our Œdipus?"

"O yes! but with this difference, that Œdipus did not know what he was doing, while the Christians premeditately commit all sorts of crimes, and are forced to it by their priests.· Before you, Lydia knows very well how to conduct herself; but let her have the ring of Gyges, which is known to make one invisible, and then she will give herself up to all sorts of wickedness."

"One solitary cause of suspicion is not sufficient, Selina, to punish the accused. If she be really guilty, it will quickly be discovered; then she can be scourged, and if that does not do, she can be put to death."

The last expression pleased Selina so much, that she ended this conversation by a lengthened encomium on Metella's severe sense of justice. As Selina herself was doubtful whether she should be able to detect Lydia again in the company of Aspasia, she ordered every slave in the house to have a sharp eye upon her. For this purpose, she related to them all that she saw with her own eyes at Adrian's Stoa, and begged them to tell at the moment, if they ever discovered her with Aspasia. The good Ophne was zealously occupied in trying to persuade Selina that there was not an atom of injustice or wrong in the matter. But in order that Lydia should be able to defend herself, she informed her of the reports that were in circulation about her. When Lydia received the information, she expressed herself in gentle terms, as follows, "I must remind Selina not to spread false reports concerning me;" but for the rest she remained as quiet as before, and gave all to understand that she did not bear the slightest revengeful feeling, nor even a dislike, towards her. "Sensitiveness," she used to say, "belongs only to little minds. A good sword and a pliable heart will bear bending without breaking, but an untempered blade snaps when used in battle. To me the saying is as precious as gold, 'Act well, and suffer blame.'—It is possible," she added to herself, "that it was a ridiculous notion of mine to loosen the bands of a sinner; if Polycarp had met this sinner, she would scarcely have deceived him.* Possibly he would have called her in his short way, the first-born of Satan. Perhaps she is so, and that I have greatly deceived myself. But there are errors which tend more to the honor of man than to his shame; yes—'more precious than wisdom and honor is a little foolishness for a short time.'† Therefore I shall be able to bear my error in this case."

Nevertheless, she began sometimes to think the language of despondency. "You have lost your country, your mother, your master, your freedom," would she

---

* St. Polycarp one day met the heretic Marcion, who asked him if he knew him. "Yes," said Polycarp, "you are the first-born of Satan."

† Eccles. x. 1.

say;—"one thing only remained of your temporal
goods—your reputation,—and this seems also to have
vanished." But she would quickly reproach herself for
this language, and call to mind how much the disciples
of our Lord had suffered. She would cast a look
through her open window at the Areopagus, where St.
Paul once stood and preached to the Athenians the
"Unknown God," and say to herself, "What did not St.
Paul suffer? Four times he suffered stripes, three times
he was whipped with rods, once he was stoned, and at
last ended his life by the sword: and shall I feel oppressed, when I receive an injurious word? Ought I
not to tread joyfully in the blood-stained footsteps of
my Redeemer, who was condemned by the Jews as a
blasphemer, and by the Romans as a rebel against the
authority of the state? Therefore, poor heart, seek thy
consolation, not from the lips of thy fellow-creatures,
but from the sufferings of thy Creator and Redeemer!"
In this reflection she found continued peace. Thus has
the sight of our crucified Lord through centuries comforted the oppressed and raised their courage; and as
the dove, when chased by the eagle, saves herself in the
crevice of a rock, so the persecuted heart flies from the
calumny of the world, and seeks peace and comfort in
the sacred wounds of her dear Redeemer.

Months had passed away, and Metella could discover
no fault in Lydia, not even that she had become less
friendly,—when the old Selina, one day, sought again
to rouse the suspicion of her mistress against Lydia, by
saying that her silence was a proof of her guilt.

Metella lost all patience: "I know," said she, "your

venomous sting, and know also what to think of you. Guilt tries to defend itself, but innocence prefers to be "silent."

Metella was perfectly convinced, from that moment, that there was no truth in the vile accusations against Lydia, and came to the conclusion, that, just as her Christian slave was calumniated in her own house, so Christianity was calumniated in the world; and as she bore all these accusations with equanimity, nay even with cheerfulness, she won the increased affection of her mistress, who thought that Christianity was best known by the life of a good Christian; and the Pagan esteemed it so much the more, the more beautiful the virtues were that she saw practised by her Lydian slave.

A few weeks later, Metella visited one of her friends, and saw, to her great astonishment, the silver mirror she had given as a present to her slave, lying on a small table. With an impatient curiosity, she sought to discover how her friend had obtained it. She said that it was brought to her by a certain person called Aspasia, and offered for sale.

So, thought she angrily to herself, my slave is really then in connection with this wretch! "Oh, I beg of you, let the girl be sent for who sold it you! She will tell us how the mirror came into her possession." A slave returned in a few minutes with Aspasia, who related that a Christian girl made her a present of the mirror, on the condition that she would, without delay, enter upon a previously intended marriage. "This, and the petition of a Christian maiden quite unknown to me, that I would change my course of life, not a little

10 *   H

surprised me, and I shed a flood of tears. Then I vowed to the gods to reform my life, and what I have vowed, that I will conscientiously keep."

Metella listened to this declaration, and felt abashed that even for a moment she had suspected her virtuous attendant, who had borne so much in silence. She returned home, firmly resolved never to utter a sentence of what she had just heard. She acknowledged herself conquered by the virtues of a slave, for she could not believe herself capable of practising such greatness of soul. Yes, she even doubted if in all the heathen philosophy a solitary example could be brought forward to compete with the modest virtue of her Lydia, and was at a loss to know which most to admire, the delicate purity and patience, or the strength of character displayed in observing a profound silence in the midst of her persecutions. The last quality, bearing wrongs patiently, appeared to her, without doubt, the pearl of Lydia's virtues.

How beautiful is chastity, when she lifts her clear eye to Heaven and feeds on the contemplation of her God! How admirable is meekness, that rewards hatred and contempt with prayers and charity! But it is not to be denied, that doubly to be appreciated, as the queen of virtues, is silent innocence crowned with the thorns of calumny.

A few weeks after, while Lydia was reading, one evening, to her mistress, the sounds of music reached their ears; they found that it proceeded from a bridal party, which was just passing under the window where they were sitting. Both stood up to see it more distinctly, Metella leaning on the shoulder of her slave. The bride suddenly stopped and drew aside her veil:— it was Aspasia, who cast a look at Metella's palace, and perceiving her benefactress, waved her hand; then dashing a tear of gratitude from her eye, she covered her face again with her veil, and passed on.

Metella thought she recognized in the features of the bride the girl for whom Lydia had so nobly suffered, and turning quickly, perceived by her slave's countenance, that she had conjectured rightly. Fearing to be questioned, and unable to disguise the joy of an approving conscience, Lydia asked permission to retire. She sought the solitude of her chamber, and kneeling before her cross, offered up a fervent prayer for Aspasia's perseverance in a virtuous life, and in gratitude to God, for having made her the humble instrument of drawing a soul from vice.

CHAPTER X.

NEWS FROM THE SEAT OF WAR.

A. D. 171.

HE termination of the war with the Parthians, A.D. 166, brought with it a lamentable evil. The soldiers returning from the East, carried with them the plague, and infected all the provinces through which they passed. Even distant Gaul suffered under this pestilential devastation; and it was so dreadful in Italy, that in several parts, as contemporary writers relate, agriculture was abandoned, and famine had set in. In Rome, the dead bodies were conveyed out of the city in immense numbers, and interred at the public expense. Athens also, and the whole of Greece, experienced the horrors of this evil, in greater or lesser visitations, which returned for several years together.

The cases of death, this summer, were so numerous, that Metella determined at once to remove from Athens to one of her estates in the country.

Previous to her departure, letters from the seat of war

were brought by carrier-pigeons to Aquileia, where they were detained and copied, as the delivery was doubtful. The originals were kept, and the copies attached to the pinions of these peaceful messengers, which were allowed to continue their journey to Rome or Athens, laden with the tidings of war

By this means, Metella received intelligence from Lucius. Sitting, one calm evening, at her open window, occupied only with the thoughts of her absent son, she heard a gentle fluttering, and raising her eyes, she beheld the faithful little courier waiting to be relieved of its burden. With the letter in her possession, she retired to her apartment, to enjoy it undisturbed,—where we shall leave her for a time.

The sun had sunk to rest, and night was closing in, as Lydia, in her little chamber, finished her task of writing. While the leaves were drying, she advanced towards her lightly curtained window, opened it and gave herself up to meditation.

All around is still, save the slight rustling caused by the waving of the palms, with their long and graceful branches, bending till they kiss the earth, and bounding back again upon the bosom of the jealous breeze. In the court-vestibule are heard the soft murmurs of the gurgling fountain. High in the wide expanse of heaven, Night, the silent widow of the Day, is seated on her throne. Her face is hidden by a veil of stars, and her sable mantle hangs in graceful folds upon her darling universe. She illumines softly, with her lamp, the moon, her plague-infected client, and bedews her with her widow's tears.

To return to Metella, who, having finished her letter, leaned her head carelessly on a cushion, and began to reflect on the contents. At length she closed her weary eyes, and sank into a gentle slumber. The letter, which lay beside her, commenced with the words: "From the camp;—Lucius to his beloved mother, health and happiness."

"Many months have passed since I have crossed the Alps, and saluted the clouds of heaven so near at hand. But, dear mother, believe me, that not a day passes without my thinking of you. I remembered you particularly, when first I beheld the Danube from Noricum.* You once read to me, as a boy, from a Roman historian, that towards the end of the world, this river will no longer flow at the foot of the mountain, but will swell to the summit, tear up rocks, and carry with it chains of mountains. You can imagine with what ideas I reached this renowned river, yet notwithstanding its great breadth, I was still disappointed when I saw that it was no wider than our flower-garden at Kephissia. You have already heard how matters stood in our tedious war, before we reached Aquileia, and that the Marcomanni had gained a victory over the Prefect Vindex, who, with twenty thousand Romans, was killed, and the retreating army pursued as far as the Adriatic Sea. This had all occurred previous to our leaving Athens. It is now nearly five years since the Emperor entered Pannonia,† and we have been waiting, week after week, expecting to come to a decided engagement,

* The land to the east of the river Inn in Bavaria.
† A part of the present Styria as far as Hungary.

which is to conclude the campaign. Our conquest over the Jazygan was accomplished in a droll manner. The barbarians held us at bay upon the frozen Danube, trusting that they could fight famously on the masses of ice, their horses being much better accustomed to slippery ground than ours; but we threw our shields upon the ice, stood on them, and then drew over to us our horses and riders at once, and we fought a magnifi-- cent battle. Also in the two succeeding battles the Marcomanni and Jazygan were well humbled. Another time, when the Danube was free of ice, we wished to frighten the barbarians, and sent amongst them some lions we had just received from Rome. The animals crossed the stream and attacked the enemy, who bravely met their antagonists, killed them with their clubs, and stood laughing and exulting over their newly acquired booty.

"You can scarcely believe, dear mother, how difficult it is to conquer such an enemy. The trumpets of war are to them an agreeable music; they intrench themselves behind their fortifications, and wait courageously for the attack. To fear, they are strangers. They tie up deserters to the enemy, as cowards, and those who take to flight are suffocated without mercy in the swamps and morasses. But incomparably worse than all this is their climate, which is so cold and damp, that we have a fog nearly every day. At home in Athens, months pass on and the heavens cheer us with their clear blue, whilst in Germany we find, even in the midst of summer, scarcely a cloudless day. O how I now prize our clear Grecian climate! The fur cloak you sent me by Bogus

is of the greatest service to me, particularly when we
sleep in the cold camp. We fought our best battles in
the hot summer days, for, though the Germans bear
hunger and cold with heroic patience, they succumb to
thirst and heat much quicker than we do. Their food
would not suit our Athenian epicures. Many of them
are satisfied with crab-apples and thick milk. But if
they had as much beer to drink as they can take, we
could vanquish them easier by their drunkenness than
by our arms. In their time of peace, they give themselves up to idleness or to the chase. The principal
difference existing between the Romans and Germans is,
that the former are masters in eating, and the latter in
drinking. Not long since, we discovered in a field a
large mound, and on a nearer approach, we curiously
examined it, and found beneath, huge stores of apples,
pears, and corn. Suddenly the ground gave way, and
some of the soldiers fell into a subterraneous cave,
whence, alas! they never more came out. We were
obliged to leave them behind us, and discovered, when
too late, that the Germans, with wives, children, and cattle, frequently dwell in such caves, to protect themselves
from the inclemency of Winter. Dear mother, would
you could see these gigantic, hardy men, one like the
other! Their clothing, and the effects of the climate,
render them insusceptible of sickness. They generally
die of old age. They are trained up in such endurance
and hardihood, that for the most part they never spend
a thought on either their clothing or their food. May
those souls and bodies, which know nothing of effemi-
nacy, riches, or debauchery, receive wisdom and well-

ordered armies. Perhaps, dear mother, you would like to hear a little about the religion of these barbarians? I regret that up to the present time I have been able to learn but very little on the subject. They have ancient poetry from time immemorial, and this is the only trace of knowledge they possess. They sing of a god, Tuisko, who sprung from the earth, and that he had a son, called Mannus; and these they style their ancestors. Also Mercury is held by them in great veneration, and they bring into their dark forests and sacred groves all those taken in war, to offer them to him in sacrifice. The reputation they have gained for morality is well founded. A female may be as beautiful and rich as you please, but if her reputation be once sullied, she falls into general contempt. There are tribes amongst them that only marry virgins, and the widows after the death of their husbands remain single. Should a married woman injure her husband's honor by incontinency, the husband cuts off her hair, and whips her with rods out of his dwelling, in the presence of her relations. This morality of the barbarians, dear mother, we do not find amongst our cultivated people; but I can assure you, that in our legion, in which there are many Cappadocian Christians, quite as great a morality reigns as among the barbarians. They are very industrious; they neither drink nor swear, nor make what are called soldiers' jests. They believe in one only God, and pray to Him daily. Nothing is more interesting than to live amongst them.

"I suppose you have heard that Verus is no more? He was sitting in the chariot with Marcus Aurelius, when he was struck with apoplexy, sank on his shoulder,

11

and expired. His body was not embalmed, but buried in the land of the barbarians. The day previous to his death, I had the honor, with some Greek nobles, of being invited to dine with him. I acknowledge that I was not a little rejoiced at the invitation, after having been nearly five years without tasting a morsel of wholesome food, leaving delicacies out of the question. The banquet far exceeded our expectations; and not one amongst us could comprehend how it was possible in this country to keep so luxurious a table. The Emperor was very gay and jested with me, asking me, as each dish was placed on the table, if I knew its name; to my answers in the affirmative, he always replied, 'Ah! missed the mark!' and then gave the dish its German name; so that we always doubted what we were eating. Still more choice were the wines. Verus had three cups beside him, — one was of Alexandrian crystal, the second of Oriental Myrrha, a material unknown to any of us, the third was of gold, and set with precious stones. When we drank the health of the Emperor, he gave us a sign to keep our cups.* After wine, we played at dice till the morning dawned. Claudius Pompeanus, son of a Roman knight, was my companion at table. He was astonished when he heard my name, and assured me that he had known you in Rome. That must certainly have been a long time ago; and when I told him that I intended to send you, my dear mother, a present of my valuable cup, he begged that I would afford him the pleasure of having some verses engraved on it.

* It is related that this Emperor once before presented his guests with a chariot each, and also with chariot-drivers.

"Bogus, who arrived here two months since, and offered himself as volunteer in the cavalry, could relate to you what beasts there are in the dark forests. Not long since, he was dreadfully beaten through mistake. Being very cold, he sought to bring down a bear for the sake of the skin. On our arrival at the camp one evening, after an engagement, Bogus, with some others, returned again to the hills, where we had left some dead bodies. To entice the bears out of the adjacent forest, he cut the head off a German, and seizing it by the hair, threw it down the hill, and it rolled to the edge of the forest; he repeated the experiment, and at length he succeeded, for a hungry bear made his appearance. As soon as he attacked the head, Bogus laid him low with an arrow. He stripped off the skin and clothed himself with it at once. So muffled up, he arrived at the camp towards dusk. The soldiers were taking their evening meal, which consists of bread and cheese, and beer, a beverage which the Germans prepare from barley and corn. Suddenly seeing something approach that had the appearance of a bear, they started up, rushed out upon him, and did not discover their mistake till he had been severely beaten. He was dreadfully injured, and I doubt much if he will ever recover.

"But now, my dear mother, I must conclude; the cold prevents me from writing more. What should lie nearer to my heart than to assure thee of my unbounded filial love! O how great is the distance between thee and me! —yet my mind, that travels without the aid of bark or wing, is ever near thee. You are in the south, and I, in all probability, am on the northern boundaries of the globe. The human race has only extended itself as far as here. It may be possible that, after a few hundred years, these forests may be cleared away, and cities be reflected in the waters of the Danube; and that civilization will extend from one end of the world to the other. For the present, I believe, with our poets, that Delphi is the central point of the earth, and that there mankind thinks and works longer, and therefore they are more cultivated. What a secret, dear mother, lies in this growth of nations, and what an answer our mind receives, when it returns to the cradle of our origin, and asks itself as to the beginning and end of the world's history! But where am I?

"I hope a few months will see me return rich in years, in experience, and in the deeds of a brave soldier, to give a lasting proof of my filial gratitude to thy loving heart. Farewell!"

Such were the contents of the letter that Metella had lying before her on the table. She is dreaming,—she starts, and shrinks as it were from an invisible hand. She raises herself from her couch, and quickly gives a sign for Lydia to enter.

"Have you not just heard the angry screaming of an owl?" said she, as Lydia approached. Lydia answered in the negative, and added that she had been standing at the open casement of her little apartment, listening to the playing waters of the fountain, and admiring the majestic silence and beauty of the night.

"I must have dreamed then that I heard an owl cry. Do you understand the interpretation of dreams? Perhaps, as a Christian, you can explain to me the meaning

of mine. Listen to me: After having finished reading
my son's letter, I sank into a soft slumber. It appeared
as if everything were dark around me. I wished to go
forward, but I was without a light, and I could not find
a road, because of the darkness. You were near me,
and were my only guide. Over my head I observed a
light, which gradually increased in brightness. This
light proceeded from a mountain; at its foot was a flight
of marble steps, which appeared to reach to the summit.
I perceived at a great height a magnificent garden, in
which were an immense number of female forms clothed
in white, and they appeared to be in constant motion.
Far beyond these, I saw a most dignified being,
clothed as a shepherd, and seated on a magnificent
throne. His appearance, though imposing, had nothing
in it to terrify. His throne was so high, that the white-
robed multitude appeared far beneath him, while they
with uplifted eyes gazed unceasingly on his loving
countenance. His garment changed suddenly to that of
a dazzling white, his heart was visible, round which
were rays far brighter than the sun, which cast streams
of light upon the worshipping multitude, who sank ever
and anon upon their knees before him, and looked like
little lambs round their shepherd. But what was most
strange, at his feet I saw a youth who resembled my
son Lucius, and who beckoned me to join him; a naked
sword lay by his side, and he was reclining on his
shield. Then a longing desire seized me to climb the
marble steps. I pressed forward, but I felt as though
my feet were bound to the earth. You then conducted
me to the steps; but as I approached, a dragon, with

11 *

eyes flashing fire and licking a deep wound on his left side, prevented my ascending. Retreating with horror, I perceived an owl perched on the protruding branch of a decayed tree; it flapped its wings and screamed angrily at me; my strength failed, I lay prostrate on the earth, and awoke with the screaming of the owl still ringing in my ears.

"Now tell me what is the meaning of that magnificent being and the heart surrounded with rays; and why did I see my Lucius reclining at the feet of that shepherd?"

Lydia did not dare to trust herself in giving the signification of this dream, and therefore answered, "My good mistress, pardon me if I do not feel myself capable of interpreting your dream. I beg of you to request the explanation of it from those who are more capable than I am. According to your description, it was, perhaps, the Son of God Himself, who has revealed to you his magnificence. He was designated, while on earth, as the 'Good Shepherd,' and his followers flocked round Him like lambs. Once they beheld him on the summit of a mountain and shining like the sun. But I am quite unable to explain the entire vision. We have in Athens holy men, true disciples of their Master, who know their Lord, and can tell you much of Him. They will also be able to explain your dream correctly."

"Do you believe, Lydia," said Metella, "that the philosopher Athenagoras, who became a Christian, and who formerly visited me, would still consent to hold converse with, and advise a heathen?"

"Dear mistress, as a Christian he is more at your service than ever."

"Then, if you think so, send to-morrow early and invite him. He is certain to be found in Plato's academy: I meet him there sometimes, standing at the tomb of the immortal philosopher."

CHAPTER XI.

ATHENAGORAS.

YDIA was only too happy to convey Metella's desire for an interview to the renowned philosopher, who cheerfully and promptly accepted the invitation, and at the appointed hour he found himself seated by the side of the illustrious matron. This learned man was as well read in polite literature, as in the Eastern and Grecian philosophy. He hung so ardently on Christianity, that some years later he advocated the cause of the Christians with the Emperor Marcus Aurelius. A philosopher of the Eclectic school, he collected from all systems what agreed most with his ideas. He besought the Emperor to observe the same clemency towards the Christians he exercised towards the religions of so many other nations under his sway. Metella commenced the conversation by assuring Athenagoras, that she did not belong to those who despised Christians, for she had often heard from her deceased father, that the Christian doctrine made those who lived according to its dictates, moral and happy;* and that lately she had an opportunity of becoming better acquainted with it, and her esteem for it was increased. She said that one of her slaves was a Christian, and she had often related to her about the Founder of her religion. "But yesterday, having had an extraordinary dream, which my slave would not undertake to interpret, I availed myself of an assurance she made me, that you would solve its meaning. It appeared to me as though I saw a shepherd, who was at the same time a king, in the midst of a host of beings clothed in white. I felt a holy awe before this shepherd, I worshipped him in the distance, and felt that I loved him. Oh teach me to know him!" After having related to him her entire dream, she begged the philosopher to explain to her its meaning. After a moment's reflection he told her that he considered her dream as a favor from God, and one which in every respect would carry that good with it, that from the present time forward she would entertain a new interest for Christianity. From the details-of her dream he took occasion to speak to her about Christ, who is truly the Shepherd of his flocks, and to describe to her the happiness of the life to come.

"Do you know," said he, "that that king is the only Son of God, and of the same nature with the Father and the Holy Ghost. Are you acquainted with the doctrine of the unity of God in the Trinity?"

Metella replied, "I know the Platonic doctrine of original existence; and I know also that Plato com-

* Atticus was obliged to declare in writing to the Emperor Antoninus Pius his approbation of Christianity.

I

manded us to swear by God, the disposer of all present and future things. I am aware, also, that the Christians consider that the statue of Jupiter at Elis, with its three heads, has some signification. But allow me to say what I think of such doctrines. I think that no mortal is capable of comprehending the existence of the Divinity. Is not that a beautiful inscription that the Egyptians have written over the statue of the God at Sais:—'I am the All that has been, that is, and that is to be, and no mortal has yet raised my veil'?*

"You ask me if I know the Christian doctrine of the Triune Deity. It could not have been explained to me in fewer words, than I heard it not long since, by a comparison from my Christian slave. 'God,' said she, 'is one in His nature just like the tree; the roots, stem and branches of which are penetrated by the same existence. As the stem proceeds from the roots, so is the Son generated by the Father, and as the branches of the tree proceed from the stem and roots, so does the Holy Spirit proceed alike from the Father and the Son.' —But, Athenagoras, how many things can be made clear to us by comparisons! Allow me to expatiate a little longer on my comprehension of the Divinity. Man is the world in miniature, his body is the picture of the earth, and his soul the reflection of the Divinity. Whoever has formed the human body has taken the earth for his model. We have a proof of this in our own members,—our bones and flesh are of earth, our veins are the streams, the waters of which are called blood. The air is converted into breath, and in order that the

* Plutarch Is. 9.

sun and moon may enlighten all this, and be reflected in the human body, he has given us eyes. But one remark more, Athenagoras, and then I conclude. Of this magnificent body, this masterpiece of visible nature, an invisible spirit takes possession, governs it and penetrates it in all its parts, and this spirit is one. And so it may be one, and only one, who created this visible world, and this one we call Jupiter—Jupiter with his divine spirit and divine understanding. So you have another comparison, or, if I may say so, more than a comparison—a proof of the unity of God."

"You are right," said Athenagoras, "and I participate in your views. We Christians say also, there is only one God, as the soul of man is one; but have you forgotten that this soul of man is a three in one?"

"How so?" asked the heathen.

"One," replied Athenagoras, "is the memory, another the understanding, and the third the will of man; and yet our thinking, understanding and willing, though three, are only one."

Metella reflected:—"Oh yes, I remember Plutarch also defended the three powers in man. If the soul be created after the image of God, so also can the Trinity be already in the Soul, an ordering, willing, and loving God. Possible also that our own hearts are a reflection of the heart of that loving son, who out of pity for sinful man, as you say, took our nature upon Him, and became the Shepherd of the people. But let us return to this shepherd whom I saw in my dream. Oh, He looked so mild upon those who stood round Him! and so lovingly on my son, who clung to his feet! Tell me how did my Lucius obtain admittance into this divine company?"

"Perhaps," replied Athenagoras, "that your son, during this campaign, has made himself acquainted with Christianity, and has united himself with confidence to its Founder, by which he enjoys undoubted peace and feels himself supremely happy."

"But what does this mean?" said she, "I saw him raise his hand and beckon to me so earnestly as if he would say, 'Come to me.' Durst then a heathen enter where those blessed beings are crowding round their king?"

"When he beckoned, he thereby expressed his happiness and a wish for you to participate. To attain the height on which Christ had His throne, two things deter you; and it appears to me that now I come nearer to the meaning of the vision. By the dragon that you perceived on one side, and the owl on the other, the first signified, according to our books of revelation, no other than the origin of all evil from the beginning of the world, whom we call Satan.* He tries to hold man down to the earth, leads him to sin, and tempts him to it; and those who give themselves to his service, he brings at last altogether in one place, where they are perpetually tormented like your Tantalus.† He also seeks to deter you; he does not wish that you gain Christ and the happiness of Heaven. The Redeemer has weakened the power of Satan, but has not entirely

---

* Apocalypse, c. K. 22, 2.

† Tantalus tormented with a parching thirst bends to the wave, which each time recedes from his lips, and returns as he removes his head. Odyssey, XI, 5822.

destroyed it; and therefore Satan resembles a wounded dragon, as you describe. But it is not he alone that separates you from Christ; there is also another hinderance which makes your union with Him difficult; and this is signified by the owl. Minerva, the goddess of wisdom, and the guardian of this our city, which is acknowledged to be the asylum of the intellectual, is represented by the owl. It signifies human wisdom, which is folly before God. Philosophy endeavors to acknowledge this contest, and would like to attain, through its own strength, the altitude of truth. But for this its wings are too weak. O, how modestly Plato expresses himself when he says, 'One must bring together the best of human proofs, and then venture upon them as on a raft through the tide of life, but still he thinks one can sail more securely, and with less danger, in a stronger ship on a Divine Word.'* This divine word, Christ has spoken, and this firm ship is the Church."

"You must pardon me, Athenagoras, if, just like an ignorant child, I ask you many things about your system. What did you mean when you spoke of a bad principle and of a Tantalus torment prepared for the wicked?"

"As the good," answered he, "will be once with God, the source of good, for all eternity, so must the wicked be with the father of wickedness, for all eternity, and for ever separated from God. As the reward of the good will be without end, so will the punishment of the

---

* Semmias to Socrates in Plato's Phædon.

wicked be everlasting; and this is one of the most important dogmas of Christianity."*

"In this respect," replied Metella, "Christ and Plato quite agree; both teach, that the good will be happy, and the wicked unhappy. Plato says: 'Those who have led a pure and well-ordered life, receive the gods as friends and guides, and dwell with them; while those, who on account of their greatness of crimes remain impenitent, sink their fate in the well-merited Tartarus, whence they never more return.' But Plato mentions another place, Acheron, whither all the imperfect were sent. 'Those who are there,' said he, 'will do penance for their faults, and when they are purified will be liberated.'* If then there are those different places, do you not believe that, according to my dream, my son will one day be counted among the blessed? for you know I saw him near your God." "No doubt," replied Athenagoras. "And I," said Metella, "if I attend to the advice of Plato, where he wills that no one shall change the religion of his ancestors, and remain a heathen, do you believe that I shall one day be received into the kingdom of Light where my son feels himself so happy?"

"When you have once learned what Christianity is, and by the means of grace have acknowledged it as the one truth, then, Metella, the Divinity and your own understanding will require from you to proclaim this truth openly, and not till this happens can you hope to attain this heavenly enjoyment; but if after this you persevere in error through a vain fear of man, you will never be one of that company in which you beheld your son."

* All these three states are taken out of Plato's *Phædon.*

"What, Athenagoras, do you think it possible that a son could feel himself happy if he thought that his mother were in eternal misery? Oh what a sorrowful happiness would that be for my Lucius, to know that his mother was in a place of torment!"

"As the rain falling into the ocean partakes of the quality of the water with which it mingles, so do the souls of the just partake so much of the qualities of the Divinity, and consequently of the love of justice, that they hate what He 'hates, and love what He loves, and it would displease them as much as God Himself, if the wicked were to be rewarded with eternal happiness."

"I do not understand this exactly, but I think I can guess what you mean: that there is in the other life merely a relationship either with the good or the wicked. But how could I avoid drawing down upon me the hatred of some one or other of the divinities, were I to worship the God of the Christians, and thereby fail in my fidelity to the religion of my ancestors?"

"You speak now, Metella, of several divinities, which you confidently look upon as servants of the great Jupiter: there are no *gods* — therefore no hatred amongst the *gods*. You are still unable to attain the conviction that all power, in Heaven and on earth, streams forth, not from a plurality of gods, but from one God alone, and just in that respect is the difference between the faith of the Christian and that of the heathen. According to the views of the heathen, Heaven has its Jupiter, the sun his Helios, the sea its Posidon, the fountains their Naiades, the tree its Dryas, and even the reed its Syrinx. On the contrary, according to Christian doctrine, there reigns in Heaven and on earth but one Almighty God, and the spirit of this same God shines forth in the sun, and moves upon the face of the waters. He has care for the tree and the flower, and forgets not, in His fatherly protection, the smallest•blade of grass. The thoughts of God are shed in millions of beams on all creatures; He is the centre whence all proceeds. Yes, Metella, God is only one, and this one God requires from you that you acknowledge Him with your whole heart."

"Beautiful and dignified as this doctrine is, Athenagoras, and though it agrees so much with my spirit, I feel myself as yet too weak to acknowledge it openly."

"Faith," continued Athenagoras, "is a gift of Divine Mercy; but to obtain this gift of Faith, it is necessary that you should withdraw yourself from the pleasures and distractions of the world, and give yourself up to prayer in silence and solitude. Thus have all those done who strove after the Truth,—yes, even the disciples of our own great sages. The voice of God allows itself only to be heard in the soul of man when all is still; but if God has once commenced to speak, His voice is as loud and audible as the rolling of thunder in a spacious and desolate mountain valley."

"Athenagoras, can you answer me one question more? I see that those who call themselves Christians are ready to sacrifice their lives for their faith. With the cool blood of the Spartan, and the tranquillity of a Socrates, they undergo martyrdom and death for Christ. Whence comes this resolution, this living conviction?"

"You put questions, Metella, which convince me that

this is not the first time you have spoken on Christianity. All those who seal their Faith with their blood, are fully convinced that Christ is truly the Son of God. Christ gave proof of His mission, as clear as the sun, often during life, and particularly in the last days before His death. He told the Jews publicly that He was the Son of God. He said to them beforehand that He should be put to death, and that on the third day He would rise again. Yes, and He was brought before Pilate, and conjured by the living God to say if He were really the Son of God.* He maintained it, although He knew that his death would follow the declaration. After His death, His side was pierced with a lance, and His body laid in the grave, and that grave was guarded by soldiers. But on the third day, as He had already said, He rose again by His own power, appeared to His disciples, and showed Himself on many occasions to several hundreds of His followers. All those who saw Him believed in Him, and they preached Him to the world; and not alone those proclaimed His doctrine, but all whom He had strengthened, previous to His death, by the numerous miracles He had worked. Therefore, as Quadratus, the former Bishop of Athens,† declares in one of his writings, the sick whom Jesus healed, and the dead He brought to life, were not a passing vision, for those very persons remained with Him upon earth; and some, added

---

* The High Priest said to Him, "I conjure Thee by the living God that you tell us if you are the Son of God." Jesus answered him, "Thou hast said it." Matt. xxvi.

† This Bishop Quadratus is not to be understood as the Quadratus of a later period. The above was the successor of St. Publius, and was appointed to the Episcopacy of Athens 125 years after the birth of Christ.

12 *

the same Bishop, lived not only after the ascension of our Lord, but even up to his own time. We all acknowledge this belief with joyful hearts, and it affords us comfort in this life, and a happy assurance of a better."

"Not so fast, Athenagoras; but so far you may rest assured, that I will follow your advice with regard to retirement, to help me in reflecting diligently on the dignified doctrine of Christianity, and daily beg of the unknown God, to whom you have drawn me nearer, that He will make Himself known to me."

CHAPTER XII.

THE COUNTRY SEAT AT ELEUSIS.

EFORE the rich Domina arrives at her country-seat, which bears the simple appellation "Theretron," or "Summer-Seat," we will invite our gentle readers to visit this magnificent Villa, situated at a short distance from Eleusis. It is only half a day's journey from Athens, and can be as easily attained across the Piraus and the sea, as by the so-called "Holy Street" or "Sacred Way." Outside Eleusis is a rich and well-watered plain called the "Thriasische Field;" and although not a drop of rain has fallen for some months over this land, still the corn, refreshed by the night-dews, stands in all its rich beauty, and the country has not yet exhibited that weary, desolate appearance which in Greece returns every year with the beginning of the second harvest. Upon this plain stand various-sized statues of Pan,* twined with the Acanthus and wild flowers, which the artistic taste of the Greeks knew so well how to arrange, and which thereby diversified

* Pan, the god of the fields.

the otherwise monotonous appearance of this flat country. Countless numbers of sunburnt hands are everywhere occupied in collecting the gifts of Ceres, to store them up for the Winter. Here we meet beasts of burden, watering in the cisterns, and drawing their heavily-laden wagons. In the distance are to be seen herds of goats, feeding on the rich pasture; while the goatherds are playing cheerfully on their reed pipes. On the sides of yonder little green undulating mounds, long terraces are erected, for the cultivation of the vine, of that peculiar sort which grows in Corinth, and the fruit of which is exported to different countries under the name of currants. On the top are dirty little fellows, dressed in goat-skin, lying lazily about, under the shade of the elm-trees, and refreshing themselves occasionally with the first-fruits of the vine. The higher hills towards the North are covered with palms and other forest-trees; and in the background, the scene is completed by the "Höhenzug of the Katharon," uniting itself to the rugged and light blue Parnassus with its cloud-capped summit.

Metella's charming Villa was situated on a gradually sloping hill; at the foot flowed the silvery waters of the Saramanta, on whose fertile banks flourished in abundance, the laurel and the dark myrtle, and the slopes were studded with clumps of the Tamarisk and box-trees. The Villa was surrounded on every side, except that facing Eleusis, with groves of palms. From the centre of the building rose a high turret, whence a charming view of the surrounding country could be obtained. On one side, the level plain opened to the sea, on whose shores stood the rich trading-town of Eleusis, in the centre of which rose, in imposing grandeur, the renowned temple of Demetrius, famed for the so-called "Eleusian Mysteries." Every year, at the commencement of October, a great procession was formed at Eleusis: and four days previously, the festival of Demeter was celebrated at Athens. On the sixth day, the child of the goddess was, in the midst of rejoicing, carried out through the sacred gate in a wicker basket. Priests and officials accompanied the statue, and those in the procession bore agricultural implements and ears of corn. On the seventh night of the festival, the form of consecration took place, and the vows of those about to be initiated into the Eleusian mysteries were received. The charm of this worship lay in the mystery of it, — in the lively dramatical representations, — in the co-operation of all the arts and artistical enjoyments of music, song, and dance, — in the dazzling illuminations, — in the effective decorations, — in the most refined enjoyment of the senses, — and above all, in the promises of a happy future after death. If you ask in what these mysteries consisted, antiquity gives no satisfactory answer. It was strictly forbidden to reveal them; and whoever did so, had every reason to dread the punishment of death. Plato was suspected of guessing the mysteries, whereby we may infer that the doctrine of his philosophy resembled that of the Eleusian. So far, it is certain that the foundation of this ancient worship, which existed as far back as the time in which the Ionians moved from Attica to Asia Minor, rested on a certain belief in a future state. "In the Eleusian," says Cicero, "one learns not only to

live happily and holily, but to die with a cheerful hope."
"Thrice happy," says Sophocles, "are those mortals who
have seen these consecrations before they descend to
Hades. For them alone is life in the next world; for
others, only sorrow and afflictions." The more noble
and refined were of opinion that their happiness would
consist in being constantly occupied in sweet devotion;
but the greater number thought, with Plato, that they
would have a continual enjoyment of the senses, and
endless intoxication. But we cannot be very far wrong
in concluding, that those mysteries took their origin
from the ancient Patriarchs, and that corrupt actions and
doctrines mingled later with the original true worship.
No wonder then if the ambitious Romans, such as Octa-
vius, Adrian, Antoninus, and Marcus Aurelius, had
themselves initiated into these mysteries. In Athens,
according to Lucian, A.D. 176, there was but one man
at that time who did not belong to this worship.*

Westerly from Eleusis, expanding wide, are fields of
rice, with its dark-red blossoms, which add to the
beauty of this flower-enamelled plain. Like a sheet of
silver in the distance, shine the smooth waters of the
lovely bay of Salamis, and the blue mountains of this
charming island rise in majestic beauty, thinly veiled
with the vapors of the sea.

* As the Christian Emperor Valentinian, A. D. 376, forbid the heathens to
hold their nocturnal solemnities. Prætextas, Proconsul of Greece, petitioned
that the Eleusian Mysteries might be an exception. The reasons he gave
were, first, that without these mysteries, the people would lead a comfortless
life, a life that would be no life, because it would be deprived of those cere-
monies which were a symbol of a future and everlasting life. Second, that to
separate the life of man from the comforting belief of a future, was only to be
compared to a living death.

To the East is the "Sacred Way," that leads from Athens, and winds itself, serpent-like, along the shore. Where it once lay, are now, in many parts, impassable swamps. Here and there, at prominent points of view, could be seen magnificent monuments containing the ashes of renowned Greeks. Those tombs in the "Sacred Way" extend as far as Kerameikos, interrupted now and then by little oratories to Jupiter, Phœbus, Aphrodite, and to some of the great heroes; so that this scene transported the traveller to the "Via Appia" in Rome, so great was the resemblance.

How deceptive is the sea! It smiles at times as friendly as a lake. There was a day on which the waters of Salamis ran red with the blood of the Persians. Thousands of them found their death in this bay,— their iron, their gold, and the Eastern decorations of their generals, lie buried in its depths, whence no hand can draw forth the sunken treasures.*

To the present day, the Greeks look down proudly from the heights of Salamis, when they think of the conquests of the ancient Hellenes, without which the entire history of Europe would have had quite another aspect. And yonder, where now the light-hearted fisherman tunes his song, thoughtless of the past, once flourished, on the shores of Corinth, the two cities Helice and Buris, which in one eventful day vanished from the earth, and sank beneath that blue sea, leaving not a trace behind.†

* On the last day before the final battle, Themistocles took three captives, nephews of Xerxes king of Persia. At a sacrifice not long after, he drank a quantity of ox blood, to which Plutarch ascribed his death.

† This event took place A. D. 370.

To observe some order on our entrance to the Villa, let us first visit the Urbana or Castle, then the Rustica or Stabling, and lastly, the Fructuaria or Granaries.

The entire front of the Villa presented to the view a princely palace built in the form of a hollow square, and bore a strong resemblance to Metella's mansion in Athens. The windows were of a transparent material,* and sheltered from the sun by framed blinds.

The gate-keeper was standing near the Corinthian pillars, which were twenty feet in length, supporting the vestibule, and beside him was a majestic watch-dog of the favorite Eperean race. The dog appeared to be a vigilant guard. Over the entrance was his likeness in Mosaic, and under it the following inscription, "Protect yourself against the Protector."

The entrance-hall was profusely ornamented on each side with numerous busts. To the right were the ancestors of Atticus, on the left, those of Metellus. Those in Parian marble, and particularly the ones of more recent date, were finished in a style worthy of a Scopas or a Praxiteles. Peeping from behind the statues, were the laughing faces of lovely little boys, painted on the Lotus flower, with the finger on the lip, and with an expression of caution on the countenance, which clearly conveyed to the visitor the idea that the statues of those great men must be approached in silence. In another part of the Hall were copies of Polygnots, from the Stoa Poikile in Athens, amongst which stood the Philosopher Zeno, who, when living, might have been seen in that gallery of paintings.

* A mineral called moonstone was used by the ancients for windows, previously to the invention of glass.

Alabaster statues, crystal vases, large candelabra of white marble, numerous smaller figures in transparent stone, or the famous Corinthian bronze, stood here and there in this richly decorated hall. After having passed this hall, which ran right through the front portion of the palace, we enter the square court-yard which was enclosed on every side by the wings of the building, and with a treble pillared colonnade all round. What a mass of curiosities here present themselves!

Inside the fluted pillars were to be seen a little forest of the choicest shrubs, varieties of grasses, cool mossy turfs, and rustic seats. The centre of this square was occupied by a fountain, whose playing waters rose to an immense height, and falling again into an expansive basin, refreshed all around. In smaller basins, supplied by water from the fountain, were sparkling gold-fish, sailing about in the cooling fluid, and turning to the sun in playful gambolling their fiery scales. Birds without number, warbling in the shrubs, and bathing in the cool waters of the fountain, completed the charms of this little paradise.

Over the grand hall which projected from the house, was a spacious dining-room furnished with slanting lounges, upon which those at dinner could recline at full length, leaning their elbows on a high cushion, and supporting the head on the hand, according to the ancient custom. Together with this dining-room, the entire story was called "cœnaculum." The third story, except the Sacrarium, in which a light was kept constantly burning, was occupied by the slaves. It consisted of a number of little rooms, the front windows of

13   K

which looked out upon the open country, and the back upon the court-yard already mentioned. Those looking towards the court-yard, reached the floor and opened on a terrace which ran the whole length of the wing.

Independently of this court-yard, the edifice boasted of a second one, of the same size and somewhat further back, separated from the first by an intermediate building called the women's department. In this second court-yard was an elaborately finished marble bath, sheltered from the sun by an awning. The pavement round the bath was Mosaic, and represented animals, fruit, and flowers. Generally speaking, the principal floors of this Villa, particularly of the reception-rooms, were of mosaic workmanship, which had the advantage of keeping the apartments cool.

We next visit the out-offices adjoining the palace. What most attracts our attention in those, are the numerous rows of windows. This portion was occupied by Metella's male slaves who had the charge of the flower-gardens, meadows, olive-gardens, and flax-fields. Under this dwelling were the stables, the doors of which we only open hastily here and there. They were filled with an abundance of horned cattle, horses, and a sort of black swine with soft shiny skins, such as can be seen at the present day lying about in the streets of the Grecian cities. Then again there were vaults for hares and rabbits, and others for geese, turkeys, and all sorts of poultry.

After this, follows the "Villa Fructuaria," which excites in many respects greater interest, for it contained large and various wine-cellars. In the back cellar were

several goat-skins filled with the wine so much valued
by the Greeks, called Lesbos; these were sealed with
pitch. Rhodian and Lydian, and also the beloved Fa-
larian, were not forgotten. Other cellars of the Fruc-
turia contained stores from Metella's olive-gardens,
which were partly delivered to the great merchant-
ships, and partly sold at the new Market of Athens.
The store-rooms for corn, hay, and garden-fruits, occupied a large space in the Fructuaria, and enclosed off
this part of the Villa. Lastly, one look at Metella's
garden. It may appear strange that, two hundred years
after the birth of Christ, one met with the same artistic
ornaments which are to be seen in the nineteenth century, particularly in France and Holland, where the
tasteless custom prevails of cutting one tree like a pyra-
mid, another like a lion, and a third like a crowing
cock, so that one imagines he is entering a menagerie
rather than a pleasure-ground. The peacock, the favorite bird of the ancients, struts about here in all his
pomp, and proudly swings his tail on high and spreads
it out in the form of a fan. The villas of the rich are a
clear proof of the extravagance of Greece, which, with
sculpture and all works of art, gave occupation to the
greater number of the half-freemen.

Every flower-bed had its peculiar attendant, a white
or colored statue. The flowers change according to
their species, and their quantity and variety would
have embarrassed a Greek of ordinary education, to
name only one of these children of Flora, so foreign
were these plants to that country. The ever blooming

gardens of Egypt provided nearly all the country villas of Greece with bulbs, seeds, and cuttings. Italy also sent her charms here;—a soft breeze waves its balmy perfume from the flower-beds of Sicily; and Metella's garden offers you a bouquet of spikenard, Myrrh, and the lovely Acanthus.

CHAPTER XIII.

THE POTTER AND HIS CHILD.

I N a magnificently gilt chariot, drawn by white horses, Metella drove up to the entrance of her Villa. Could we then have seen the number of her attendants, standing on the marble steps, and the majestic form and haughty look of this noble dame, as she gracefully ascended, recognizing neither to the right nor to the left a single slave amongst those who stood in crouching servility, with arms crossed on the breast, to welcome her arrival, a doubt would have passed through our minds, whether this proud lady would ever tread the thorny path of our Faith.

But Divine Providence has always means at hand to humble our pride. As the autumnal winds strip the trees of their withering foliage, and mingle it—aye, that of the mighty oak—with that of the meanest shrub, and leave them bare and desolate till the coming Spring, so the Providence of God is wont to blow away, with the winds of affliction, all the vanities of man, and level his proud heart to the dust, leaving it for a time empty, desolate, and bereft of all consolation.

We see here but slight grounds for supposing that Metella will ever become a disciple of Christ, or a lover of self-denial. Yet a few days later she made a slight beginning, by a sort of condescending benevolence, of which we shall give an example.

On the following morning after her arrival, as she was walking in the court-yard, and, fanned by her maid with an artistically woven peacock's tail, she saw, at the end of the interior court, which was somewhat hidden by an ornamental shrubbery, a poor, but very cheerful old man, sitting near the kitchen-door. His flowing hair and peculiar woollen mantle bespoke him to be a sort of artisan.

He is a potter by trade, and his name is Hyllos. While sitting on the cool Mosaic pavement, and leaning against a pillar, he little thinks that a stranger is observing him closely.

Poor Hyllos had just brought to the palace some kitchen-utensils from his work-shop, and had ardently hoped that he would have received payment for them on delivery. But it was not so, and after his long walk, he had only received a piece of dry bread from one of the cooks. A little annoyed, as he had not had anything to eat that day, he seated himself down close to the kitchen, and commenced talking to himself. "Well, Hyllos! but you are a poor, pitiful old blockhead! you have overworked yourself the whole week, and now you have nothing more for your trouble than a bit of dry bread. Oh, hunger bites! but stop! you growling old fellow! don't you smell an amazingly good odor from the kitchen? what more do you want?" and taking a long sniff,—"oh! tit-bits! roasted or steamed!—ah! if you were not a discontented rascal, you would be satisfied with your share of the feast!" So saying, he took his bread from his bag, and with a long draw, sniffed up the good smell, and then ate his morsel of bread, and after a pause, as if to test the quality of taste and smell, said, "Of course you've had a good dinner!—You old fool, to be grumbling for nothing! Why the bread dipped in the smell from the kitchen is quite another thing. Ah! we have only to sop it in the delicious broth of a healthy imagination, to enjoy it with an understanding." He repeated the bite and sniff several times, and by the help of his imagination, began to feel himself not only satisfied, but satiated,—so much so, that he seemed to fear it was amounting to gluttony, and rising from the ground began to admonish himself. —"Come, Hyllos, don't gormandize, you have had more than enough for this day;" and throwing his bag over his shoulder, commenced his journey home with a cheerful countenance.

Metella was forcibly struck with the piteous scene she had just witnessed. This poor man, thought she, is contented with the odor that proceeds from the food preparing for my table. What wealth lies in contentment! and yet what wealth can purchase it?—She firmly resolved to visit the poor man without delay, in his own humble dwelling.

It was on one of those hot, dry harvest-days, such as are often experienced in Greece, when the heat of the sun, the wind, and the sandy dust, vie with each other which shall conquer, when Metella gave orders for her favorite

slave to hold herself in readiness for an evening walk.
Ophne brings with her a long-handled sun-shade, which
with the ancients played so important a part, and which .
has been handed down to the Greeks of the present day
in a smaller form.   She cannot help feeling anxious
whether she will be able to move it about with the
necessary agility, in order to protect her mistress as well
from the rays of the sun as from the thick clouds of
harvest dust.   She consoled herself with the reflection,
that latterly her mistress had become far less sensitive,
and that very day, during the entire walk, she did not
hear from her a single complaint.

"Ophne," said Metella, as they had been walking
for some time in the hot valley, "do you know the
house of poor Hyllos, the potter of Corinth, to whom I
sent Lydia not long since?   He has a little sick boy,
and, if I do not err, yonder is his poor, clay-built dwelling.   I should like to visit the old man and give him a
little present."

Ophne was not a little astonished to hear from her
gracious Domina, that she was going to the house of a
poor potter, and to bestow a charity with her own hands.

"Undoubtedly," said Ophne, " Hyllos dwells there on
the other side of the moor.   He was once well off, and
used to provide the potter market at Athens with his
goods.   But since he has become old, his strength and
activity fail him, and he finds great difficulty in supporting himself.   In addition to his poverty, he has a child
to provide for, whom he also instructs in his trade, and
in the rudiments of reading and writing."

Hyllos, who was just then in his work-shop finishing

flower-pots, saw the gracious lady with her slave, while they were still at a good distance, and hastened to thank her, as she was passing by, for the many blessings she had sent him lately. But how great was his surprise on seeing her approach his humble dwelling. She entered smilingly, and inquired after himself and his son. The little Askanus, who was scarcely six years old, sat in a corner on a broken flower-pot, and held in his arms a young rabbit, which he was sleeking down with his hand.

"Are you contented, Hyllos?" asked Metella; and before the potter could give an answer, Askanus frightened his little rabbit away by whispering in his ear, "Are you contented, she asks." Then the child ran behind the wooden pillar or support of the house, and every now and then stole a glance at the lady, when he thought he was unobserved.

"What have you had for dinner to-day, Hyllos?" asked Metella.

"A cake of bread, madam, onions and watercresses, a little salt, and a drink from the wine-pipe fountain in the pine forest."

"You have a sick boy, I heard lately; how is he?"

While the potter commenced to relate all the particulars of his child's illness, the little fellow sought to conceal his face behind his bound-up arm. Metella then called the little boy from his hiding-place. He approached the strange lady bashfully, and endeavored by retreating slowly to hide himself behind his father.

Metella drew from her girdle-pocket a piece of gold, and held it up before the boy. At the sight of the gold,

all embarrassment vanished, and calling his healthy
arm into action, he eagerly seized the offered gift. The
tears of the potter showed Metella the joy she had
afforded a poor old man.   He continued to relate how
his little son's malady had fallen into his hand and arm,
and ·that the doctor declared amputation was indis-
pensable.

At these words, Metella showed a decided repugnance
to the operation. "Yes, yes," said little Askanus, "the
horrid man said that, and went away, but shortly after
the good Lydia came and brought me a large sweet
almond-cake."   Metella laughed at the childish prattle,
which brought to her mind that of her darling Lucius
at the same age.

"And then," continued Askanus, "the good Lydia
said to me that cutting off my hand would not be so
dreadful, and that she would · come herself to me, that it
might not pain me so much."

·"And then, did the good Lydia really come to help
you?" asked Metella.   The boy nodded silently and began to cry.

The old father answered for him, dried his tears and
said, "Oh, of course, gracious lady, or we could not have
gone on with the operation, if your servant had not
helped us.   To us poor people, such a help comes seldom.   I am a poor, ailing old man, and I could not possibly have held the boy when he put his hands implor-
ingly together, begging that we would not hurt him.
How also could a father look on at a sharp knife passing
through the arm of his dear child?   I still tremble at
the remembrance of it.   Oh, no! your Lydia kept her

word, and came at the stated time, and was here before
the doctor arrived."

"Yes," added Askanus, "and brought father a
couple of red herrings, and some grapes and sweet seed-
cake."

"But still sweeter were the words of comfort," continued the old man, "that she brought to the sorrowful father and his child. Ah! poverty seldom finds
a friend! but the few friends it does find are as
true as gold, for they do not love us for the sake of gold
or honor, but for one's own sake. Such a friend your
servant has been to us. When the doctor began his
work, she told the boy to be firm, and held him during
the entire operation with a heroic courage. How affectionately she wiped the perspiration from his brow, and
how piously she prayed to the highest God! For she
had other gods as well as we, and called the highest
God,—not Father Jupiter, but God the Father, and his
attendant gods, — not gods, but angels. Then she repeated so often to the little fellow, 'Patience, only another moment's patience, — we have just finished!'"

Metella felt herself touched by this description, and a
sensation passed over her cheeks like a cool breeze; but
as old Hyllos was about to show her the arm, that she
might see how nicely it was healing, she quickly gave
him a sign not to remove the bandage. "No, no, Hyllos,
let it be, we must go now."

Askanus stood quite close to the strange lady, his little
rabbit jumping about at his feet. The boy looked embarrassed, first at his little pet, and then at Metella, and
on his blushing cheeks could be read that he had some-

thing else to say. He cast an inquiring glance at his father, and twisted his fingers in his nut-brown locks.

"Well, little one, what is the matter now?" inquired Metella, in a most amiable tone. With increasing confusion, the boy stooped down, took his dear little rabbit on his arm, and thinking the lady would be pleased with a present of his favorite, offered it to her. She accepted the little animal, gave it to Ophne to carry, patted the boy on the head, and hoped that Heaven would always preserve to him his good heart.

Had Ophne been told that Thrax had become a giant, she would have believed it sooner than that Metella had become condescending; but seeing was believing, and her own eyes were witness to the fact. At the commencement of the scene, she was seized with convulsions of laughter, which she concealed with difficulty from her haughty mistress. This was soon changed into silent admiration, and ended with veneration and love.

Metella, on her way home, was lost in thought, which allowed her lively little slave to indulge in her own reflections also. The tongue not being called into action, left the thoughts a double duty. The interview she had just witnessed filled her with admiration and astonishment. The *self* that twines round our best thoughts and actions intruded here. "Dear Lydia is so perfect," thought she to herself, "that everything I did contrary to her notions of right and wrong, I was snubbed for, often enough in the day; but mercy on me, what is to become of me now, when my Domina begins the same sort of life! It will be, — Ophne don't be too curious, — Ophne, keep your temper, — Ophne, a silent tongue is an ornament in a woman, — till, at last, poor Ophne might as well be one of the statues in the pleasure-ground, looking at everything and saying nothing. Well, I think one Mentor is enough for any poor slave, and I am quite satisfied with Lydia. However, too much thought injures the health, and I shall have plenty of time to think of the troubles when they come;" so, casting off care, she began to fan her mistress with redoubled zeal.

But to return to Metella. This evening her respect for Lydia, whom she usually called the bee of Hymett, on account of her many acts of virtue, rose higher and higher. She felt an ardent desire, not only to be esteemed by such a soul, but to be ardently and sincerely loved. Though she believed her slave was attached to her, still she thought that she was not tenderly beloved by her. In any case, the love that she received from her was not of that enthusiastic expression which she looked upon as true friendship. She then reflected on the two sorts of benevolence which the poor potter had received through her and her servant. "I gave him gold," said she to herself, — "a small gift, which has made me nothing poorer. Lydia, on the contrary, had no gold to offer, but she gave what was more valuable, her personal services. I would rather have given the unhappy father ten pieces of gold than do for him what she did, and therefore her acts of benevolence are far greater than mine, and certainly before God her work has by far a greater merit. Oh, if I were so ardently and sincerely beloved by her as that child of Hyllos! The old man was right: friendship to the poor is without self-seeking;

14

but the more riches and earthly greatness raise us, the more reason we have to mistrust the love of man. The higher those lofty mountains raise their heads, the more densely are they enveloped in fog and vapor, while the darting rays of the genial sun pass them by unheeded, to reflect themselves in the modest valley. What signifies this bowing and cringing servility bestowed on us by mortals like ourselves, when we don't possess either a true friend or a single heart to love us?" Such reflections rendered her melancholy and dejected, for when she looked back on her past life, she found that all her good works grew on no other soil than that of her wealth; and because those riches were not her own merits, but, at the most, the mere possessions of her ancestors, it appeared to her as though she had passed a useless life. She therefore saw herself in effect poor in good deeds, and a feeling of shame and sadness took possession of her. It appeared to her, that great souls must think little of her, as she had nothing else to offer for another life but fleeting treasures. Then she understood, for the first time, that there could be that man who would look upon riches as an imperfection, and that the gospel was right in connecting perfection with a renunciation of temporal goods. Even a Roman noble, Minutius Felix, expressed the same sentiments. Whence all at once would such an honor come to the poor, that the greatest among the inhabitants would visit them, and try to comfort them?

The rich matron does this merely because she begins to experience a pleasure in a doctrine that commands us without distinction to love every one as we love ourselves; still more willingly would she hasten to the poor, if she knew who He is that says, "What you do to the least of these my brethren, you have done to me."

So poverty in the Christian world has quite another position than that which it had in the Pagan. Poverty gives virtue a patent for nobility, love, vassals, and in the naked God-man on the cross she beholds her oldest and most renowned Ancestor. The poor themselves have at all times acknowledged this privilege through the Redeemer, and have therefore been from one century to another the most affectionate and faithful children of Christ and his holy Church.

CHAPTER XIV.

SAD INTELLIGENCE.

N a shady part of the extensive garden is a bower formed of majestic palm-trees, and their projecting branches fall in graceful profusion over the arched roof, and mingle in pleasing contrast with the lighter green of the Acacia, and the blooming roses of Pestum, which with their full buds insinuate themselves through the dark foliage of the interior.

In this lovely spot, surrounded by a wilderness of beauties, was Metella, reclining on a soft couch, and taking her morning repast. Close to the sofa sat Lydia, reading to her mistress. She held a portion of the Gospel of St. John in her hand. Although the early Christians carefully preserved the Gospels from the heathens, still Bishop Quadratus allowed Metella to read all their religious writings. At her feet, on the skirt of her robe, lay her little Maltese dog. It had its little brown paws stretched out at full length, on which it rested its tiny black nose, and settled itself snugly to sleep. Selina is seen approaching up the shady walk, accompanied by a sweet-looking boy. She carries in her hand a perforated.

silver fruit-basket, in which are beautiful peaches arranged on fresh vine-leaves, and surrounded with blue and yellow figs and Arabian dates. The boy carried a fine towel of Pelusiam linen on his arm; he held in his right hand a tankard, and in the left a massive golden cup. Behind Duranus stood little Thrax, bearing a muscle-shaped dish of rose-colored Sardonyx, filled with clear ice. All were laid on the black marble table; the slaves bowed themselves backward with arms crossed on the breast, and retired.

"My Lucius is a good son," said Metella, taking the golden cup in her hand. "He sent me this cup lately—the present of the Emperor Verus, and he begged me to use it daily until his return. Also Pompeianus, whom I knew in Rome, and who now fights on the Danube with Lucius, guessed what would please me. He has had some words of comfort, touching the death of my beloved husband, engraved on it. Before you pour in the beverage, you may recall the verses to my mind."

> "Amidst the busy hours of life's routine,
> Oft hast thou joyful raised the veil, and seen
> Laborious Tyke, grand in her gilded plough,
> With toilsome pain, thine acres furrow through.
> Thus suff'rings mix with state, and through the mind
> Wail in sad accents, like the moaning wind.
> Death forced thy noble spouse from thee to part,
> And in the dark tomb sleeps his faithful heart.
> Metella, still thou 'st joy amidst thy grief,
> Bloom to thy cheek, and to thy heart relief:
> Ah! may not that joy thou 'st gained be brief.
> May Lucius' face thine eyes delight, for there
> Strength, courage, virtue, in bright traits appear,
> Proud ornaments of that afflicting Bier."

14*   L

After Lydia had repeated them, she poured the red wine into the cup, and dropped in a few crumbs of ice to give it an agreeable coolness.

Lydia related, as an introduction to the paragraph, that she was to read that morning, that Jesus returned willingly to his friend Lazarus, who lived at a short distance from Jerusalem. Lazarus was at one time dangerously ill, and his afflicted sisters Martha and Mary sent a special message to Jesus, to obtain His Divine assistance for their sick brother. After this introduction, she began to read the touching account of the raising of Lazarus, and added that this resuscitation stood in close connection with the imprisonment of our Lord.

This wonder, and the solemn reception of Jesus into Jerusalem, roused the envy of the High-Priest, and the death of our Redeemer was the result. But just as Lazarus was only a few days in the grave, so our Lord was but part of three days in the tomb, when by His own power He rose from the dead. So will our souls be united to our bodies, never to be separated. The hope of meeting again is a consolation to us, when standing by the side of those graves that contain all we loved on earth.

While Metella interrupted her frequently with questions, she perceived that in front of the garden, coming towards her with hasty steps, was a man of rank. As he approached, she recognized him as her old domestic friend Pausanias, and her father's most grateful disciple. He commenced, with an agitated voice, to say, that the Proconsul in Athens had just received news from the seat of war, and that the conquest of the barbarians was at last completed, which conquest was particularly attributed to the bravery of the "Legio Fulminatrix," which many Greeks had joined. The wonderful assistance of the Divinity was everywhere spoken of, without which the whole army must have succumbed to the savage force of the barbarians. Also news of Lucius, who fought bravely, was contained in the accounts to the Proconsul. He had scarcely said these words, when, with extraordinary haste, he drew forth a note, and laying it on the little table, took his immediate departure.

"News of my son?" asked Metella, and cast an anxious look upon Lydia.

"Probably joyful news," replied she, "for he fought bravely."

"I scarcely dare break open the note, — Pausanias departed so quickly, what can it signify? I tremble! Oh, withdraw to the shady walk and pray to your God for me. In the meantime, I will occupy myself a few minutes with my darling Lucius." Lydia obeyed. "The opening of that little missive can give me unbounded joy, or plunge me into the deepest grief! — There it lies in prophetic silence, bearing in its simple folds a secret to me, yet the knowledge of which may for ever dash from my lips the cup of joy. It still says nothing, and yet contains what? — perhaps more than I shall live to bear."

The longer she delayed opening the missive, the greater became her anxiety. Pausanias stood ever before her; — his mien, his confused look, his hasty departure, were all doubtful omens. She seemed incapable of thought, not even one to Him on high, to grant a gracious termination to her melancholy fears. "My darling son, what shall I know of thee now?" and with one desperate struggle she broke the seal.

A considerable time had passed, and Lydia heard no sound; she began to look impatiently towards the arbor. She heard the little dog barking piteously as if he had been hurt. Whining, and with sunken head and soft steps, the little animal ran along the walk, and scarcely had he joined Lydia, when he began to retrace his steps, drag his tail along the ground, and now and then looked back to see if Lydia were following. Lydia concluded that the dog's howling signified something, and she resolved to return, though uncalled, and drawing aside the branches, looked into the arbor, and uttering a cry of horror, exclaimed, — "My dear, dear mistress!" She entered, and called her again and again by name, but received no answer. She then raised her head gently, but her eyes were still closed, and she held in her half-opened hand the little missive. Lydia now guessed all. The deadly paleness of Metella's countenance told her the contents of the letter. Lucius was slain! At this moment a feeling pervaded her entire frame, to which she had hitherto been a stranger, since her painful separation from her dear mother.

Placing Metella's head upon her arm, she took the napkin from the table, poured on it a little wine, and with it chafed her lady's temples. The little dog sprang anxiously upon his mistress, and dragging with his paws. endeavored to arouse her. Lydia knew that a

cry for help would be useless at this moment, she therefore remained supporting the head of the afflicted
mother, awaiting the return of her senses.

The good slave continued long in this position,
anxiously looking for a change. She pressed Metella's
head to her heart with tender affection, that she might
once in her life have the happiness of being near her.
At last she observed her breathing softly, and her eyes
gradually opened.

Metella cast a vacant look around, and knew nothing
of the past, but inquired if she had been dreaming.
Lydia answered, "No, dear mistress,—it is only a little
weakness that will quickly vanish." She then offered
her the golden cup, and begged of her to drink. The
lady sipped a little, and looked inquiringly into Lydia's
eyes.

"My child, I believe you are crying? Say, has anything happened to you? Ah! I feel as if I should cry
with thee! Oh, let me rest a little on thy arm!—Has
not some one been here with us?" she asked, after a
long pause;—"was there not a stranger here, and I
imagine he said something about Lucius? Oh, yes—I
remember now—he said that all was well with him."—
Lydia turned aside to conceal the bitter tears that flowed
without ceasing.

"Child," said Metella, "why are you silent? Why
do you not help me to remember what is passing?

"Lucius fought bravely—of course he fought bravely,
or he would have been an unworthy scion of a noble
stem! But—there is something more. Some one spoke
of defeat. Lydia, why are you silent?—again this

letter! Lydia, am I in my senses, or does this letter speak of my son?"

Lydia dares not trust herself with one look, but supporting her dear mistress still on her arm, remains motionless.

Metella again seized the note, and with a fixed gaze reads on. — "My child fallen? Lucius slain? The desolate widow without a son! The hope, the joy of her widowed life, to come no more! Is she then never more to hear that voice again? — that buoyant step, that spoke the gladness of the heart, — that honest tongue, its truth speaking from his flashing eye! — that docile will, bending always in obedience! — and does that loving filial heart beat now no more? Alas, poor mother, thy only hope is slain! Thou hast nothing more to love! All, all is desolation here," placing her hand convulsively on her beating heart. "The link that bound me to this fleeting world is broken! I have nothing now to care for!" Metella was roused from her anguish by a voice outside the arbor weeping like a child. A little form sought to get a glimpse between the foliage: it was the Thracian dwarf, the most faithful follower of the fallen Lucius — little Thrax. Then came Ophne, and cast herself at the feet of her afflicted mistress, pressed her robe to her face, and sobbed aloud. Thrax hid himself behind her, and took the letter from the table. He appeared by his imploring countenance to ask if he might read it. Metella by a slight inclination of the head gave assent, and he and Ophne were motioned to leave the arbor. In a few moments loud lamentations were heard through the villa, for Pausanias had informed the gate-keeper of the news he had brought. The letter that the dwarf took from the arbor passed from hand to hand, but no one ventured to approach Metella, who had just been carried to her apartment by her sympathizing slaves.

After the violent grief had a little subsided, Lydia sought to stammer out a word of consolation, but as often as she tried to speak, her voice failed her. Metella saw that her affectionate servant wished to console her, and she discovered, in the midst of her sorrow, that her wish to be·loved by Lydia as a dear friend was more than fulfilled. It was difficult for Lydia to utter a word. " Dearest lady," said she, "your suffering is great, but you do not bear it alone, — those who know the secrets of thy noble soul suffer with thee, and share this pain with an intensity that you would scarcely credit." By her affectionate attention she changed her mistress' pain into sorrow, and the tears began to flow.

" My eyes," said she, "will become a dried-up spring."

" Till the God of comfort," added the Christian slave, "makes the eye clear again to see the dear departed one. Between the present and that moment, there is only a little space, then the mother will be united to her child: what a treasure of comfort, my dear mistress, lies in this truth !"

"Did I not believe this," replied she, "my grief would annihilate me, — I am fully convinced of the immortality of the soul. Oh, it is a melancholy Religion that places in the hand of a sorrowing mother the shroud of her son, and in it buries her last consolation. The belief of again seeing the lost one,"— and suddenly starting up, she continued, "Lydia, Lydia, my dream! perhaps Lucius was then dead."

"And at that time already happy," replied Lydia, "for he was reclining near Christ the Son of God; and that same Christ that gave back to Martha her brother, who had been four days dead, can also heal thy wounds and give thee back thy son."

"I wished to go to Christ when I saw Him, but I was not able; you sought to help me — you were also too weak.   Who will lead me?

"Oh, if I never could approach my son, how hard — how dreadful would it be! I should be the most miserable of mortals! I should wander about lamenting through all parts of the heavens and the lower world. I should sob and call for the child of my heart — never tire calling for him, if even for an eternity. Oh, dear child, do you lead me to my son!"

'My arm," replied Lydia, "is too weak; but grace, when it enlightens you, can send you a strong angel from Heaven, who will drive away all hinderance, and lead you to the happiness of your son."

Up to this time, the Christian slave shared the sufferings of her mistress, not like a servant, but like a faithful friend; for without knowing it, she was no longer the servant, but the comforter of Metella.

CHAPTER XV.

DIONYSIUS OF CORINTH.

ETELLA was too well known in Athens, not to excite the deepest sympathy amongst her friends, at the melancholy tidings from the seat of war. Some of them started for the Villa, to express in person the share they took in her afflictions. Amongst these was the venerable philosopher Athenagoras, whose condolence fell on the withered heart of the noble sufferer like a mild sunbeam. Although Athens, where she had her numerous friends, was not far distant, still she did not carry her sorrows there; for in misfortune, the heart of man prefers solitude, and finds but few friends to keep it company. Athens was the last place she would wish to visit, as there were preparations making there to celebrate the conquest over the barbarians, and these would have opened her wounds anew.

Athenagoras promised to introduce her to a man who was honored by the faithful of Greece as a worker of·

miracles.   He lived in Corinth, and therefore was not
very far from the Villa.

Metella accepted this attention with gratitude.

The Legends introduce to us two Bishops of Greece,
who bore the name of Dionysius.   The oldest is the well-
known Dionysius, the Areopagite, who, through the
address that St. Paul made A.D. 51, before the Areopa-
gites, was converted to the Faith, and became his disciple.   He was the first Bishop of Athens, and died A.D.
117.   Centuries later, a church was built to his memory
on the Areopagus, but it is now in ruins.

The Dionysius of whom Athenagoras spoke, flourished
in the reign of Marcus Aurelius at Corinth, and distinguished himself by his great zeal and brilliant oratory.
He was not contented to live solely for his church, but
wrote several epistles to distant congregations, the most
renowned of which were those to the Lacedemonians
and the Athenians.   Those to the churches of Nicomedia,
Gortyna, Amastris, Gnossus, and Rome, — letters full of
Apostolic zeal, wherein were frequently exposed the
errors and heresies of that century, — are for the greater
part no longer extant.   Eusebius has only saved some
remnants of them in his Church History.   Dionysius
encouraged the Athenians, in his epistles, to a firmer
faith and to an evangelical life; he mentions their former
Bishop Publius, who was martyred, and his successor
Quadratus; and of the latter he gave testimony, that he
had again lighted up the sinking faith of the Athenians.
This holy Bishop opposed those heresies which arose in
the first and second centuries, and was renowned for inquiring into every particular of each sect that started

up, from what writings their founders drew them, and in what they consisted.

Some of his writings were wilfully misrepresented by his opponents, of which he complained. "I wrote some letters," said he, "at the petition of my brothers, but they have been falsified by the messengers of Satan, who found it their interest to make additions and omissions. If they cannot pass unimportant works without injuring them, it may not be much wondered at, if from the same source, the text of Holy Scripture becomes hacked and maimed."

With just this view, to face the faith and plant Hope in a soul weighed down with grief, the saint found himself urged on to suspend his widely spread activity for some days, and visit Metella. Detached as he was from earth, this visit was to perform no earthly duty. Nothing but an immortal soul found value in his eyes; and little did it trouble him, whether he had to seek it in a palace, or in a wretched hovel. Let us follow the holy man, bent with the burden of age and heavy duties, wending his way slowly towards Theredron.

In his aged countenance shines forth a soul, inflamed with the love of God. With a magnetic power he draws all to Him, and gains the esteem and love of those with whom he converses.

As much as Metella had been accustomed, from her earliest years, to mix with those of the highest rank and deepest learning, she had never met one who had made so great an impression upon her, or who had inspired her with so much awe, as this venerable man.

It appeared to her, as if a more than ordinary spirit was concealed within his breast.

She expressed her gratitude that her afflictions were shared in so sincerely from the side of the Christians. "My mind," said she to him, "is in the same wrecked condition as my body. It appears to me as if the God of the Christians, whom I saw in a vision, was drawing me up to His glory of streaming light. But scarcely had I raised my thoughts to Him, when I seemed to behold the gods of Greece looking angrily at me, and that Jupiter on that account has allowed this lightning of misfortune to strike me, for having forsaken him and turned to the God of the Christians.

"I totter like a child who is just learning to walk, first leaning to one side, and then to the other.

"And yet there can be but one true God,—either the God of the Christians or the god of the heathens. For the truth has this peculiarity—that no second truth stands near it.

"Revered master, unloose this knot, and give my mind a rest after which it has so long sighed! Give me the true faith."

"It would be a vain thought," said he, "if a Christian were to believe that it is he who gives the Faith. Faith comes from God alone, and is the greatest gift He can bestow on mortals. To some he gives it in a greater degree, to others in a lesser. Faith is a light that illuminates the spiritual darkness, yet in each it is but a weak lamp till lighted up in the great Luminary— Jesus Christ Himself.

"For some, the oil is scarcely sufficient for their own necessities, to pass through the dark labyrinth of life; they can scarcely see a few steps before them on their pilgrimage to the other world, much less to light them selves with it into the glory of Heaven. Should the fuel of this heavenly light fail, and the lamp threaten to extinguish, we must not lose courage; even the Apostles experienced this, as they once expressed it: 'Lord, increase our faith!'

"Concerning the question of whether misfortune comes from the God of the Christians, or from the highest god of the heathens: suppose that Jupiter sends the misfortune,—is it not incomprehensible why he does not punish all the Hellenes that do not believe in him, insomuch that many of the learned have forsaken the religion of their forefathers? But above all, Jupiter would have to punish the Christians who intend to annihilate his altars and temple. If your misfortune be sent to you by the God of the Christians, it is easily explained."

"How! Does your God then, who is called the source of all good, send misfortune and affliction to them?" asked the heathen.

"God is a vine-dresser," said Dionysius, "who lays the knife to the vine, and cuts off its withered branches, that it may bring forth stronger fruit. We feel the wounds he inflicts, 'tis true; and they press out most bitter tears, like the drop that falls from the pruned vine: but we must bear in mind that this Vine-Dresser cuts off that only which is hurtful and unfruitful.

"If you will raise the veil of your conscience, you will discover that the divine love has seen also something in you that must be pruned, to make you truly fruitful."

15 *

"What do you mean, revered master?"

'Perhaps it was the love of the world, or the love of riches, or the love of the creature, that held thee enchained, so that the thought of eternity was stupefied by that of time.   Perhaps, since this trial has happened to you, that you think much oftener on the God of Heaven, on your last end, and on your son, who has found peace by the side of his God."

"O how truly have you spoken!   Does then the Divinity send sorrow to lead us to truth and happiness?— That is an act worthy of the highest Being.

"But Plato did not suppose that, when he said that the human mind stands still when it reflects on wickedness.   Am I right, Dionysius, to believe that the Divinity in thus afflicting me, loves me more than ever?"

"Without doubt, Metella;—whom God punishes, He also loves."

"O how willingly would I bear each punishment, were I certain that the Divinity would thereby lead me to the happy plains!

"But do you believe, revered master, that God sees through the immeasurable extent of my anguish?   No language on earth is capable of expressing the misery of a mother's sorrow at the loss of her only child."

Dionysius now drew forth a scroll, upon which he had written some words, with the intention of giving them to the afflicted matron.

They were taken from the Gospel of St. Luke, and were on the touching sympathy our Lord expressed towards an afflicted widow.   He read aloud:

"As Jesus came nigh to the gates of the city of Naim, behold a dead man was carried out, the only son of his mother; and she was a widow: and a great multitude of the city was with her. Whom when the Lord had seen, being moved with mercy towards her, he said to her, 'Weep not!' and he came near and touched the bier. And they that carried it stood still, and He said, 'Young man, I say unto thee, arise;' and he that was dead, sat up, and began to speak. And He gave him to his mother."

"That same Lord," said Dionysius, "who felt pity for the afflicted widow of Naim, feels also for thee, and the moment will come in which he will say to thee, 'Weep not,' and He will restore to thee thy beloved son."

Metella felt herself gaining new strength, as she heard of this wonderful event, and with the saint's explanation. "You give me also the same hope that Athenagoras did. He said that I should yet be united to the blessed in Heaven."

"Certainly, if you fulfil the conditions on which God grants the crown of happiness.

"Faith and virtue unite themselves in our Lord, like the two sisters, Martha and Mary; while one sits at His feet, the other is anxiously occupied about Him. Whoever is acquainted with the one sister, will most certainly be introduced to the other. Form a friendship with Christian virtue, and that virtue will soon lead you to faith. 'Will you know if my doctrine is from God,' said Christ, 'so observe it.' It is something beautiful to occupy one's self with study, and to refresh one's self in the treasures of knowledge as in a cooling spring. There is something dignified in reflecting on the things we have read, that we may come nearer and nearer to the truth. But virtue leads you higher than wisdom. Worldly wisdom is a deep sea, many draw from it the pearl of truth, but many, death."

"But what virtues do you recommend to me in particular, in order that I may secure for myself the happiness of Heaven?"

"A holy pope," said he, "sent a letter once to our Church in Corinth, which we still read on Sundays. It commences thus:

"The all-wise Creator of the world knows the multitude and beauty of the Heavenly enjoyments. Let us strive to be found amongst the number of those who wait to partake of His promised gifts. How shall we attain thereto? If we in the faith hold fast on God, if we reflect upon what is pleasing and agreeable to God, that we may accomplish His holy will. Let us walk in the path of truth, and cast aside all injustice, covetousness, discord, wickedness, lust, loquacity, hatred, arrogance, pride, vainglory, and self-sufficiency."*

Metella listened with profound attention, and on the venerable man rising to depart, she promised him to practise zealously all the virtues he had just dictated.

Report soon circulated amongst her friends and acquaintances, that she was about to adopt a religion which was nothing short of folly. They used their utmost endeavors to dissuade her from such a step. Her ancient nobility, her dazzling wealth, the fame of her learning, the displeasure of the Emperor,—all

---

* Pope Clement, in his letter to the Corinthians, Chap. xxxiv.

these, they said, should deter her from becoming a Christian.

She was placed in the most agonizing position Doubts gnawed again upon the freshness of the soul, and it appeared to her as though she must sink under the combat that was passing within.

CHAPTER XVI

THE CONVERSION.

ONTHS had passed since the Greek matron had received the melancholy intelligence of her son's death. Harvest and Winter had come and gone, and she was still at her villa. Pale and reduced to a shadow, she wandered through her costly apartments, clad in deep mourning. Nothing could charm her now. She often sat in the courtyard for hours, gazing listlessly on the waters of the fountain, or wandered by moonlight, seeking consolation in the soothing and melancholy strains of the nightingale. Dionysius endeavored to raise her depressed spirits by letters, but his pious sister, Chrysophora, as he called Metella, could not be comforted. What he built up, Metella's friends would pull down again,— and particularly the intellectual Lucian, just returned from Egypt, did not fail to set up Christianity to ridicule. He compared the Christians with the inhabitants of Aldera, who, by listening to a single Grecian declaimer, became so insane, that they spoke ever after in the spirit of Sophocles, and even in the streets talked only in Iambic measure. Such derision had a paralyzing effect on Metella's soul, and she longed for nothing so much as death; and then she knew not whether she should die as a Christian or as a heathen. So far, doubt had brought her to the brink of despair.

The human mind has a natural desire for truth, and as long as it finds it not, it has no rest, and feels only melancholy and a death-like anxiety. The mind of man strives after truth as his heart does after love; but when a doubt is in the case, two elements mingle together, error and truth, which form such a miserable state in the mind, that it can only be compared to the chaotic mixture of earth and water. Metella's corporal strength sank under such sufferings. She scarcely touched food, and medical aid was resorted to in vain. She wasted away, and was no longer able to leave her apartment without the assistance of her attendants.

"I feel it," said she one day, "that surly Charon is pushing off his bark and waits for me at the sea of Acheron. Do not forget to put the Obolus (penny) under my tongue. The light of my eyes, the flash of which has made hundreds of slaves tremble, will soon be extinguished. Existence here below has no charm for me. Sorrow has one advantage—it frees us from the fear of death."

In this state she had but one wish left—to see Dionysius. He also had an intense desire to see Metella converted before he died; and he was convinced that she would be a pattern for the Christians of Greece; and therefore he besought God to spare her life, for the honor of His Son, and to grant to the much-tried one her health, as well as a believing heart. On his way to Eleusis, he continued his fervent prayer, and ascended the steps of Metella's villa absorbed in meditation. On entering her apartment, he found her lying on a sofa, apparently at the point of death, and the slaves sobbing round their dying mistress. Theirs was not the grief of hirelings, for she had lately won their tenderest love. Amongst them stood Lydia, a monument of silent resignation.

No one could discover whether Metella was in a swoon or sleep. She lay there like a fallen oak, that once stood proudly on the hill, till the storms came and laid it low.

Dionysius wept as he beheld this fading hope of the Church. Casting himself on his knees, he continued long in prayer, and all the slaves knelt with him. At last he rose, as if he had received a command from above. He raised his eyes to Heaven, and passed his aged hands noiselessly over the sick-bed. The bystanders felt a holy awe, as they saw the trembling hands and uplifted eyes of the saintly man. He then uttered aloud: "In the name of our Lord Jesus Christ."

At these words, Metella's eyes opened, and a delicate blush suffused her cheeks. She sat up, and seized the hand of the Bishop and kissed it. "Oh, I have much to say to you, my venerable friend, before I pass away! Faith in the Divinity of Jesus Christ is the broad chasm over which I can find no bridge. Human wisdom has its limits. She can imagine the Divinity, but cannot prove it, because she is human. Oh, Dionysius!

who will cast this bridge across, if God Himself will
not; in a wonderful manner, let me know Him. Yes,
show me the Divine power of miracles of which you
have so often spoken, and I will believe—believe as
no heart has ever yet believed."

Dionysius replied, with a heavenly calm, "God has
just given you a proof."

Metella looked round, and could not describe how she
felt. All present were trembling, for they saw the wonderful effect of God's power with their own eyes.

She gazed around as if about to ask how she was
cured; the saintly man quickly answered her inquiring
look. "Not by human, but by Divine aid you have
been restored to health." Metella now perceived for the
first time, that she had risen as if from the grave, and
that a new life had diffused itself through her entire
frame. She arose and walked without any assistance.

The astonishment of all present was a pledge to her
that she did not dream. She confessed that her lost
strength had been restored to her in the name of the
Redeemer, and she began to praise and glorify Him.
This is the signification of a miracle that it is performed in the name of Jesus Christ,—a proof to man
that He fulfils His own promises, and that whatsoever
is asked of the Eternal Father in His name shall be
granted.

"From this moment I believe!" exclaimed Metella;
'yes, I believe that Christ is more than man, and I will
preserve this belief to the end of my days." Dionysius
made the sign of the cross upon her forehead;—she
knelt down, and that once proud head bent humbly,

16

and petitioned to be numbered amongst the followers of
Jesus Christ, and to receive baptism. It was the custom in the Church from the very commencement, that
those who wished to receive baptism were obliged beforehand, as Tertullian says, to prepare themselves by
diligent prayer, fasting, nightly watching, and the con-
fessing of their sins.* Dionysius decided that the neophite should be formally received into the Church on
the coming Easter eve, and ordered her to prepare for
the solemn occasion by religious practices. Every day
enriched her in works of perfection ; clearer and clearer
rose the heavenly truth out of the chaos of her former
ideas. God created the world and man through love,
and through that same love He sent His only-begotten
Son for man's redemption. To allow God to love us,
and to love Him in return, form the Heavenly bond on
earth, which we call religion. Love is all the issue,
means, and aim of all things.

A few days before Easter, Metella assembled her entire household of slaves, and presented them with their
freedom,—that treasure so much prized by man, and
after which many of them had sighed for years, but
never had hope of obtaining it in this life. Many of
Metella's inferiors had already enjoyed these first-fruits
springing from the soil of a believing mind. Some returned to their longed-for homes, and to their families,
but the greater number having no homes, offered their
services anew for the same wages as before. As soon
as Lydia heard of this gracious act, she was not a
moment in doubt as to what she would do. She had

* Tertullian on Baptism, Chapter ix.

already been many years in slavery, and had saved as much of her wages as would have purchased her freedom. With this money she now intended to seek after her mother in distant Rome. Then she resolved, that if her money were insufficient, to offer herself as a substitute for her mother, thereby to release her and secure to her a quiet evening of life.

Metella asked her, one day, what her views were for the future; and she answered, with an embarrassed air, "It will cost me much to leave my present home, but the duty I owe my mother requires this sacrifice, and therefore I am resolved on journeying to Rome."

Concealing the indescribable agony that this separation was causing her, Metella, although it appeared to her to be the greatest she could offer, was still willing to lay this sacrifice on the altar of her God. Placing her hand on Lydia's shoulder, she said, "Do not let us think of anything sorrowful during these days of peace. I never supposed that so many ties of gratitude and friendship could ever bind me to a single mortal. What was I before the grace of God brought you into my house?—a foolish creature, shining like a gilded statue of the gods, and worshipped by many fools. Indeed, I resembled that colossal statue in the Temple of Jupiter at Athens. From without, it appears to be composed of nothing but gold and ivory, and before which each one stands in astonishment and awe, but bend yourself and look into the interior, and what do you there behold? Nothing but wooden rafters, nuts, wedges and clumps, pitch and clay, and a quantity of such stuff, not to say anything of the rats and mice that

take up their abode in the vacuum. Such was I, my
very dear child, in the hidden depths of my soul. If I
am otherwise now, the merit is thine." She broke off
the discourse, and hastened to her apartment, deeply affected with gratitude and sorrow.

As she had been for some time ranked amongst the
number of the catechumens, she fulfilled the duties and
sometimes visited the place of meeting at Corinth, where
the Christians assembled. It is known that, in the first
centuries, those who sought to be received into the communion of the Church were divided into three classes:
those of the first class were called "Listeners," because
they had only permission to be present at the sermon;
those of the second class were called the "Kneelers," as
they knelt for a time after the sermon, to receive the
prayers and blessing of the Bishop; the third class was
called the "Elect." The last-mentioned remained in the
church till after the Credo, when, at the command of the
Deacon, "Go, the mass commences,"—*"Ite missa est,"*
they were obliged to leave.

The Spring approached,—that time of grace in which
the Church celebrates the greatest of her festivals. The
Resurrection of the Son of God coincides with the
resuscitation of dead Nature, and the conquest of the
heavenly Paradise by the second Adam is yearly announced by joyful verdant May, which animates again
the mountain valley, thicket, brake, and forest. This
rejoicing of Nature strikes in each breast the responding
chord, but where is it so vividly and melodiously en-
toned as where it thaws the ice-covering of self,—and
when a new life of grace begins to bloom over benumbed

egotism, when the angels unite themselves as guides, and begin to announce to the awakening soul their songs of the heavenly spheres.

These days, previous to receiving the Sacrament of Baptism, Metella summoned all her servants to attend.

It was an ancient custom that on the feast of Saturn in December, and on the first day of the month of August, the slaves were served at table by their masters. Since the death of Metellus, this feast had not been celebrated in Theredron. It was now going to be solemnized in a more touching manner. Our Divine Lord, King of Heaven and earth, had, a short time before Easter, prepared a feast for His disciples, and showed himself as the servant of all. He washed their feet and waited on them. In commemoration of this, Metella ordered her servants to sit at table, took, according to the custom of a server, a towel, girt herself therewith, and waited on them. The feast at an end, she begged pardon of all in general, and each one in particular whom she had offended through her natural hastiness of temper, and she practised thereby one of the most beautiful virtues; these acts of humility being most painful to nature, are therefore the most meritorious. It is a noble act to acknowledge our faults, and for a noble action no one is too noble.

We will now accompany our neophite to the threshold of the church at Corinth. There she stands like the lowliest among the petitioners, asking to be received into the communion of the Church. The Bishop reminded the supplicants of the persecution that awaited them on earth, and of the triumph that awaited them in

16*

Heaven. He then stepped forward, — as in former times Baptisms were only administered by the Bishop, — and laid his hand on the head of each, as Ananias did once on the blind Saul, and signed each one on the forehead with the sign of Redemption; — as the faithful pronounced the words which a noble neophite once said to Philip, "I believe that Jesus Christ is the Son of God." They then abjured the devil, after which they were exorcised and reminded of the words: "Heal the sick, raise the dead, cleanse the lepers, cast out the devils." While repeating the Credo, the catechumens entered the church, where they were anointed with oil, and they then proceeded to the Baptistry, which in ancient times was very capacious, and amply provided with water. Each one was taken separately by a deacon or deaconess and immersed three times: so the expression, "Bath of Regeneration," signified, in the actual sense of the word, a bath of water. This immersion required fresh garments, and it was then the newly baptized received the white robe, — the figure of a spotless soul, — which garment they wore till the eighth day after Easter, which is called "Dominica in Albis," or the "Sunday in White."

Metella was instructed in each particular ceremony, until her regeneration was perfected in water and the Holy Spirit. But the new covenant into which she had just entered, must now be sealed by that most dignified of all mysteries, the holy Eucharist. "The body of Christ," said Dionysius, and he placed the Blessed Eucharist in her hand. He then took the golden chalice and held it to her lips with the words, "The chalice, or cup of life," and Metella deemed herself truly blest to drink of the blood of the Redeemer. This heavenly beverage brought her into a new affinity, — the blood of the Messias flowed in her veins. What delight sparkled in her eyes, and what joy diffused itself over her countenance! Her past sufferings and her agonizing doubts were at an end! How rich did not the Faith render her! What life with its sorrowful events had taken, grace had indemnified in rich measure and flowing over. Death deprived her of a husband, and grace bestowed upon her in the Redeemer a heavenly Bridegroom. Death tore from her a dear son, the only hope of her future life; grace opened to her the prospect of being united with him again.

The prayer of the venerable and saintly Dionysius was heard, and the precious soul was after great wandering brought into the one true fold. The joy that beamed on his aged countenance expressed the feelings of his heart. He raised his hands on high and invoked a blessing on Metella, and on the humble Lydia, whose virtuous example urged her to seek after, and find the Way the Truth, and the Life.

CHAPTER XVII.

MARCUS AURELIUS' CONQUEST OF THE MARCOMANNI.

HILE Metella was enjoying this peace of soul, to which she had till then been a stranger, the troops returned from the distant campaign, and were received amidst the rejoicings of the people. In Rome, a magnificent triumphal procession was prepared for the Emperor, and in all the other cities of his vast dominions the conquest was celebrated with public feasts, processions, sacrifices of thanksgivings, and bull-fights. Athens also opened its numerous temples, and offered sacrifice. Public games and festivities continued for several weeks without intermission. The Athenians even thought of introducing the combats of Gladiators, but old Lucien said to them contemptuously, "Don't resolve on this till at least the altar of commiseration be done away with among you." *

Before we relate anything of this memorable conquest, which the Romans gained over the Germans, and which was much more a conquest of Faith than of arms, let us

* Lucien, D. N. 57.

introduce a few remarks on the character of the Emperor. At an early age, Marcus Aurelius distinguished himself by the qualities of his mind and heart. He was but a boy of eight years when he was received into a particular confraternity of priests, in whose society he received his first religious impressions. He always declared himself to be an advocate for public worship, and on that account he is sometimes compared with the pious Numa Pompilius. Once weeping over the death of one of his teachers, to the astonishment of those present, and of which some of the youths complained, the Emperor Antoninus, his adopted father, beautifully replied, "Allow him to be human, — neither philosophy nor imperial dignity ought to deprive him of feeling."

In the second year of Antoninus' reign, he married him to his daughter Faustina, and took him shortly after into the consulship. Marcus was only twenty-six years old, when the Emperor bestowed upon him the honor of the Tribuneship, and even the Regency, which, though not publicly proclaimed, still was actually so. His affection for the Emperor was so ardent, that he never once left him during the twenty-five years which elapsed from his adoption to his death. He was forty years old when he began first to wield the Roman Sceptre. He was an Emperor, favorable to philosophy, and thought, with Plato, that those people were happy whose philosophers were kings or whose kings were philosophers. According to the wish of the new Emperor, the Roman Senate took his adopted brother Lucius Verus as colleague, but he troubled himself more about his eating and drinking than the happiness of the people.

Aurelius was most intent on preserving the old religion and encouraging learning. If he were in anything blameworthy, it was in his great indulgence to his son Commodus, as also towards his wife Faustina, and the absolute authority which he allowed his officials in the provinces to exercise. Neither can he be exonerated from cruelty during the war with the Marcomanni: some of his officers with their men stood once before him, and informed him, that they had killed three thousand of the enemy, and had taken great booty; but as they had received no commands for this, the Emperor ordered them to be crucified for having broken military discipline. There arose amongst the soldiers loud clamors of displeasure, but the Emperor sprang into the midst of them unarmed, and cried, "Well then, put me to death, and add a new crime to the one already committed." He also ordered many thousands in Selucia to be executed during the Parthian war. His reign was a most unquiet one. The Catti, the Marcomanni, the Scythians, and other people were constant disturbers, and in addition, several cities in his dominions were desolated either by earthquakes, plagues, or famine. The heathen priests sought in every possible way to appease the anger of the gods, but without effect, and at last they threw all the blame upon the Christians, who were consequently delivered up to public persecutions.

Amongst the wars which Marcus Aurelius had conducted, the one against the Marcomanni and Quadi was the most stubborn. No battle that was ever fought since the foundation of Rome was so remarkable as that over the Marcomanni. The following is a short account of it, and is taken chiefly from Dio Cassius.

In the year A.D. 174, Marcus Aurelius, with his soldiers, found himself in the heart of Germany. The barbarians pressed his army into a deep valley, that was surrounded on all sides by quarries and steep rocks; having completely hemmed them in, they ascended the heights and looked down upon them with savage exultation. The courage of the Romans sank still deeper, as the dreadful effects of the climate added to their distress. They had, already been for five days without water, so that they were almost consumed by a burning thirst. In this extreme distress, the commander-in-chief of the Prætorean Cohort sought the Emperor and said to him, "Cæsar, a portion of our troops, the Melitani Legion, consists of Christians; to them nothing is impossible."

"Let them pray," said the Emperor, and in an instant the Christian soldiers to a man fell upon their knees. They conjured the true God to let his name be known and glorified in that hour. Their prayer was scarcely ended, when dark clouds collected, the thunder rolled in the distance, and peals re-echoed against the rocky walls of their mountain valley. The lightning, in vivid flashes, accompanied by a heavy hail-storm, struck the rocks where the barbarians were posted. The flashes were so terrific, and followed each other in such rapid succession, that in a few minutes the enemy fell into disorder. But in the valley, a soft rain fell upon the parched Romans, who held out their helmets to receive it, and drank in copious draughts of the refreshment sent them from Heaven. Dio Cassius, a heathen writer, has assured us that fire and water descended from heaven at the same time. Our army, said he, was refreshed, the other was consumed; for the water that fell upon the Romans in refreshing showers, fell upon the barbarians, with the fire, like boiling oil. Although inundated, they cried loudly for water, and at every attempt made to extinguish the fire they received great injuries. In their despair they cast themselves into the midst of the Romans, where alone the water was capable of refreshing them, and the Emperor exercised the greatest clemency towards them.

In memory of this battle, Marcus was proclaimed Emperor for the seventh time. He issued commands, that the Melitani Legion should be called from that time forward the "Legio Fulminatrix," or "Thundering Legion;" and not contented with this, he imparted the wonderful event to the Senate, and published an edict whereby he put a stop to the persecutions of the Christians. The edict, the force of which lasted but a short time, is still extant, and it gives us the title of the then Lord of the world:—

Imperator Cæsar, Marcus Aurelius, Antoninus, Augustus Parthicus, Germanicus, Sermaticus, Pontifix, Maximus, Tribunitiæ Potestatis.

As a memorial of this remarkable battle, the Roman Senate had a colossal pillar erected, on which the event was depicted in bas-relief. On the top was Jupiter, with a long beard and extended arms, bearing the thunder-bolt in his hands. A little lower down were the two armies, one in disorder, the other pressing forward, sword in hand. The pillar is preserved to the present day, and is one of the greatest ornaments of Rome. It stands on the Piazza Colonna, in the northern part of the city, and consists of 28 blocks of marble, which extend to a height of 135 feet. It was restored in the time of Sixtus the Fifth, and a statue of St. Paul substituted for that of Jupiter. Peace being concluded with the people of the Danube, the attention of the Emperor was drawn to the province of Syria, where the General Avidius Cassius had usurped the imperial purple. He set out immediately for the East, but Cassius had already been murdered by his soldiers. He pacified the provinces, and hastened back through Greece towards Rome, there to celebrate a glorious triumph. In the midst of such a variety of affairs, and during the most fatiguing journeys, he wrote "Meditations on Self," in twelve books, which was a rich treasure, containing the moral maxims of life, and which won him the renown of being the most famous of the sages of antiquity. In the first book, he related how he learned to conquer his passions, and particularly anger, from his parents, friends, and teachers, — and how he labored to attain each virtue. He kept in view, in a most attractive manner, temperance, and the reigning virtues of Antoninus Pius, whose adopted son he was. He then offers a rich collection of the most beautiful moral instruction, such as never emanated from the pen of a heathen. "Virtue," said he, "constitutes the fame, the perfection, and the happiness of a nation. Nothing is more dignified than the divinity dwelling within us. As soon as nature has become master of the passions, and knows all that could excite them, she has, according to the words of Socrates, torn herself from that which chains her to sensuality,

17   N

and charmed, she submits herself to the gods, and has for mankind a tender solicitude." He defines as the original destiny of the soul, knowledge and love of God, to have but one will with God through resignation, and a constant practice of virtue. Man must do what is his to do, just as the fig-tree or the bees perform that for which they were destined. A virtuous man never troubles himself about what people say of him, think of him, or do against him, but he is contented when his actions are upright, and accomplishes with love what his vocation requires of him. Free from all excitement, he has no other will than the law of God. What a falsehood it is to say, "I will act openly!" What do you mean by that, my friend? One must read in your eyes what rests in your soul, just as a lover reads in the eyes of his bride what is passing in her heart. A hypocritical openness or candor is a concealed dagger. One can be a pious man, and yet be unknown to all. Never lose sight of this principle, that the happiness of life consists in a little. Make use of the short time you have. Yet a little while, and the time that is given you to do good will have passed away. Perform each action as if you were to die at the same moment. It sits badly on a wise man to express a talkative contempt for death.

Through the entire collection of his moral maxims, Marcus Aurelius showed that he was far nearer to Christianity than he himself imagined.

CHAPTER XVIII.

LYDIA'S DEPARTURE.

N the first days of May, a season in which the southern clime pours forth its blessings, the Greeks begin, according to the ancient heathen custom, to prepare for their processions in honor of their gods on all the cross-ways, to petition for a plentiful harvest.

Wherever a statue was to be found, either in the cross-streets or in the fields, there the people assembled in holiday attire, to make their offerings. This feast was called the Compitalien, because it was held in the cross-ways (in Compitis). Metella and Lydia, who had just returned from Eleusis, were standing at a window, looking down upon the altars of offerings and on the Pagan processions. Before the portico of the house, a servant is seen arranging luggage for a journey; on the opposite side of the olive-groves, in the distant harbor, flutter the pennant and flags of a large merchant-vessel, which is preparing to set sail in the evening, and is the one destined to carry Lydia to Rome in search of her mother.

"Good child," said Metella, "I was lately at the cemetery of Kerameikos visiting my father's grave, and my
thoughts turned on the changes and trials of my eventful life. I reflected on the melancholy hours that the
future promised me, and could have wished to lame the
wings of time, to postpone this our separation for a little
longer. While thus thinking and wishing, my eye fell
upon the trunk of a pine-tree, on the bark of which I
perceived something inscribed. On a closer inspection,
I discovered it to be the initials of my beloved son's
name, and from each letter the gum of the tree fell down
in golden tears. This made me feel your departure
doubly heavy. Every one whom I prize leaves me:
Father, husband, son, and friend; and I hope also to
depart soon, and then at last I shall find a resting-place.
But one thought comforts me, — that perhaps a great
joy awaits you, when you again meet your mother. Oh
tell her that I was often very unkind to you, that I
often grieved you and not seldom treated you badly.
But you must not refuse me two requests: they are the
most earnest I have ever made. The first is, that you
accept the means for your journey. The distance is
great, and the time of your sojourn in Rome very uncertain. I have placed amongst your effects a sum of
money, sufficient, not only for yourself, but to purchase
your mother's freedom; which, when you have purchased, then, my beloved child, — and this is my second
petition, — return with her to Athens, and you shall
spend happy days with me. — I know," continued Metella, "that you have a longing to return to your native
land, but for a widow who has much sorrow, Christian

friendship will not hesitate to deny itself a satisfaction in the cause of charity."

Lydia took the hands of her mistress reverently within her own, and lifting her eyes to heaven, sobbed forth, "May God bless you according to the goodness of your noble heart! Nothing but the duty I owe to my beloved mother could sanction this separation, and nothing but death, dear mistress, shall prevent our return." At this moment, Duranus struck the hour, and Metella and Lydia retired to the oratory, to pass the last moments together in prayer.

In the Lararium the lamp burned, as in former years, but the protecting house-gods had disappeared, and their place was occupied by the true and living God, Jesus Christ, under the species of bread. An emblematic picture concealed the tabernacle, wherein reposed the treasure of the faithful, for it was allowed to the early Christians to keep in their own homes this heavenly manna, particularly in troubled times, and to commune themselves. Metella advanced reverentially towards the tabernacle, opened it, and drew aside the curtain that concealed the Holy of Holies. From the tabernacle shone a silver dove, whose wings were raised as if in flight, and the breast was richly set with sparkling diamonds. Within this was the holy Eucharist, and near it was lying a reliquary and chain of gold; the centre of the case was set with one magnificent, large pearl. "In this little reliquary," said Metella, "I have enclosed a portion of the sacred bread. May our God accompany you on the waves, and protect you from the scoffs of the heathens!" At these words, she

17*

placed the chain round Lydia's neck, and concealed the case in the bosom of her dress.

.Lydia observed the pearl, and drawing forth the reliquary again, kissed it and said to her mistress, "It is a thought full of meaning, that you to the gold which encloses the great pearl of divine love, have added, on the exterior, a pearl, as a type of the interior. But, dearest mistress, it is the most costly of all your jewels, and perhaps a remembrance from your ancestors;—may I return it?"

"Do so," replied Metella,—"in Rome, if the price of thy mother's freedom will not be so great as I expect; but thou hast merited infinitely more, as you have led me to that field in which I discovered the great pearl of our holy faith.—I was as a beaten way," continued she, sighing, "till your prayers and tears loosened the soil, and placed within its bosom the seeds of faith. I was a cast-off piece of rough marble, in which a noble image slumbered, but which could only be brought to light by a good chisel. Dearest child, thou art that chisel, never to be forgotten. The artist that guided it is the Creator of the world, who formed the body of Eve, and placed it at the head of the creation. Blow after blow fell upon thee, thou patient instrument, and upon me, the hard unformed stuff. Still, the longer our martyrdom lasts, the nearer we are to its completion. Now the work is finished, therefore the chisel is to be put back to enjoy its well-merited rest."

After a most affectionate embrace, and with heart-felt thanks, Lydia tore herself from the arms of her benefactress. She departed from Athens, after having passed in it ten eventful years. Metella ascended the pergula to have a last look at the dear traveller. The sun sinking in the west, cast a rich glow on the distant Piræus; a soft evening breeze rose, and gently swelled the sails of the vessel.

Lydia was accompanied to the harbor by several of the domestics, all of whom loved her tenderly; and close to her side was the faithful Ophne, whose loquacity never ceased till they reached the harbor, nor would it then, had not the noise and confusion attracted her attention. The sailors were putting all in order: some were hauling in the ropes and unfurling sufficient sail; while one, with more authority than the rest, calls those to order who have the care of stowing in the luggage, to keep a sharp look-out for goods still left on the landing-place. A tight little fellow, although one of the crew, slips from the labor and confusion to a distant part of the ship, to hold converse with a friend on the opposite side of the water, — which seemed no easy task, as their questions and answers were almost drowned by the noisy waves and the freshening breeze. The hour for departure at length arrives, and the sailors are bustling to and fro, shouting with all their might, to tighten up and clear decks. The farewells were of a varied description. A mother could be seen parting with her only son, and in floods of tears, invoking for him the protection of the gods. Husbands taking leave of their wives and families, to seek in a foreign land a support for them, which was denied at home. Men were amongst the number, who by their countenances clearly showed that loss and gain were the sum-total of their existence here. They were alone, for when the heart is absorbed in the goods of this life, it closes itself against the tender ties of family and friends. Wealth is their god, and every sacrifice is made to the deity of their sordid minds.

The principal passengers consisted of rich merchants, trading between Greece, Rome, and Italy. Jews also, with their merchandise, and invalid Greeks, who then, as now, sought the restoration of their health in the balmy climate of Malta. Lydia joined herself to some Christian families who were bound for Rome. The decks being cleared, the trumpet blew the signal for departure, and Lydia waved her last adieu to her friends on shore.

"A happy journey!" screamed out little Ophne, "and a quick return;" and she dried up her falling tears, and returned pensively to the palace, regretting the loss of her dear friend. The second signal sounded, and, loosed from its moorings, the vessel floated on with swelling sail. They anchored at Delos. This island of the Grecian Archipelago, and so famous in ancient history, is said to have been at one time a floating island. Being the birthplace of Apollo and Diana, it was always held sacred on that account by the Pagans, and used as an asylum for all living creatures. In the distance was lovely Syra, rising above the blue waters like a citadel on a rock. This friendly and well-known island, famous in ancient times for its commerce, has even in our own days become a place of staple commodities. From Delos the ship sailed by the most southern point of the Morea, —so called from "Morus," a mulberry-tree, which abounds in that part of Greece, and is appropriated to the support of the silkworm. They then struck out on the high seas in the direction of the distantly situated Malta.

During the last months, the crowd of circumstances in Lydia's life had so oppressed her, that she was glad to be alone and unobserved, that she might recall to her mind the events that had so quickly followed in succession. She would sit for hours on the deck, apparently watching the foaming waters, but her mind was far distant, and busily occupied taking a retrospective view of the chequered scenes of her own eventful life. How much richer was she now in experience, after having passed through such a school of affliction! At the time she was captive in Smyrna, every pulse throbbed for martyrdom. Now experience taught her, that there was a still greater martyrdom than that of the sword or fire; and that to a certain extent, her life as a slave had been nothing but a continued one, which had ended in the conquest of the Faith. How unmistakable did the loving dispensations of Providence present themselves before her mind! She had been appointed as an humble instrument towards the conversion of one of the most illustrious women of Athens. God had prepared this soul to embrace Christianity by the death of her husband and son, — trials over which her wealth had no control; but these drew her to the possession of that which neither temporal prosperity nor the gifts of the mind could purchase for her—the one Faith. The human heart has a necessity to communicate with those after death whom it loved in life, and this communication is only possible when the belief is in the immortality of

the soul. This was the first motive that attracted Metella towards conversion. But what Christianity was,
and in what manner it was to be practised in order to
prepare man for a supernatural life, she learned from her
slave. At length, God showed her the truth of His revealed Religion, by His holy servants, and confirmed the
doctrine of the same by the wonderful interference of
His own divine power.

If a voyage be long, and for the greater part monotonous, how can a meditative mind fail for a subject, when
it beholds, in the immeasurable waters of the deep, the
beauties of nature in their wildest form. The sea itself
gives ample scope for contemplation. Is it not in its
calm, as well as in its loud anger, in its immeasurable
extent, as well as in its unfathomable depths, a type of
the Divinity? And is not the vessel that sails on the
bosom of the waves, between the blue firmament and
the yawning, unknown abyss, a figure of man who wanders through life between the haven of grace and the
depth of depravity?

When the great luminary of the day sinks in the
west, and leaving to the wide expanse of heaven his
reflective rays, almost as varied in color as the rainbow,
does it not give the soul a longing desire to wing its
flight above and bask in the eternal sunshine of its
Creator!

What loving soul that has ever gazed on the starry
heavens when on the sea, can say that he was ever more
deeply impressed with the majesty of God, and his own
nothingness, than at such a moment? He is as a mite
on the face of the waters, wondering at the immensity

of its Creator. It seems as though the soul would burst its earthly bondage, soar on high, and mingle with the starry host. That milky way, where the stars roll as in a cloud of vapor, draws our mind along, higher and higher, until it arrives at the palace of the Almighty. It is only a heart full of faith that can appreciate all this. Just as in the darkness of night a million of worlds appear to man, which by the dazzling light of day are to Him invisible, so the dispensations of the power and wisdom of God disclose themselves to the single eye of the believer in the hidden darkness of life —a government of which the enlightened minds of the wise ones of the world have not the slightest conception.

The passengers could as yet see nothing of lovely Malta, save the tops of the sloping hills that were just appearing above the horizon. As they approached nearer, its steep and rugged coast excited no small degree of alarm among the passengers. On those rocks, thought Lydia, the vessel that was conveying the great St. Paul as prisoner to Rome, was shattered by a storm, leaving its crew, pensioners on the bounty and hospitality of its benevolent inhabitants, who first looked upon the great Apostle as a murderer, on seeing a viper cling to his arm, but on beholding him cast the reptile from him, into the fire, without his having received any injury, they looked upon him as a god. While the vessel anchored, to land the passengers destined for the island, Lydia felt a strong desire to place her foot upon a soil hallowed by the presence and miracles of such an illustrious convert; but as she could not gratify this laudable desire, she implored the protection of the saint for the remainder of the journey to that renowned city, where he was twice imprisoned, and sealed his labors by his martyrdom. As the vessel receded from the shore, Lydia gazed on the watery element that lay before her,—and never did the providence of God appear to her greater than at that moment, when she reflected that a number of human beings were assembled together in a fragile vessel, moving upon the face of the unfathomable waters, with nothing but a few planks between them and eternity: Land had again entirely disappeared, and nothing could be seen but the blue vault of heaven, closed in on every side of the horizon by the expansive waters. A few birds of passage were the only living creatures to be met with,—untiring travellers! they cut through the air and seek but a moment's rest, on either the masts of the vessel or a water-plant. Unwearied as these birds, does Time also fly, and when we think he lingers with us, we find ourselves carried away by him much quicker.

In Syracuse, the passengers received a more exact account of the glorious conquest by the Emperor, and the soldiers returning home to Sicily, lauded Marcus for his extraordinary generosity in bestowing presents on the troops. Between hope and fear, the vessel anchored off the eastern coast of Sicily, where, not far distant, rose in gigantic heights the imposing Ætna, which sent forth, in deep draughts, black clouds of smoke in graceful curls, darkening the blue ether. Pretty little barks, with their dazzling sails, were to be seen in numbers floating by, and stopping at the several places of their destination along the shore. Dolphins bounded over the surface of the waters touching the sides of the vessel in their playful gambols. Higher up, the anchor was dropped at the famous city of Catania, so beautifully situated at the foot of Mount Ætna, and which to this day ranks as one of the elegant cities of Europe, though it has frequently suffered from the volcanic eruptions of its majestic neighbor. Having landed the passengers bound for that city, they steered their course to the Straits, that passage so much dreaded by the ancients, but through which they passed in safety; and leaving a cluster of islands to the west, they found themselves again on the broad waters, making rapid sail for the coast of Italy. They passed by the matchless bay of Naples, with its city partly seated on the declivity of a hill, and its broad shores studded with beauteous villas and lovely gardens, — presenting an unrivalled assemblage of the picturesque and beautiful, and bearing a strong contrast to the rugged Vesuvius in the background.

Few voyages could present more interesting variety than the one our travellers had just completed, and yet it was with joy that they saw themselves nearing their destination.

Those for Rome were landed at Ostia, a distance from Rome of fourteen miles, and Lydia for the first time set foot on Italian soil. After having passed a day at Ostia, she proceeded to Rome by land. The nearer she approached its walls, the more intense became her feelings, and alternate hope and fear agitated her breast. With a holy awe she approached that city, which was even

18

then the centre of the Christian world. And who could not feel a more than ordinary interest on finding himself in the city of the Cæsars? Rome, as a late writer of this "Eternal City" expresses himself in one of his works, is the mysterious link between two worlds, wherein is represented the history of man under the influence of Paganism and of Christianity; and as on earth all rivers flow towards the ocean, so run in the divine, as in the human order, all events of the ancient, as well as of the modern history, out of one city,—and this city is Rome. Rome can therefore say of itself, "I am the world!"

11 *   H

CHAPTER XIX.

THE TRIUMPHAL PROCESSION.

A. D. 176.

HEN Lydia landed in Italy, she heard that the Emperor, who had already returned from the campaign, had, after a short stay, departed again, accompanied by his wife, Faustina, on a visit to the East; but was expected back to Rome in a few days. On his arrival he was to celebrate his conquest over the barbarians. The feast promised to be one of extraordinary magnificence: first, because he had been so little in Rome for the last eight years; and secondly, because, on his recent journey to the East, he had suffered a misfortune in the sudden death of his wife Faustina, who met her fate at the foot of the Taurus mountains. The sympathy of Rome upon the death of this woman, renowned for wickedness, was in the exterior only, for in private they congratulated themselves upon the happy event.

Marcus Aurelius gave himself up to intense grief, and had a temple built in her honor.

The Emperor was waited for by the Consuls and Prætors in Brundusium, one of the most renowned seaports of Calabria.

Thus Rome, "City of the World," expected with impatience and anxiety, from one day. to another, the arrival of its Emperor.

A violent storm was the cause of the delay, which, as the historians relate, placed the vessels in the most imminent danger. Commodus, the Emperor's son, was at that time sixteen years old, and for his age remarkably tall and robust. He and his eldest sister Lucilla, the young widow of Verus, went to meet their father, with a numerous retinue, and congratulated him at Præmeste. In this very place he invested his son with the dignity of the Tribuneship, and commanded that he should stand beside him on the golden chariot during the triumphal procession.

Upon the Campus Vaticanus in Rome, where now stands the Pope's Palace, the procession was arranged. All the Senators had assembled there to receive the Emperor. Behind them were numerous animals for sacrifice, — white bulls, with gilt horns. The spoils of war were dragged along; then came the inscriptions, and figurative representations of the generals and the conquered Germans. Then followed the unhappy captives, who were brought to Rome when the campaign had terminated. "Have you already heard," was the saying, "that it is actually true, what Tacitus relates, that Helusians and Oxioners have heads and faces of men, but that the remainder of the body is a wild animal? Come let us see them!"

Bands of musicians were filling up the time with their drums and fifes, and changing alternately with the singers. The Lictors then arrived in their purple tunics, and their fasces were entwined with laurels; they took their places immediately behind the captives. A great company of jesters filled up the rear, and immediately before the triumphal chariot, which was still unoccupied, stood rows of priests attired in all their festive solemnity, and carrying the insignia of their gods, the vessels for sacrifice and for incense. Masses of people from the city and from the country, forced themselves into all the elevated positions where could be had a clear view. The field of Mars, as well as the Vatican Hills on the other side of the Portus Triumphalis, — then the hill of Marius, — the bridges and all the surrounding heights, were crowded with spectators. The public places where the procession touched at, and the windows of the houses in those streets through which it passed, were filled with people of all ranks.

The musicians commenced anew, when a hollow sound, that aroused attention, passed through the dense crowd, and shouts reached them from the distance announcing the arrival of the conqueror.

"*Io Triumphe! triumphe!*" cried out the people.

"*Vita et victoria magno Imperatori!*"— Life and victory to the great Emperor!

The triumphal car was drawn by richly caparisoned elephants. Marcus Aurelius wore a purple mantle bordered with gold, and a toga embroidered with stars. He held in the left hand an ivory sceptre headed with the Roman eagle, and in the right, a palm-branch. The

18 *   O

crown that encircled his brow was of gold and precious stones, and made so as to represent laurel-leaves. Commodus was dressed precisely similar.

A herald went on before, commanding silence; and behind him were boys who sung the song of triumph, and men repeated each time the last words of the strophe. The hymn lauded the bravery, the paternal care, and the immortality of their divine ruler.

The car had not yet reached the triumphal arch, when young Commodus was seen looking several times up at the heights of the newly built Moles Adriani, now called Angel's Mount, and laughingly drew his father's attention to a sight that presented itself there. It was Brutus Præsais with his daughter Crispina, who occupied magnificent seats under the imperial tents. The daughter, who was about thirteen years old, uttered a cry of joy as the procession approached, and waved a flag unceasingly, until she drew upon her the eyes of Commodus. But when she saw his face painted with vermilion,* she burst into loud laughter, and ran to conceal herself behind her father. That very Crispina was Rome's future Empress, and was married a short time after to Commodus. How little did she suspect at the time, what her fate would be!†

The more the Emperor and his son enjoyed the scene, the more did the African, who stood behind the Cæsars, fulfil his duty. According to the ancient custom, a slave, who held in his hand a golden crown, and who

* The face of the conqueror was painted with vermilion, like the statue of Jupiter on feast-days. Plin. xxxiii.

† Crispina was later banished to the Island of Capri, and there murdered.

stood behind the car, had to call out frequently during the procession, "Remember that thou art mortal."

As the African crown-bearer repeated these words several times in the ear of Commodus, he pushed him back in his rough manner, with the words, "I am no common mortal."

The procession had turned round the Via Triumphalis, where Adrian's Mausoleum could no longer be seen. But tears so bitter as those that fell from the captives, the soil of Rome had seldom drunk. That the pain and sacrifice of a tedious war should end for them in such disgrace! The captives walked along, carrying on their arms heavy chains, and derided and mocked by the most flighty and contemptible men in the world. Their dark blue eyes, shaded with bushy eyebrows, were cast to the earth, and only raised to throw an expression of the deepest hatred on their deriders. Their auburn hair flowed proudly down their muscular backs in natural curls. Their national costume, a simple woollen mantle, or the skin of a beast fastened on the breast with a buckle or strong clasp, increased their herculean appearance. Young Commodus almost envied them, as he liked so much to be compared with Hercules.* Some of the barbarian generals and princes had on a richer costume, and by their mien, and every motion of their body, showed the proud national feeling that pervaded their whole frame. Women and children were also amongst the captives. The women wore the same

---

* When Emperor, Commodus called himself the "Roman Hercules," ran about at night dressed in the skin of a lion, and struck all those he met, with a club.

costume as the men, except that some of them were clothed in white linen, which here and there was colored fancifully with red. Their garments closed tightly round their shoulders, leaving part of their arms uncovered.*

The cries of the children were most touching, and they were clinging closely to their mothers and calling for help, thereby redoubling the pain of their parents. To increase the hatred of their captives, there was a pantomimist, who in the midst of leapers and jesters, ornamented with golden chains and manacles, mimicked all the gestures of the barbarians;—the grinding of their teeth, the thrusting with their clenched fists, and the whining of the children. He runs first before, and then behind, depending upon the protection of the Lictors. On the bridge crossing the Tiber, one of the scoffers got a blow from an iron chain in his face, with such force, that the blood streamed down, and he had to thank his red mantle for not being himself a subject of laughter. No wonder that the cithern and pipe-players who surrounded the pantomimist, moderated their leaping. What was taken from the enemy in helmets, arms, and vessels of the temple, in gold and bronze, was of little value. Amongst their arms, the native spear of the conquered excited some attention. It was of small, short, but very sharp iron. The shields were also considered remarkable, because of their form, and rare variety of ornaments.

The distinguished Romans, who accompanied the triumphal car, were a cheerful contrast to the despairing

* Tacitus Germ. a. m.

gloom of the captives. Immediately behind the nobles, the cohorts of the victorious soldiers followed; the foot and cavalry were crowned with wreaths. They sing songs in praise of their arms, and seize the wine and delicate morsels which were now and then offered them by the nobles. Whatever houses the procession passed, were ornamented with garlands, flowers, and tapestry, on which the initials of the Emperor's name were richly embroidered. The cries, "*Io triumphe! Vivant Patres Patriæ!*"—"Triumph! triumph to the father of the fatherland!" echoed from all sides.*

The pavement of the different streets was thickly strewn with flowers, so that Rome resembled a flower-garden. In addition to this, the air was heavy with perfume,—for from every temple the incense rose in clouds, but from the Pantheon of Agrippa, and from the Capitoline Hill it was dense.

The Emperor was so affected at his reception, that he called out to the people several times, "This is the happiest day of my life!" and he kissed the golden bull that hung upon his neck as a preservative against envy.

* Young Commodus, nearly a year later, as Marcus Aurelius had him titled Augustus and partner in the government, received from the Senate the honorable title of "Father of the Fatherland," a title of which he was as unworthy as the Senate who conferred it. How Commodus, who was sole Emperor at eighteen years old, treated the Senate, can be seen by the following example. Once he killed a bird in the amphitheatre, cut off its head and returned to his seat with his bloody sword; then he showed the head of the bird to the Senators, who were sitting near him, and gave them by menaces to understand that he would treat their heads so. Dio Cassius, who relates the circumstance, sat under them, and declares they could only suppress their laughter at the comic scene, by stuffing their mouths with the leaves of their laurel-wreaths, which they pulled from their hair. The laughter would have cost them their lives.

At the foot of the Capitol a large statue of Faustina was erected, before which the procession halted, and the Emperor descended from the car of triumph and offered incense. Then he ascended the marble steps of Jupiter Capitolinus; when ascending, the Moor presented him with the golden crown, and the conqueror laid it at the feet of Jupiter with the words, "The gods have conquered: to Jupiter Pluvius belongs the crown."

The animals that followed in the procession were here offered in sacrifice. At the same moment sacrifices commenced in all the other temples. The procession at an end, the feasting commenced. On this, and on the following days, public festivities of all sorts were celebrated, whereby old and young, high and low, and particularly the common people, gave themselves up to all sorts of gaming, and the most far-fetched revelling and gormandizing in the customary way, and which were indigenous to the Roman people. The plays, says an ancient writer, which the Emperor had provided for the people, were magnificent, and at one of them appeared not less than a hundred lions for combat. Notwithstanding his great efforts to make himself pleasing to all, still he opposed them in their desire of gladiatorial combats. He took their swords, and exchanged them for the rapier, and maintained that they could prove their skill equally with them, and that the murders would be less frequent.

The feast was concluded by Marcus making presents to the people: no Emperor, in fact, held them in so much consideration as he did. He mentioned, in a speech to them, his several years' absence from Rome, and some who were listening to him held up eight

fingers and called out, "Eight years." The Emperor
gave immediate orders for each one present to receive
eight pieces of gold of the value of a ducat, in remembrance of those eight years. The provincial towns, as
Dio Cassius remarks, and particularly Smyrna, that had
just risen from its ashes, were richly gifted by the Emperor. Through such munificence, the coffers of Marcus
Aurelius were so much exhausted, that at last he had
no money. He therefore put up his imperial jewels, his
plate, and even Faustina's jewels and wardrobe, for public sale.

Inasmuch as Marcus Aurelius gained the favor of his
people by his generosity, and as much as he labored to
establish his dignity, so much the more was Commodus
hated by them; so that all the intentions and labors of
the noble father were wrecked on the worthlessness of
the son. He was wanton, cruel, unjust, and rapacious,
and in every respect bore a striking resemblance to his
tyrannical and depraved predecessor, Domitian, and his
greatest ambition was to be styled, "The conqueror of a
thousand gladiators." Commodus' wicked career was
terminated by a sudden and violent death, in the thirty-
first year of his age, after a reign of thirteen years.

CHAPTER XX.

LYDIA IN SEARCH OF HER MOTHER.

UCIEN remarked once, in speaking of the Christians: "It is scarcely to be believed how these men, so indifferent to the duties of the state, can run, the moment the neck of one of their own sect is in danger; they assemble together like ants to save him. They are persuaded that they are immortal in soul and body, and are taught to believe that they are all brothers."

How could it be difficult, under such circumstances, for one of their faith, entering the imperial city as a stranger, to find a hospitable reception with sympathizing brothers.

Even as it is to this day, where the members of that community settle themselves near the church, so we find that the Christians of that time placed themselves near the sanctuary, and that too on the east side of the city.

The Viminal Hill could perhaps be called the first spot where a colony of Christians settled. "Already in the time of the apostles there were in Rome, places consecrated to God,—by some called oratories, by others churches,—where, on every first day of the week, a meeting took place, and the Christians who prayed there heard the word of God, and received communion."*

At the foot of the Viminal stood the church called the "Church of the Shepherd." In this church, which was afterwards called St. Pudentiana, St. Peter had officiated a hundred years previous, and there celebrated the sacred mysteries. S.S. Peter and Paul, during their sojourn in Rome, converted to Christianity the Senator Pudens and his daughters; and those two daughters, Pudentiana and Praxedes, who clung to the Faith with a holy zeal, appropriated not only their dwelling-places, but the entire of their fortunes to religious purposes.

At this day, eighteen hundred years later, strangers find in Rome, not far from the famous Basilica of S. Maria Maggiore, two churches called St. Pudentiana and St. Praxedes.

Although Lydia was a stranger in Rome, still she found in these oratories several Christians, who with the greatest kindness assured her of their services, for they were at that time, as in the apostles', "One heart and one soul." She hastened to impart to her first acquaintance, how her mother had been torn from her, several years back, at Smyrna,—that she was a Christian, and her name Charitana, and that she was probably a slave in Rome. The number of the Christians was then so great, that it would have been difficult in so large a city to find a slave, who had in all probability changed her former name. Besides, the rich families were, for the most part,

* C. f. Proprium Sanctorum in dedicut. Basil S. S. Salvatoris.

19

in the country during the summer months, seeking change of air, either in the mountains or at the sea-side, where they were attended by the greater number of their domestics.

Lydia resolved to remain in Rome, and to seek her mother unceasingly until she had found her, or till she had received certain news of her fate.

She was told that in a few days the feast of St. Magdalen would be celebrated, and that for this purpose many of the Christians would assemble in the Catacombs near the Appian Way, for divine service, and that she would probably then receive more certain news of Charitana.

At these words, Lydia's countenance brightened; she felt herself the happiest of mortals, and imagined herself already in the embraces of her dear mother, from whom she had been so long separated. This hope did not deter her from making inquiries of all the Christians she met, asking them if they had seen or heard anything of Charitana. She went first of all to a pious and wealthy matron, named Felicitas, to whom she was recommended by Bishop Dionysius, and was received by her as if she had belonged to the renowned family of this much-tried woman. The circumstance that she was the daughter of one sold on account of her Faith, was a sufficient recommendation. Felicitas promised that she would introduce her to the Roman Bishop Soter, at the next meeting of the Faithful, and added that perhaps he could give her some intelligence.

We will now accompany the Christians to the nightly

meeting, which on the above-named day took place in the Catacombs in the Appian Way. It is two hours past midnight, and Rome is sunk in sleep; but here and there can be seen a straggler, who has been tempted to linger with his dissolute companions far beyond the hour prescribed by usage. Approaching footsteps echoed along the deserted streets; some females from the house of a wealthy Roman solicitor, Minitius Felix, were wending their way in profound silence along the Esqui-line Hill, and passing the Coliseum. This gigantic structure, erected by order of Vespasian, is said to have been built in one year, by the forced labor of 12,000 Jews and Christians. It consisted of three orders of architecture, the Doric, Ionic, and Corinthian, and was sixteen hundred and twelve feet in circumference. It contained eighty arcades, and was capable of accommodating a hundred thousand spectators. Their road led to the new and extensive baths built by Antoninus, and then across to the Via Appia towards the Almo River. The females to the left advance towards some villas in the valley of Egeria, where were some monuments to the departed Romans, and a temple to the Deus Ridiculus.

The pious company had not yet reached the Catacombs, when Lydia interrupted the long silence of her companions by remarking, "I wonder if I shall see my mother again in this world! Now that I expect to hear something of her, I feel myself oppressed with an unusual heaviness and anxious sorrow. Our wandering here in the first dawn of morning, as well as the tombs here in the Appian Way,—yes, the memory of the saint herself, whose feast we are going to celebrate,—all re-mind me of the journey of those holy women, who, be-fore it was yet day, departed from Jerusalem to visit the sepulchre of our Redeemer. Perhaps our way will also lead to a grave."

"Why such melancholy thoughts," interrupted Feli-citas; "remember that Magdalen found Him living, whom she sought in the grave. We are also going to the graves of the saints, who lie in the Catacombs, and perhaps you will find her, whom you seek amongst the dead, also living." The nearer she approached the en-trance, the more animated became the streets which led to the subterraneous churches. Christians from all parts were assembling at that early hour, to join in the solemn service. The women passed through a door to the sub-terraneous streets and to the last resting-places of so many thousands of the faithful departed. A youth was keeping a careful watch at the door, and offered them a taper. The air was thick and oppressive, which the heat of summer did not tend to lessen, and the smell of mouldering bodies was scarcely to be borne. The gray walls of the alternately small and large passages, which crossed each other a hundred times, were full of aper-tures in the form of open coffins; some of these apertures, which were carried up on each side in several tiers, were covered with stone slabs, on each of which was an in-scription in Latin or Greek. In some places, a little earthen vessel was placed before the inscription, a sign that a martyr rested there. There were in several places, sacred emblems under the inscriptions,—such as a deer thirsting for water, or a pair of palm-branches, or a ship

in full sail. On many of the slabs the initials of our
Lord's name could be seen.

They had already gone through several of these subterranean passages, when at length the sound of music
fell upon their ears. Further on, the space widened,
and a subterranean church, lighted up with lamps and
wax lights, opened to their view. The length of the
church was considerable, and contained two divisions,
one for the clergy and men, the other for the females.

At the conclusion of the singing, an aged priest advanced towards the altar, and turning from the people,
commenced the divine sacrifice. The arrangements of
the prayers were, for the most part, as they are now.
After the holy sacrifice, a great number of those present
retired to an adjacent hall, to hand to the Bishop charitable gifts, or to consult on the affairs of the faithful.
Lydia had looked round in vain to see if her mother
were among the number of those present. Felicitas
turned to one of the Deacons, and begged his permission
to speak to the aged priest who had just celebrated
mass. Her request was granted, and she informed him
that a Christian from Smyrna had arrived in search of
her mother, who was also a Christian, and named Charitana, and after whom she had, up to the present, made
fruitless inquiries. At this, joy and pain were alike
depicted on the priest's countenance, for he doubted not
being able to give the information she required. The
young stranger stood motionless before him, her eye
anxiously fixed upon every movement of his lips. She
expected that the thousand conjectures which had so
often harassed her mind were now about to be con-

19*

firmed. "O thou happy child!" said the old man,—
"happy in having been in the school of St. Polycarp,
and threefold happy, because thou art the daughter of a
Saint!"

His voice began to falter, which Felicitas perceiving,
understood at once what was to follow, and turned aside
to conceal her emotion. Lydia did not understand the
meaning of his words; her heart beat violently, as the
old man rose and motioned to them to follow him.
They went through long passages that crossed each
other at intervals, till they came to one somewhat
wider; here the priest stood still. He brushed away a
tear, and motioned Lydia to approach. With deep emotion, he drew her attention to a square stone, upon
which the light of the torch fell, and helped her to
perceive, though indistinctly, the name of her beloved
mother.

"Charitana the martyr lies here, as a saint among the
Saints. She died on the Ides of April. Rejoice in the
Lord, and pray for us!"

Lydia read the inscription, and turned with a look
full of vague sorrow towards Felicitas. Her eye betrayed a doubt as to whether she was not mistaken; and
looking at her friend, she suddenly uttered a loud scream
that echoed through the vaults, and cast herself convulsively into the arms of Felicitas, where she remained
motionless for some minutes. At last she began to
realize her position. She was standing at the grave of
her mother, Charitana;—in that very hour in which
she had hoped to find her living, she had found her
tomb. A phial of the Martyr's blood stood near the

slab. What hast thou not to suffer, much-tried daughter, before thy body sinks beneath the burden of thy
trials! Thou camest from Athens to Rome to seek thy
long-lost mother, and thou hast found nothing but her
tomb! O that thou also couldst rest here in peace!
Faith and affection struggled within her,—affection
grieved at not having her beloved mother on earth, but
Faith rejoiced at her triumph. The latter conquered,
and the daughter sank upon her knees and pressed her
hands upon the stone that covered the remains of all
she held most dear. Many and strong were the feelings
that agitated her heart,—sorrow and pity struggled for
mastery, but the joy that the departed one had gained
the crown of martyrdom, silenced every other emotion.
At that time, as well as now, a lively faith penetrated
the hearts of the believers, and the separation between
the living and the dead did not appear so dreadful.
Fervent Christians considered a good death as the greatest gift from God; and what can any one wish more for
those he loves, than the possession of the highest of all
gifts—God Himself!

Therefore, great as Lydia's joy would have been, had
she found her mother amongst the living, still she was
no less delighted that she had suffered death for the
Faith, by which she had secured the immediate possession of God. Charitana, as we have already related,
was shipped for Rome on the night of the earthquake
of Smyrna, and was there purchased by a former Prefect. As long as the persecution was quiet, Cresentius
would not betray that she was a Christian.

The philosopher Justin wrote a letter of defence

about this time, and addressed it to Marcus Aurelius, and the Senate. Soon after he was cast into prison, together with several other Christians. Cresentius, in order to ingratiate himself with the Proconsul Rusticus, sent his slave Charitana to him, telling him that he might do with her what he liked. The Proconsul ordered Charitana, whose strength was already greatly impaired by anxiety, to be sent to the same prison with the other Christians. When Justin, with six of his companions in the Faith, was brought before the judge, he commenced speaking, and declared openly and frankly that they would preserve their faith to their last breath. To offer sacrifice to the gods, as the Emperor had commanded, Justin held to be in opposition to the commands of the Redeemer. Rusticus questioned him as to what sort of learning occupied him. Justin gave the answer that is to be found in the acts of his martyrdom: "I exerted myself to attain knowledge of all sorts, but as I could not therein find the truth, I at last devoted myself to Christian philosophy, although it displeases those who allow themselves to be blinded by error and prejudice. I glory in it, because it has afforded me the advantage of walking in the way of truth."

When asked by the Prefect about the place where the Christians usually assembled, he answered, "They assemble when and where they can. Our God is not bound to any certain place, as he is invisible, and fills Heaven and earth; He is praised and worshipped in all places."

The judge put similar questions to the others who

were imprisoned with Justin, and they all answered that they were Christians by the mercy of God. "Are you convinced," said the Proconsul, turning to Justin, "that you will ascend to Heaven if you be scourged from head to foot?"

Justin answered in the affirmative. "Our sufferings will hasten our happiness, and carry us to that judg-ment-seat before which all will have to appear." The others added, "It is useless to keep us longer waiting. We are Christians, and will never sacrifice to the gods."

As the Prefect saw that they persevered undauntedly in their refusal, he condemned them to be first scourged, and then, according to the Roman method, he com-manded them once more to sacrifice to the gods: but all refused. The martyrs were then led to the place of execution where they received their glorious crowns.

Justin had already fallen, and five of his companions had shared his fate, leaving Charitana alone standing in the blood of her companions. She bent her head to the earth in all humility, crossed her arms upon her breast, and remained in prayer. As she returned no answer to the many questions put to her by the judge, Rusticus gave a sign to the executioner, and immediately his rough hand seized her fainting form by the shoulder, cast her to the ground, and in a moment her head lay severed from her body.

The legends have preserved to us the names of these six martyrs who suffered with Justin, and they are: Charitana, Euclipistus, Hierax, Pæon, Liberianus, and Chariton. The year of this event is given as A. D. 167, 13th of April. Justin is honored by the Greeks on the 1st of June. **P**

After this short digression, let us return again to the grave of Charitana. He who led her daughter to it, is already departed to join the meeting which was usual after the sacrifice. He is no other than the kind and pious pope, Soter, who is like the Good Shepherd in the midst of his threatened sheep, and whose bare appearance is a loud exhortation to all to stand firm. Church history praised this holy pope in a particular manner, on account of his mildness and fatherly tenderness. Not only to the members of the Church in Rome did the Pope extend his care, but also to each one individually, no matter whence he came. That same Dionysius whom we before mentioned, sent his thanks to the Faithful in Rome for the donations they had forwarded to him at Corinth. "From the beginning of Christianity," he wrote to them, "you were accustomed to assist the faithful in every possible way, and to supply the wants of many churches. You have also provided for the support of the poor brethren in the mines, and thereby proved yourselves true imitators of our great Master. Your bishop, the highly venerated Soter, far from preventing this praiseworthy custom, has himself, on the contrary, given it a fresh impetus, and he is not only careful to distribute alms collected for the support of the Christians, but he comforts with the tenderness of a father all the Faithful who go to Rome."

How consoling it was for Lydia to witness the truth confirmed of all she had heard in Greece of Soter's goodness. There was not one in the whole assembly for whom this holy man had not a word of encouragement and edification. None amongst them is truly in need, because all are rich in love. It was one and the same faith which called the Christians of the only true Church to such meetings, and if they were threatened with worldly power, so one and the same hope made each danger small, nay, insignificant. But that the calumnies which were to be met with everywhere in the heathen writings were without foundation, we can see already from the letter which Pliny the younger addressed to the Emperor Trajan, in which amongst other things he says: "The Christians assure us that their entire guilt consists in this, that, on certain days before the rising of the sun, they assemble to sing a hymn in honor of Christ the Son of God. Therefore they would not have solemnly bound themselves to treason, but on the contrary refrain from theft and adultery, and the denial of that which is intrusted to them."

The Faithful withdrew separately to return to the city. The pope still remained in the meeting-hall to arrange the collections. Lydia advanced to the holy father, cast herself at his feet, and thanked him for what he had done for her mother. At the same time she had learned that, as Soter had been a friend of St. Polycarp, and in consideration of Charitana having been his spiritual daughter, he gave orders himself for her burial and tomb. The kind pope exhorted Lydia to imitate the virtues of her mother, and to persevere with firmness to the end, in imitating her Divine Master. She then visited the tombs of Anicetus and of several other popes, and returned with her companions through the entrance of the Catacombs to the Via Appia.

CHAPTER XXI.

SOLITUDE AND HOLY PLACES.

YDIA, after the events of the last few days. sought retirement in a little room appropriated for her use in the house of the pious Felicitas, there to recover her strength in silence, and to impart the results of her visit to Rome to her much valued and now only friend on earth, Metella. She felt it her duty to give a detailed account of everything she saw and heard to her dear mistress. After God, it was the only solace left her, to communicate her inmost thoughts to one whom she so tenderly loved.

Rome was at this time peopled by nearly a million of inhabitants, and although its magnificent palaces and temples, its public baths and pleasure-grounds, could not be surpassed, still Lydia preferred to renounce the immediate seeing of those great sights, that she might reflect on the wonderful ways of God, particularly as they had been revealed to her within the last few days. She was accustomed at all times, as often as a remarkable event occurred that broke through the monotony

of her hidden life, to retire into herself, and seek to discover the cause, by a close union with God. The sweet
remembrances of her joyful childhood passed like
phantoms before her eyes. She thought of the time
when, as a cheerful, happy child, she sat on her mother's
knee, and listened to her pious instructions, and the
raptures with which she spoke of the happiness that is
prepared in Heaven for those who serve God faithfully
on earth. Then, the remembrance of the sorrowful
hours she spent at the bedside of a dying father, whose
pious exhortations sank deeply into her youthful mind.
Then, how she sat at the feet of those holy men, filled
with the Divine Spirit, to be instructed by them in the
faith, and who afterwards shed their blood in its defence.
But she became doubly afflicted when her thoughts
turned upon the last meeting she had with her dear
mother. But this was now at an end, and her heart
beat with emotion as she looked heavenward, and represented to herself the glorious triumphs of the saints;
and she knew that in the number of the elect she had
an advocate that would never forget her. If a breath
of temptation passed over her pure heart, the bare
thought of this, her advocate, was a strong shield
against all the suggestions of the Evil One. So should
all Christian mothers become the guardian spirits of
their children here on earth, and if the heart of a well-
trained child find itself inclined to commit sin, the
remembrance of a mother's pious admonitions will
never fail to warn it against the seductions of the
common Enemy.

The beloved parent of Lydia had given her, during

20

life, a perfect model of what a Christian ought to be, and confirmed it by her holy death. God did not accept the sacrifice of Lydia's freedom, which she had come from Greece to offer; but the merit was not less, for God accepts the will, and in that the sacrifice was included. Therefore the pious daughter could from that time forward perfectly enjoy her freedom, the greatest amongst all the temporal blessings, and that which is the most difficult to resign.

No Christian would leave Rome without visiting the tombs of the saints. "In my youth," said Hieronymus, "when I studied in Rome, I used to spend my Sundays at the tombs of the Apostles and Martyrs. How often have I visited the crypts, where their sacred remains lay side by side, and surrounded by a darkness that impressed the visitor with a holy awe!"

The tombs of S.S. Peter and Paul first claimed Lydia's attention. According to Pope Gregory, the two Apostles were first buried in the Catacombs, two miles distant from the city. Soon afterwards, the body of St. Peter was brought to the Vatican Hill, and that of St. Paul to the Ostian Way. After Lydia had visited the tombs of the Apostles, before which so many thousand Christians had had their faith strengthened, she then desired to see the spot where her mother's blood had been shed. Felicitas, who accompanied her on the way, showed her the temple of Jupiter on the Capitoline Hill, under which were the dark prisons, where so many Christians, Lydia's mother amongst the number, had suffered imprisonment. These vaults were hewn out of the Capitoline Hill, and to the deepest there was not even a passage, and the condemned had to be slipped into the vault on planks; this can be seen at the present day. In one of these subterraneous prisons, was also St. Peter, wherein he baptized a jailer with water from a spring, which he in a wonderful manner, like a second Moses, brought forth from the rock. What a multitude of thoughts did not the sight of the Roman Capitol occasion! Above, was the temple of Jupiter, surrounded by a multiplicity of little shrines dedicated to the numer- ous idols; beneath, as it was then thought, was the tomb for Christianity;—above, the signs of unlimited self- love, which, as St. Augustine says, reaches to self-deifi- cation; beneath, the signs of the love of God, which humbles and annihilates self. At a short distance is the Forum. Who then can describe the glorious combats that were here fought, and who could name the thou- sands that heard their sentence here? On reaching the Forum, Lydia knelt down and kissed the marble flags which covered this memorable place, for from that spot her mother's soul had ascended to heaven. Felicitas advanced a little, and showed her where the Prefect's seat was at that time,—where Justin had stood, and where her mother had shed her blood.

"When Rusticus saw," continued Felicitas, "that Chari- tana would not sacrifice to the gods, he ordered her to be scourged,—a punishment, my child, that a greater than we had to bear, long before us. She then placed herself close to her companions, and prayed unceasingly, with bowed head. She was so lost in prayer, that she never moved her position when the head of Justin was held up to the applauding multitude. At last when her turn came, she stepped forward, and answered the two questions: 'For whom do you die? and, does death appear so agreeable?' Her answer was: 'For my Faith in Christ, who is my Redeemer and my all. It is sweet to suffer for a friend, but to die for God is heavenly delight.'"

Lydia, with tears in her eyes, looked at one time on the earth, at another towards heaven. How willingly would she not have resigned her life at that moment, to be happy with her mother. Occupied with these thoughts, she left the Forum, and Felicitas led her to the great amphitheatre of Nero, which from the adjacent high Collossus was called the Coliseum. How many hundred Christians, true to the faith, have stood on this Arena,—how many lions and leopards have here lapped up the blood of the martyrs,—and how did the applause of ninety thousand spectators thunder forth, when such amusements were granted to pagan Rome! There were still two other tombs in which Lydia felt the deepest interest, although in later centuries the veil of oblivion has passed over them.

About twenty years before Lydia's birth, there lived, in a province of Umbria, a noble and richly endowed widow, named Sabina. This pagan matron had a Syrian slave, who with a rare zeal clung to the doctrines of the Gospel. She never ceased, so says the legend, praising the beauty of Christianity to her mistress; and as she exemplified it in her own pure and chaste life, she overcame the prejudice which her mistress had for many years entertained against the Christians. Sabina became a Christian, and by the brilliancy of her virtues was one of the brightest ornaments of the Church in the second century.

The Emperor Adrian published an edict for a persecution of the Christians, and in consequence of this, the Governor of the province of Umbria imprisoned Sabina and her slave, Seraphica; and as the latter was the cause of Sabina's conversion, he had her beaten with rods till her tender body sunk under the cruelty, and she was finally beheaded. Seraphica's mistress, who was released from prison in consideration of her high rank, procured the body of her martyred slave, and gave it honorable interment. After this, she led a more retired life than ever, and night and day besought her departed friend to obtain for her the grace of martyrdom. Her prayer was heard, for in the following year she was summoned by Elpidius, the new Governor of Umbria, to appear before him; and he having shamefully maltreated her, ordered her to prison. When she arrived there, she found herself filled with a holy joy. "And is it then possible," she exclaimed, "that I am to be admitted to a participation of the glory enjoyed by my Seraphica? She has obtained for me this great privilege." She was again summoned the following day, but Elpidius finding all his entreaties vain, condemned her to be beheaded. She suffered on the very day upon which, in the preceding year, her companion gained the crown.* Although this Syrian slave bore a great resemblance to Lydia in her glowing love for Christ, and by the conversion of her

---

* Not far from the Sulpice Bridge, there was a beautiful church built to St. Sabina some hundred years later, and near which the Dominican monastery now stands, commanding a lovely view of the magnificent city. The erection of the church is dated as far back as A. D. 430.

20*

mistress, still she had another tie upon her affection — having been baptized after that saint, whose name, it will be remembered, she bore, till she became a slave in Athens.

Lydia was seldom so oppressed with sorrow as now, standing before the tomb of this much-tried virgin who bore the miseries of slavery to her last breath. She cast a look upon her own interior, and read therein what her patron must have suffered, and also the joy she must have experienced when she saw her mistress one of the "True Fold." With what ardor did not she thank St. Seraphica for the protection she had afforded her through her past life, and recommended not only herself, but also her newly converted mistress, to the powerful protection of both martyrs.

Before the tombs of these holy women she took a vow of perpetual chastity, and resolved, as a handmaid of the Lord, to devote herself to His service.

CHAPTER XXII.

IRENÆUS.

YDIA was now occupied in making preparations for her return to Athens, as she was
receiving letter after letter from Metella, en-
treating her to delay her departure no longer;
and urged by this last request, she sallied
forth at once, to make inquiries on what day
the next ship would sail for Greece. On her
way, she was surprised to meet one whose features were
familiar to her, and on a moment's reflection, she recognized no other than the priest Irenæus, whom she last
saw on the ruins of Smyrna.

For many years he had preached the faith in the south
of France, by the side of the aged Pothinus, bishop of
Lyons, who, like him, had been a disciple of St. Polycarp. Immediately after the persecution had commenced
in Smyrna, a number of Christians from Asia Minor
wandered to the south of Gaul, and Irenæus was one of
the number. Trade and traffic had made their way between these two distant lands, where, as the seed of

Christianity began to shoot, a tempest of persecution threatened to destroy it forever.

Notwithstanding the Emperor's decree, A. D. 177, in favor of the Christians, the Roman Governor, and the people of Lyons and Vienne, still raged against them with dreadful cruelty. Roman justice, as church history informs us, was, in the first three centuries, very vacillating, and the immense extent of the Empire easily explains how the Emperor's decree was carried out in distant provinces, with greater or less exactness, according to the dispositions of whatever governor was in authority. The position of a governor depended more or less on the favor of the people, who, it is well known, had a downright passion for sanguinary combats, and that their cry became, *"Panem et Circuses!"*—"Bread and the Circus." During war, Rome stained its sword in the blood of its enemies; during peace, in that of its own citizens. These were the gladiatorial combats and the persecutions of the Christians.

We need not doubt that some Christians were to be found earlier in Gaul; still it is worthy of credit, that no Christian blood was shed on the soil of France before the reign of Marcus Aurelius.

The lights of the new faith were Pothinus and Irenæus. These two great missionaries of Gaul carried the faith thither from Asia Minor, where they received it from St. Polycarp; and because Polycarp had been a disciple of St. John, it might with truth be said, that they received it from the Apostles themselves. The labors of St. Pothinus were carried on almost in silence, and he was already a venerable man of ninety years when the persecution commenced. Except in the church records in Smyrna, wherein there is an account of the death of St. Polycarp and his companions, we have not so remarkable a memento of Christian antiquity, as the famous account which the churches of Lyons and Vienne have left us, upon the persecution of the Church in Asia Minor. It is thought that Irenæus was the writer of those epistles, and that in the same year in which the persecution took place, 177, he was sent to Rome to impart to the pope the minutiæ of the sanguinary proceedings. Soter was already dead, and in his place Eleutherius had undertaken the guidance of the Church.

It was the custom of the first centuries to read the acts of the martyrs in all Christian assemblies, for the edification of the Faithful, and what Irenæus had witnessed with his own eyes, he wished on his arrival in Rome to deliver verbally to the Faithful. The day on which he was to hold the funeral oration on the death of forty-eight holy martyrs, was announced in the assemblies, and the church of St. Praxedes — that asylum and oratory of the early Christians, beneath which the bodies of 3300 martyrs lay buried — was chosen for this purpose. Lydia was also there, and she took with her the precious girdle of St. Polycarp, to become the possessor of which had cost her eleven years of slavery. With anxious heart, she passed the Theatre of Flora, ignorant of the shocking scenes that took place there, — scenes that often brought the blush to the most shameless countenances, and she stands already at the entrance of the house of God.

How altered was Irenæus! Care and labor, not years,

had furrowed his countenance, and had given him the appearance of an aged man.

"It would be in vain to describe," commenced Irenæus, "the trouble that fell upon us in those latter days. The Christians in Lyons were formally proscribed. They were hunted forth from their dwellings, and the blue heavens given to them as a shelter. They were not allowed to appear in public places without being put to shame; not even the refreshing comfort of a bath was granted to them. If any of the people ill-used one of us in blind fury, the officers of justice had no ear for his troubles; on the contrary, it was the officials themselves who led the Christians to the public places, and there asked them what their faith was, and then, without anything further, had them cast into prison. On account of this treatment, one of the senators, urged by a holy zeal, petitioned one day to speak in the Hall of Justice in defence of the Christians. He did it with that vivacity which his feeling of justice and his youth dictated, and stood as witness that the Christians were not guilty of the vices ascribed to them. But the people interrupted the speaker with vehement groans, and the Proconsul, who also sat in the hall, asked the defender if he himself were a Christian. Vettius, so he was called, answered in the affirmative;—he was immediately seized, on a sign from the Proconsul, and sent to join the Christians already in prison. On this, the public judicial persecution commenced. The following days the Proconsul ordered all the prisoners to be led bound before him. He addressed them in the most violent language, upon the horrible crimes they had committed, and threatened them with the most dreadful tortures, if they did not abjure Christianity. When the executioner placed before their eyes the favorite instruments of torment, and explained the use of them, some of the Christians began to tremble and grow pale. The Proconsul profiting by their agitation, ordered incense to be placed in their hands, and, alas! many of them sacrificed to the gods. The apostates were ten. This act filled us with unspeakable grief. We suffered a further humiliation through some slaves, who, with their Christian owners, had entered the church, although as yet they were not thoroughly instructed in the doctrines. Frightened by the threatened punishments, they not only related what they saw in the Christian assemblies, but several of them hoped to gain their freedom by becoming false witnesses. They were therefore not ashamed to maintain before the people, that they saw with their own eyes how we, like Thyestes, eat the flesh of children, and practised vices that my lips would refuse to utter. At this speech, some of the people applauded, others were indignant, and also those turned against us who up to that time had some faith in our holy doctrine. The torture was next applied to many of the prisoners in the most cruel manner, and not alone the torture, but also red-hot irons were pressed down upon the sufferers in great brutality, until the bodies were no longer to be recognized. Others were put into the stocks, and their feet stretched till the sinews tore asunder.

"So passed a portion of the month of May. But more sorrowfully did it terminate. I must now speak of the death of an old man, who amply fulfilled the hopes of his great master Polycarp, and as in life, so in death he trod in his holy footsteps. Although the last events greatly affected him, still a youthful vigor seemed to take possession of his aged limbs. This was but lent to him that he might leave behind him a remarkable example. The city authorities sent armed soldiers for this old man, and had him brought through the public streets from his dwelling. An immense concourse of people, children, and the aged, followed with ferocious cries, amidst curses and opprobrious language. When the Proconsul asked who was the God of the Christians, he answered:

" 'You will know God when you are worthy of it.'

"The pagans no sooner heard this reply, than they set upon the aged bishop like wild beasts, and so inhumanly treated him, that he sank to the ground. The Governor then saw that the people were embittered, and that they were even arrogating to themselves the office of judge; he therefore ordered Pothinus to be carried back to prison. There we saw him for the last time. He signed us with the sign of martyrdom, by pressing his bleeding lips to our foreheads. Two days later, the church of Lyons had to mourn her bishop and one of her principal pillars." At these words, the speaker thought of the loss he had himself sustained by the death of his beloved and venerated friend. All present participated in his grief, and loud sobbing was heard in the assembly.

"Amongst the prisoners," continued he, "were some Roman citizens, who claimed protection from public contempt by privilege. The Proconsul sent the information to Rome, and begged a command to retain the citizens as well as the other prisoners. When we were informed of this, our hopes were raised, for we trusted that it was still fresh in the Emperor's mind in what situation his whole army had lately found themselves, and how the prayers of the Christian legion drew down the refreshing rain from heaven which saved them from a parching death. How bitterly did the Emperor's commands deceive us! Marcus Aurelius decided on the death of each one that persevered in the confession of Christ. The Proconsul resolved that at the next public sports, at which a great multitude was expected to assemble, the prisoners should be brought forth, and that the Roman citizens were to be beheaded, but that the others should be reserved for the wild beasts.

"As we saw at this investigation those also appear who had already declared that they would offer sacrifice to the gods, our hearts beat in anxious expectation. Quite close to the judge's seat we observed a doctor of Lyons, Alexander of Phrygia, who was most beloved by the people. His presence there astonished and perplexed us, for he was known to be a man of apostolic spirit. While the apostates were questioned anew, if they abided by their former declaration, some of them unhesitatingly acknowledged, that they had been guilty of great injustice by their apostasy, and were now firmly resolved to offer up their lives for the faith.

"Alexander, who stood opposite to them, bowed his head in a friendly manner, and showed by the motion of his whole body how ardently he wished them to remain firm in their good resolutions. This was a great

21   Q

comfort to us, and but few, who were never very much in earnest, remained apostates. So this admirable Alexander saved many from destruction, not thinking of the danger in which he was placing himself. The people had observed him, and were roused almost to madness, and the Governor putting the question to him if he were a Christian, Alexander answered in the affirmative, and immediately his sentence was pronounced. He who loses his life in this manner is sure to find it.

"On the following day, all met at the sports in the amphitheatre; alas! it was a sport as in Nero's time. Two from Asia Minor were to be led to death, Alexander, and Attalus from Pergamus, who was formerly so vehemently persecuted. As he was placed on a red-hot iron stool, because he was accused of being a cannibal, he turned to the spectators and said to them in the Latin language, 'Behold, this is what you may call consuming men; you are guilty of this inhumanity, but we are no cannibals.' Alexander next suffered. But now, dearest brethren, for an edifying example of two young persons;—one was a very youthful and beautiful girl, named Blandina; she was a slave, and of so delicate a constitution, that she caused in us the greatest anxiety; and yet this remarkable servant of God had from the earliest dawn till late in the evening defied her tormentors, who relieved each other at intervals, and when the savages sent her back to her prison, she spent her whole time in attending and consoling her companions to the entire forgetfulness of herself. Her death had been previously decided on, but a remarkable circumstance prevented its taking place. She had been even tied to the stake in the middle of the Arena, to be attacked by wild beasts. She stood there with outstretched arms, a true follower of her crucified Lord. At one moment she raised her eyes to heaven, at another she fixed them on the panther just liberated from its cage. The beast was less of the savage than the jailer who liberated him, for the moment he beheld the maiden, his ferocious nature gave way, he turned suddenly from her, and crouchingly retreated to his cave. This failing, she was then led, together with Ponticus, a youth of fifteen years of age, to the different altars, and they were desired to offer incense. But still Blandina thought not of her own sufferings; she pressed her chains piously to her bosom, and whispered to her youthful companion, smilingly, words of comfort. The youth suffered with a cheerful mien all sorts of torments, and terminated his young life by a heroic death. Now Blandina stood alone; that she was stronger than all the instruments of torture excited the people to the greatest fury, but the last hour struck for her also. She was scourged, next torn with iron hooks till her entrails appeared; she was then tied in a net, and dragged about by a wild bull, and at last was put sitting on a red-hot stool. Finding she still breathed, her sufferings were terminated by the sword; and it was acknowledged by the Pagans themselves, that no woman had ever been known to endure such torments with so much constancy.

· "Forty-eight martyrs thus sacrificed their lives. Their bodies were thrown to the dogs, their bones burnt, and their ashes cast into the Rhone. 'Let us

see,' said the heathens, 'whether their God will resusci-
tate them again.'—And if we were able," concluded
Irenæus. "to cast a look above the blue vault of heaven,
that separates us from our happy brethren, we should
behold on the head of each a sparkling crown.　For as
often as a persecution breaks out, the portals of Heaven
open, and the crowns of glory descend on the bleeding
temples of the well-tried combatants."

When the holy man had ceased speaking, all those
present cast themselves on their knees, beseeching the
assistance of the martyrs to obtain strength, if God so
willed them to suffer a similar death; but they were
not called upon to suffer, as the persecution ceased for a
time.

This sermon made an indelible impression on all
present, and one after the other left the church in deep
thought.　Lydia waited for the moment that Irenæus
would cross the threshold of the sanctuary.　Many
years had passed since he saw her bound with the
girdle of his martyred master at Smyrna.　This precious
relic she carried about her, and suspecting that Irenæus
would have a death similar to that of St. Polycarp, she
resolved to renounce all claim to the relic and present
it to him, who by his talents and virtue filled so high a
position.

Irenæus gazed at her inquiringly; for a moment he
appeared as if he had to recall bygone days, to bring
back her features to his mind.　Suddenly he exclaimed,
"This is a child of St. Polycarp, one whom I last saw
on the ruins of Smyrna."　Lydia was silent.　Felicitas,
who stood near her, spoke for her, and related in a few

words her sorrows and the cause of her journey to Rome. Lydia, taking courage, addressed him: "Revered disciple of our great Bishop! dare I venture to offer you a remembrance of Smyrna? Behold the girdle which St. Polycarp took off before he ascended the pile! The first amongst his followers should possess it, and when the last hour shall strike for him, may the protecting spirit of the patron saint of my native city hover round him!"

Irenæus accepted the gift, and pressed it silently to his lips. Thanking Lydia for the precious and unexpected present, he bestowed upon her and Felicitas his blessing, with a fervent hope that after the trials of this life he would meet them in the world to come, where separation is no more.

21 *

CHAPTER XXIII.

THE INVALID.

 HAT sadness filled the house of Felicitas! The dearly loved emancipated one prepares to return to Athens. Her hostess had firmly attached herself to her guest, because she had shared with her in this life the same dangers, and had for the future the same hopes. The last good wishes were exchanged, and Lydia placed the casket before her which contained the great pearl; for, according to the pious custom of those days, she commenced her journey accompanied by her God. Hark! there is suddenly a loud knocking at the gate, and Lydia distinctly hears a man's voice. He is asking, in an excited tone, if the young Athenian is to be found here, or if she is already on her way to Greece.

"Well, God be praised!" said the stranger, and entered the apartment. "God greet you," said he to Lydia. "Where is the emancipated slave who served the rich Metella. I have something to impart to her."

The rough manner in which the stranger approached

her, and, on the other hand, the look of astonishment that his features expressed, quite confused her. Still it appeared to Lydia as though she had seen the wounded man lately in one of the assemblies. "Are you," continued he, "the enfranchised of an Athenian lady, who had a son named Lucius, a blooming son, who died fighting against the Marcomanni?"

Lydia cast a trembling look at Felicitas, who whispered to her in the Greek language, "Do not be alarmed, my dear child; the man is a Christian; we can give him a trifle, and he will be contented."

"No, no!" replied the inquirer, smilingly; "I am an overseer in the baths of Timotheus, and am an invalid, but through the benevolence of the Emperor and some good people, I manage to live. My arm was wounded by the arrow of a marksman, so that I was useless for warlike service. How gladly would I engage myself again in such a cause! and find myself face to face with those rebellious people of the Danube!"

"Perhaps you knew the son of Metella?" inquired Lydia hastily, for the thought struck her that the man could probably tell her something of Lucius.

"Of course I did!" replied the invalid,—"of course I knew Lucius, and on that account I have come here to-day. Alas! alas! he died too soon."

Felicitas thought that the visit of the poor invalid was only for the purpose of obtaining a small gift, on the plea of his having known Lucius; and as the moments were precious to her, she sought to put an end to the interview by saying, "Now, good man, you are very poor, and perhaps you would like a little gift from Metella's enfranchised."

"By no means," answered he. "If I am poor, I am contented, and I comfort myself with the thought that the Redeemer of the world Himself belonged to the poor, as long as he was on earth."

"You are a Christian?" said Lydia.

"O yes!—and one of those who fought in the Legio Fulminatrix, and therefore I have the privilege to confess my faith everywhere without fear."

"You have perhaps spoken to Lucius?"

"No doubt of it: we belonged to the same Legion, and were under one commander. The son of Metella, equally enthusiastic in virtue as in the honor of war, will ever be remembered by us all. Oh, I see him still! How, after a battle was won, he rode his foaming charger over the ice-clad field of action, and so courageously, that his heart beat strong enough to burst the buckles of his coat of mail. Then flew an arrow from the secret ambush, that struck his charger, and a second brought down the rider. We hastened to his assistance. We had a Christian commander, named Cornelius; he was, alas! also left behind. This commander loved Lucius with an enthusiastic affection, and met him often during the winter-quarters, that he might explain the truth of Christianity to him.

"Oh! he was a rare youth. How often he gave us the commission, that, if he were once wounded, to carry him off the field and baptize him! For at first he was afraid to receive baptism, as he did not consider himself sufficiently instructed."

Lydia's attention was riveted, and she sent a secret sigh to Heaven as if she would now, as she had often done before, pray for Lucius' baptism.

"Continue," said she; "you speak like a messenger from Heaven."

"Oh! his life was too short! the arrow did its work quicker than we had expected. We drew it out, washed the wound, which began to bleed, and the youth then awoke as if from a sleep. He signed to us with half-closed eyes, and exerted himself to utter a few words. I did not understand him, and had, through downright anxiety, forgotten his last wish. At length one of my comrades understood him, and said hurriedly, 'He asks you to baptize him!' Oh, had you but seen the seraphic smile that played upon his dying face, when he found his words were understood! We then struck his spear deep into the earth, and raised him against it on his shield in a reclining position. No vessel being at hand, 1 took off my helmet, and his eye anxiously watched my every step, as I went in search of water. I returned quickly and knelt by his side; the dying youth summoned up all his sinking strength for one great effort; he spoke distinctly: 'I believe in Jesus Christ, the Son of God,— O baptize me in his name!' With heavy sobs I poured the contents of my helmet upon his head, and baptized him, in the name of the Father, and of the Son, and of the Holy Ghost. He smiled, bent his head in thanksgiving, and placed his hand in mine; he then fell into his agony, and seemed by the movement of his lips to be in fervent prayer. He opened his dying eyes once more, and motioned that he had something still to say. One of my comrades placed his ear to Lucius' lips and heard with difficulty: 'Love to my dear mother, and say I died a Christian.' These were his last words; he then closed his eyes and expired.

"As I heard, the other day, that an emancipated Christian slave was here from Athens, I sought you out, to beg that you would deliver the last message of a good son to his mother." The poor invalid felt deeply affected; the remembrance of his fellow-combatant, whom he had accompanied to the threshold of Heaven, and was then obliged to bid a long farewell, grieved him intensely.

"Merciful God!" ejaculated Lydia,—"how? Metella's son one of the Faithful?—Lucius died a Christian?—Baptized on the field of battle?" Her bright eyes sparkled and filled with tears.

"Yes, yes; tell his mother that she had a good and brave son, who was the darling of the whole Legion, and tell her also that this son died a disciple of Christ."

Lydia informed the invalid, that Metella had also become a Christian, and that perhaps he, who was so tenderly loved by her, had petitioned for her. "So are the ways of Him," continued she, "who carries the destiny of the world and all His creatures in His hands."

The brave soldier was taking leave and wishing the traveller a favorable journey, when Lydia considered that in the name of her good mistress she was bound to reward the bearer of such joyful tidings. She had scarcely entertained the thought a moment, when she opened the golden locket that she had suspended from her neck, and took out of it the large and valuable pearl, a present of Metella's, and offered it to the invalid in the name of her mistress. He refused to accept a reward for a service done to a dying comrade, but as Lydia had assured him that Metella would send him a reward from Athens, if he did not accept the present she offered, he then received the generous gift.

At such unexpected and joyful news, Lydia was stunned, and was obliged, as soon as the stranger had departed, to reflect a little and convince herself, if what she had just heard were a dream or a reality. Already she placed before her eyes the happiness this news would afford her mistress, and if her departure had not been fixed for that day, she would have had to summon all the strength of her will to conquer the desire with which she longed for Athens. She hastened with Felicitas to the harbor of Tiberius. The late intelligence made her separation an easy one. Both promised never to loosen the firm band of mutual love, and wished each other, if they were never to meet again on earth, a happy meeting in "the better Land."

And now farewell, thou precious Rome! Ever memorable to those who have tarried within thy walls, and offered up their prayers at the tombs of thy saints!

CHAPTER XXIV.

THE RETURN.

HERE was in the time of the ancient Greeks, a much approved of and peculiar sort of ship, of remarkable height and bulk, to which they gave the name of Kerkyra,—from the island of Korcyra, where they were originally built. Such a trading-vessel, bearing the name of Centaurus, was just launched in the harbor of Ostia, and was the one which Lydia had decided on for her return to Greece. Rich Romans came alongside in their gilded barges to visit this triple-oared galley.

At the call of the Hortators, the rowers take their seats and beat time with their oars to the flute-players on deck.

To judge by the dress and appearance, there were many Asiatics among the travellers. Some were returning from Gaul, in consequence of the persecutions there, to their homes in the East. They had not words to express the manner in which the Proconsul of that province consented to the most abominable requests of the people, and this principally to ingratiate himself with them.

Some of them carried the traces of martyrdom on their bodies, like so many seals of their faith; and as if the days in Lyons had given them no previous warning, they continued in the practice of their religion, regardless of the judgment of the heathens.

Irenæus and Hegesippus, both of whom were journeying to Smyrna, were, so to say, the spiritual pillars around which the faithful heroes crowded.

The learned Hegesippus is not unknown in the legends of the saints, although his works are not extant. He was a Jew by birth, and became afterwards a member of the Church in Jerusalem. He had travelled much, and had acquainted himself thoroughly with the most remarkable events of church history; and completed, in the year 133, a history of the Church in five volumes. He resided in Rome till the year 177,—the same year in which the persecution took place at Lyons.

Amongst the above-named Asiatics who were returning from Gaul, one claims our particular attention. He sits motionless the entire day, with a fixed gaze on the blue waters. Now and then he raises his head and sighs deeply. His strained arms, and the scorched flesh on one side of his face, clearly showed that he had suffered the torture. While all were cheerful and even gay at meals, this gloomy individual, dressed in a thin over-all garment, sat eating a hard biscuit that he dipped occasionally in a cup of wine. He touched no other food the entire day. Lydia studied this man for some time, and then .

22

took courage to address him. He looked at her frown-ingly, listened to her question, then turned himself to-wards the sea, and gave no answer. How delighted she would have been to help him, but he kept a sullen dis-tance. Some days after, she made a second attempt, asked him where he came from, and who he was. He answered with a measured voice, "I am an unhappy Christian; leave me in peace!"

He was a Christian, and in the last persecution in Gaul he denied his faith, amidst the pains of the rack; and as he was threatened with still greater torments if he refused to reveal the secret crimes of the Christians, he, against his conscience, uttered scandalous lies of crimes which he said they had committed in their secret meetings. At this acknowledgment he was liberated; he took to flight, and waited for an opportunity to leave the province for ever, and return to Asia. The heathens who were in the ship, said his name was Melissos; they knew his history, and some of them had seen him sacri-ficing to the gods. Notwithstanding, they despised his character and refused to associate with him. Of course the Christians had a still poorer opinion of him, so that the unfortunate man was proscribed on all sides. Lydia felt the deepest commiseration for the apostate. As she discovered the cause of his melancholy, she addressed herself to Hegesippus, who usually sat on the stern of the vessel, writing down the thoughts that occurred to him during the voyage. She informed him of the sad state of Melissos, and begged his sympathy. He sought to address him, spoke words of comfort to him, and re-minded him, that even the prince of the apostles three times denied his Master. But also that this denial Peter made good, by his redoubled zeal for Christ, and by his acknowledgment to his Lord, after His resurrection, in the presence of the apostles three times, to love Him more than the rest.*

Melissos replied in a hollow voice, "I hope to be freed from the wicked spirits by a baptism in the sea," and in a sullen manner turned from the historian.

There was a Christian youth on board, who, unmindful of the heathens present, went through his religious duties without fear. He was liked by all, not only on account of his wit, but also for his enchanting vòice, with which he knew how to amuse every one during the long voyage. He seemed to make a sad impression on Melissos, and to awaken in him many remembrances of the past. One morning the youth sat in the scuttle and began to sing the following, whilst the sun was rising:

> Night flees apace: lo! now the ruddy dawn
> With rising sun, breaks sparkling into morn.
> O'er the blue sea shrill winds are whistling wild,
> Whilst in the trim bark sails a lonely child.
>
> Cheerful the boy plies well the ready oar;
> "I'll turn my helm for port on yonder shore,
> Where golden Spring glows warm, and gladsome May
> Blooms without cease, and decks the glitt'ring bay.
>
> "But see! what nymph starts up, and from the rocks
> Trips on the wave, and shakes her fragrant locks?
> Enchanting songs my soul with joy so move,
> That my young heart wellnigh will break with love."

* St. John xxi. 17.

The heedless boy, though love and music mock,
Salutes the sprite, and scudding for the rock,
Spreads all his sails, and steers with eager hand,—
Then joyous sets his foot on Siren-land.

Whilst hush'd he bends to hear the warbling strain,
The deadly spell steals o'er his soul amain,
Holds him with charms bound fast to magic land,
And chains with joys unblest his nerveless hand.

Rousing at last, and trembling with affright,
He sees his doom, and takes to rapid flight, —
Seeks for his little bark, but seeks in vain :
The bark is gone, its planks bestrew the main!

The hapless boy sinks sobbing to a séat,
Beneath the rocks where foaming billows beat,
Casts o'er the sea his eyes, and wails uncheck'd,
And breaks his heart, as first his bark was wreck'd.

Watch then, O lonesome youth! and guard with care,
Lest to the Siren's song thou lend an ear,
And dire enchantments lure and love's pretence,
Thy fragile bark to wreck — thine Innocence.*

The effect of this song on Melissos was remarkable and observed by all. Night came on, and each one had retired to rest, save the helmsman and the Hortator, who stood on his elevation. A dark figure crept along the deck till it reached the end of the vessel, and began to talk aloud. "O Thou never-sleeping Protector of the universe, lend me thine ear! Thou listenest to the chirping cricket and providest for it, and even the powerless butterfly, that flutters from flower to flower, is an object of thy tender care. Thou beholdest me also.—I am the butter-

* The translator is indebted to the Rev. R. Palmer, O.S.D., for putting the above into proper metre.

fly, that should have ascended to yonder Paradise of de-
lights, but whose wings have been burnt off under
dreadful torture; now I am but a worm — a miserable
worm! I have lost faith and hope, the wings of my
soul! Bereft of these, I now crawl a pitiful worm on
the earth. Man mocks me, and thy Divinity will crush
me. Eternal God, dost Thou still know me? I am an
object of Thy hatred, and all heaven must detest me!
For whose love did I offer incense on the altars of the
gods in whom I have no faith? On whom did I think,
and who held me back in the moment that I should have
gained the crown? She who is now wandering on the
Asiatic shores, sleeplessly and anxiously watching for
the sails that are to bring to her, him she has so longed
for! *She* is the Siren that took my heart and senses
captive, and wrecked my bark when steering for the land
of the saints! *She* is the slender Roe that gnaws at the
stem of my faith, and bites off the bark. Oh that death
had pursued her, before she had annihilated my virtue!
And when I do arrive, she will no longer love, but curse
the cripple and the atheist!

"O sea, O sea, thy cool embrace, thy melodious song!
Thy liberating baptism! Dissolve this immortal being
called soul, and spread it over thy immeasurable waters.
In foaming billows will I then beat on the Asiatic shores,
kiss her feet, and cool her longing. Dissolve this immortal being, that it may rise on high over thy surface
as a mist, and, as storm-whipped clouds in myriads of
drops, fall upon the locks and robes of my complaining
Syrinx!" And then he bent himself forward lower and
lower, and vanished in an instant.

22 *   R

The Hortator near the ship's lamp was looking at the apostate, and said to the young Christian who had not yet retired, "Listen to the Phrygian fool! He is declaiming a monologue."

'I did not observe him," replied the youth, and both looked inquiringly towards the front rail, where he had been standing. They lost sight of the stranger in the darkness of the night, but on the waters they heard a gentle splashing, which ceased by degrees.

"Help! help!" cried out a clear voice from the deck. "Melissos has thrown himself into the sea," and almost in the same moment, the supple youth sprang into the row-boat, loosened it from the ship, and made towards the drowning man. By ropes thrown to the youth from above, Melissos was drawn up just as he was on the point of sinking. He lay in the bottom of the boat, without showing the slightest sign of life. His pale features, half shrouded in his dripping hair, clearly portrayed the agony of mind that drove him to the deed. The occurrence caused great confusion. They looked upon the drowned man as a madman, and complained of the imprudence of allowing him his liberty among the passengers. Others expressed the suspicion that the Christians, who did not seem to think much about him, had purposely sacrificed him.

In the meantime, they left him lying there, and returned again to rest. The deck cleared, and all restored to its former quiet, Lydia came forward from the stern of the vessel, with uplifted hands; she cast a sorrowful look around her, and wept and prayed. "Oh if I had but followed the dictates of my heart! Had I but sacrificed the least respect to the greater, you would not now lie a victim here to our insensibility! Alas, why did we not save thee! Almighty Father, if still a spark of life be in him, fan it, and give him back to Thy flock! It becomes Thee as the all Holy One to judge the sinner, but it becomes us to look upon him as our brother, and to love him."

The moon rose clear, and the waves, as if naught had happened, danced fondly in her beams. Flying fish rose from the dark waters, saluted the splashing boat and the sails of the vessel, then fluttered a little higher and sank again to their watery home.

An anxious feeling agitated the heart of Lydia. Nature looked so peaceful, the body so pale, and the deed so dreadful. Overwhelmed with anguish, she sank upon her cushion, and throwing a veil over her face, she began to reflect on the fate of Melissos. Suddenly a ray of hope darted through her frame, mild as the morning-beam that kisses off the dew from the flower. She rose and approached the body, which appeared to her as if its posture had changed. "Good Father!" she exclaims, "he raises himself; he sinks his head upon his arm! Melissos, you return again to life!"—"Yes," replied he, after a pause, and looking round,—"and again to hope. No, all is not yet lost: I feel it here,"—placing his hand upon his breast.—"Regenerated, then," said Lydia: "return back to expiate the injustice done."

Melissos recovered; his despair was conquered by the language of sympathy, and the care bestowed upon him daily by the passengers. His lost peace returned, and he sailed towards his Asiatic home another man, and with the resolution, there to be received again into the Communion of Saints.

Two months had passed, and the longed-for land was still at a distance. A cabin-boy sits above on the mast, and scans the broad sea in the direction of Achaia. He looked long in vain, but at length his clear silver voice called down from his rocking ship-cradle, "The mountains of Greece are visible!" All hastened to the forecastle, to convince themselves that the shores were near. In the greatest haste the announcer descended from the mast, to claim a reward for his joyful tidings. Although land was distant, the pilot looked around him unconcerned, for he had now another sea-mark by which to guide his ship; as long as he was on the high seas, he had nothing but the stars,—now he had the mountains, and he steered courageously by them towards Syros, where some of the passengers disembarked.

Melissos was of the number. On taking a respectful leave of Lydia, he, with tears, expressed his gratitude for her sympathy, and made a firm promise, with God's assistance, to be again of the "One Fold." Those who were journeying to the East went by another vessel, and those destined for Attica continued the voyage in the Centaurus. It was a soft, pleasant morning, such as we never see in our foggy North, when the ship arrived at Piræus. The sun was still slumbering in the East, and the Hymettus on the other side of Athens resembled a gray veil, behind which the rising sun was still concealed. At last, Aurora waking, drew aside "the curtain of the morn." The king of day scatters his golden gifts over mountain, sea, and plain, and sheds a new life upon the earth.

How majestically the Centaurus neared the shore! the morning breeze swelling every sail! The last commands given to the weary crew were in a tone that said, "Fellow-laborers, our work is done!" Lydia was almost the first to touch the land and greet the ruins of the once great arsenal, and the walls of Cyclops, destroyed by Sulla, which united Piræus with Athens; and now she pictured to herself in the liveliest colors, the meeting that was just at hand. One of Metella's servants was to be seen for some days on the heights of the Acropolis, looking anxiously towards the harbor. At length the mast of a vessel appeared above the horizon, and by degrees showed itself in full sail, steering towards the coast. When it approached near enough, he recognized in the flags and pennants the expected ship. Duranus hurried down breathless, to announce the tidings to his mistress. Metella answered with a cry of delight, and hastened to the threshold of the inner gate of the palace, where she waited impatiently the arrival of her much-loved child. Ophne was sent immediately to the harbor, and Lydia had scarcely landed, when she found herself in the embraces of her affectionate friend, who overwhelmed her with questions which she herself answered, and imparted a volume of news relative to the changes that had occurred in her absence, and ended by declaring that there was *one* secret she was most impatient to tell her, but she dared not, and so she went on, talking unceasingly till they reached the palace.

Feeling has a language in all places and through all ages, and this language expresses itself in the acts of that ardent tenderness wherewith one heart unites itself to another. When Metella and Lydia met, they lost all power of utterance; Metella stretched out her arms, and her newly found child sunk nearly senseless into her embrace. After a few moments, both retired to the oratory to pour forth their gratitude to God. Having spent some time in prayer, Metella motioned Lydia to follow her into one of her private apartments.

"How have I not sighed for this day that would bring thee back to Athens! The silent valleys, the solitary groves, the purling streams, yes, all the stars in the blue vault of heaven, can witness my longing for thee! The letters, dear child, that you sent me from Rome, were a weak indemnity for your own dear self, and still they were so precious to me, that I had them ever near me. What an interest I took in all you have gone through since we parted! and how did I grieve at the news that you could not find your mother!"

A look gave Metella to understand with what resignation and peace of soul the daughter had borne the loss of her parent.

"My child," continued she, "as happy as is the return home, so must those you have left behind feel your loss."

"I have no one now on this earth to whom I belong," said Lydia, "but I have still a mistress who, I am certain, for the future will accept my services, and who will never abandon me."

Metella embraced Lydia tenderly. "Not mistress, not lady, not friend: there is another name that stands higher than all these—that which of all the names on earth sounds sweetest, and by this sweet name you shall ever call me,—the name of Mother!

"What I offer thee now is not a thing of momentary affection; ever since I lost my son, I have thought of how I could hear again the sweet name of mother. I have chosen you, that you may be to me a daughter, a tenderly beloved daughter, presented to me by God Himself. I have always called thee Lydia, but you received another name, far more beautiful, in baptism. Therefore take back thy name—Seraphica! yes, my only daughter must be Seraphica! All that belongs to me in future belongs to thee, and as thou hast a daughter's possession of my heart, so shalt thou have the possession of all the temporal trifles that I call my own. Long did the court of Athens hesitate to acknowledge you as my heiress, because you had been a slave, but I proved that you were free-born, and never purchased in public places; that you came to my house a fugitive, and found shelter there, and that without having any right, the master of the Smyrnian vessel, on which you sought your passage to Greece, took you as captive, and sent you to my house. All is now arranged, and you are acknowledged as my adopted child, and heir to all I possess. O may you be for the inhabitants of Athens what I should like to have been for them, and you 'll be a pattern of a benevolent Christian, and when death draws near, you will look upon the poor of our city as your children."

The deeply affected Lydia composed herself, and without being asked, pressed a kiss on Metella's cheek for the first time. "My faith," said she, "left me once an orphan, and the same faith has again given me a mother

I shall never forget that it was thy boundless love that liberated the slave, and from an enfranchised raised her to be thy child. And now I can no longer suppress the joy that fills my overflowing heart. I have now to tell you the particulars of the happy death of your son Lucius!—this is not the first day that you have been a mother to a Christian child."

Metella did not understand what the words signified, "You had a Christian child before you yourself thought of being one. Yes, your son reposed in the bosom of his Redeemer before the dawn of faith enlightened his mother's heart. O remember the vision! Thy Lucius slumbered at the feet of his Redeemer."

"My son? I suspect!"—

"Your suspicions are happy truths. I myself spoke to the veteran in Rome, who baptized him. His last words were, 'I believe in Jesus Christ the Son of God, —O baptize me in his name;' and before he expired, 'Love to my dear mother, and say that her son Lucius died a Christian.'"

Metella was astounded, and a holy awe ran through her whole frame. She rose hastily and speechless, seized Seraphica's hand, and hastened with her to the oratory. He alone who searches the depths of the heart knows what she felt when pouring forth to Him the effusions of a grateful soul.

What a double joy for Metella! God had already commenced to bestow upon her "The hundred-fold in this life." She had now one child an advocate in Heaven, and another a sweet solace to her on earth. Her life was beginning to her anew, but O how changed!

The pleasures of Chrysophora were very different from those of the Christian Metella. In former years, *self* was her first consideration, now it was her last,—so wonderfully did faith transform this noble soul, that she was scarcely to be recognized. The haughty and impe-rious bearing was changed to a mild and modest dignity. The fiery Metella of former days is no longer heard to speak to the meanest of her household in aught but gentle and consoling words. She spends her days with her adopted child, doing good to all, dispensing the temporal blessings which God has bestowed upon her, like the faithful steward of a liberal Master.

Lydia was delighted beyond measure when Metella told her that Ophne had become a Christian, and that Duranus was then a catechumen; she knew immediately that this was Ophne's secret. The joy of all the domestics, on the return of Lydia, knew no bounds, particularly poor little Thrax, to whom she had always been most kind.

Metella and Lydia spent their days alternately between Elis, Athens, and Eleusis, in each of which places they had the happiness of seeing a little colony of Christians rising up around them. Lydia took upon her the laborious portion of their charitable labors, and the sick and needy were the objects of her most anxious solicitude.

The poor potter was no longer poor; he had been removed with his now dying child to one of Metella's outdwellings appropriated to the male portion of her domestics. In Lydia's daily visit to his little son, who gradually declined after the operation already mentioned,

23

poor Hyllos learned to believe—from the conversation she had with Askanus, who loved Lydia dearly, and who always entreated her to tell him something of her God —that Jupiter and Minerva were no gods, and therefore unable to help him. And when Askanus became thoroughly instructed in the duties of a Christian, and begged to be of the same religion with his benefactress, his father added an earnest petition that he might also have the same happiness. "Yes, Hyllos," said Lydia, "I shall be delighted to see you one of the true fold, but you have yet to be instructed."

"Dear Lady, have I not been present each day that you talked so beautifully to my son? Old Hyllos has still a good memory,—I don't forget a word of all you have said." To Lydia's astonishment, on questioning him, she found him thoroughly prepared to receive baptism, and promised that his name should be added to that of Askanus, for the Bishop's approval.

After having ministered to the temporal comforts of her poor invalid, she left their little dwelling, and in crossing the court-yard, on her way to the palace, she heard loud sobbing behind one of the pillars, and wondered to see little Thrax bathed in tears. "What has happened, Thrax?" Poor Thrax could give no other answer than, "I'm only a dwarf! I'm only a dwarf!" "A caged dwarf, Thrax, not one by nature."—"Oh, but I was bought only to be laughed at!"—"No, Thrax; you were sold to be laughed at, but purchased by a feeling mistress, to be treated with every kindness. Your dear young master, Lucius, was always your best friend."

" Oh, there it is! there it is! I want to see him again, but I can't, I can't,—I'm only a dwarf! Askanus told me, the other day, that if he were good, he would soon be where my young master is, and that is where I want to go; but I'm only a dwarf, I'm only a dwarf!" continued he, wringing his hands.

Lydia could scarcely conceal her emotion at the faithful and affectionate remembrance of the departed, and found great difficulty in persuading Thrax that his diminutive body was no obstacle to his being one day united to his deceased master. His countenance began to brighten up at this assurance, and he asked if he tried to be as good as Askanus, to whom he had become greatly attached; might he not soon know all about the happy place of which they were always talking?

Lydia told him that he could come with her every day to visit Askanus, and receive instructions, but that the God of the Christians was to be loved for Himself, and not for any other consideration.

We will now leave Thrax on his way to Christianity, and reflect on how faithfully Seraphica fulfilled the duties for which she had so ardently petitioned when in the dungeon at Smyrna. "Mother, I shall not die yet; I have besought our Lord not yet to call me to my eternal home. I wish to suffer, not to die; I burn with the desire of showing to the world, in the mirror of a pure life, the devotion to our Redeemer, and to relate to unbelievers what the Son of God has done for man. Not till I have fulfilled that mission, shall I be called hence. It may be long till then! God has heard my prayer,—my Guardian Angel has revealed it to me!"

CHAPTER XXV.

THE CONCLUSION.

NOSSE peræta juvat, sed præstat tradita posse.

It is beautiful to know what is noble, but still more beautiful to practise it. Thus we see in a slave, weak in sex, in age, and above all in her state of life, to what an elevation grace can raise the heart. God has chosen the weak ones of the world to confirm the strong.* Suppose Lydia had not been rewarded for this triumph of virtue by any temporal gains, by honors or dignities, what consequence?

Earthly splendor and exterior recognitions are a mere accidental gift of the interior moral greatness, which could neither be raised nor lessened by her.

Notwithstanding, it thus generally happens that honor likes to attach itself to virtue, and follows it as though it were her shadow.

This much-tried girl could tell what wisdom lies in affliction. She would never have reached that degree

* 1 Cor. i. 27.

of virtue, had she not passed through the fiery ordeal of suffering. If virtue is to appear in its beauty, she must for a time suffer oppression. The martyrs of our holy Church would never have died so resigned and joyful, if unutterable sorrows had not led them through the dark labyrinths of their lives to the open gates of justice, for them the gates of triumph.

Witness Polycarp, Justin, Blandina, Pothinus of Lyons, and a multitude of others. It is in fact the truly gifted souls which God visits, purifies, and perfects. This very truth Seneca so beautifully explained by the words: "Miserable he who was never miserable." There is not an anguish, if we begin with the blighted hopes of the youthful loving heart, down to that of treachery, torture, and the laceration of a despairing mind, which will not there find a complete expression. Every injustice is an admonishing voice in this valley of tears, and the oftener it returns, the more we long for our departure, which, correctly speaking, is our way home. But a friendship with death is the greatest triumph of the human mind over the terror of nature. How magnificent is the sun surrounded by stormy clouds when sinking to the west! But while one hemisphere admires his departing beauty, another, at the same moment, is cheered by his rising splendor,—thus sinking and rising are one and the same.—With man it is even so; his departure from this world is a hymn of joy to Heaven and a kiss to death, which eternity gives to the approaching soul as the seal of an indissoluble espousal. Through the life of our slave, a warm zeal animated her for the salvation of souls. She had the lamp of faith lighted up in the sun of revelation, and carried it as well in her humble dwelling as in the palace of the wealthy. The love by which it was animated conquered all obstacles. "I passed by thee, and saw thee," said the prophet, "and behold, thy time was the time of lovers."* She wandered on the thorny way imprinted with the footsteps of the Lord, and when she saw a loiterer, either to the right or to the left, she called to him, "Thou slow of heart, why delayest thou? come without fear, without hesitation; be not timid in treading on thorns, which fell from the crown of your King." Such are souls as God wills them, not those who loiter about inactively, counting the grains of sand. Oh how is also, in our day, the number of the afflicted so large, and our love so small! "Ye shall be fishers of men," said the Lord to His disciples, and He Himself went before them as a divine model. For He once in the fulness of time looked down from the highest Heavens on the dark ocean of the universe, where myriads of worlds were in motion;—looking also on our planet, whose inhabitants were sighing after light and truth, and He lowered His doctrine in the net of mercy, and drew us all to Him. His disciples followed His example. The Prince of the Apostles, while hanging on the cross, admonished His third successor Cletus: "Never forget to preserve your own soul, in saving the souls of your brethren." The same duty is also laid on the conscience of each one of us. *Salvando Salvabimur.*

While we describe the bitter trials of a single unbloody martyr, in that century of affliction, another pic

* Oz. xvi. 8.

ture of incomparably greater martyrdom presents itself to our eyes,—the bride of Jesus Christ—the holy Church. Was not the Church herself that slave, who already in her earliest youth carried the chains of slavery? Unsheltered, this orphan wandered about, after her paternal home, Jerusalem, was laid desolate, of which Smyrna's destruction was a mere painting. As a fugitive maiden, this same bride journeyed across the Mediterranean Sea, and entered into the service of an imperious, sensual, and crowned mistress, rolling in superfluous prosperity: and the name of this mistress is Rome. She served there nearly three hundred years, during constant ill-treatment, mockery, and persecution and tortures even to the heart's blood. Who imagined then, that from this obscurity, and after such contempt, so powerful a life, so rich in influence, would unfold itself? Then came the time in which this proud mistress submitted to be taught by the low and persecuted maiden,—a time in which princes abjured their tyranny and absolute will, and shared with the slave the possessions of the world, and both named themselves— Christian Empire and Christian Church. This remarkable day, the most important since the day of our Redemption, was the 29th of October, in the year 312. "It appears to be almost a general law," said an observer of the people, "that this prosperity or success of things is connected with a certain obscurity."* What a coming forth, after three hundred years of secrecy and silence! That effect was not accomplished by physical strength, not by the sword, but by a power

* Lasaulx' Attempt of a Philosophy : " History. 128.

called Christian charity. For this charity is of all
powers the greatest on earth, and what she fails to conquer is unconquerable.

It was a conflict to be, or not to be, which was kept
on from Nero's time to that of Constantine. After the
conquest, the last of which was gained over Maxentius
on the Tiber, he passed in triumph through the streets
of Rome, and with him brought the faith victorious to
the " Eternal City."

A lance-bearer walked before the chariot of the conqueror, holding on high the bleeding head of the conquered,—it was the head of fallen heathenism. "Not
captive strangers," remarks a writer of that time, "swell
the triumph, but armies of vices which had hitherto
filled the city, conquered crimes, perfidy, haughtiness,
cruelty, pride, scorn, voluptuousness and unlawful desires,—all these were bound in iron chains. But still
more remarkable, and less known than one would imagine, is the edict which Constantine and his partner in
power, Licinius, appointed to be proclaimed in Nicomedia."   •

"As we havé known long since," said the Imperators,
"that freedom in religion is not to be denied, and that
the practice of which is left to the will and views of
each one, so should we have sooner commanded that,
like all others, the Christians should be free to hold
. their religious views.

"But as this permission has been granted on many
and various conditions, so it has perhaps happened,
that, by a constrained practice of their religion, many
have been repulsed. As .we therefore, I the Emperor

Constantine, and I the Emperor Licinius, arrived happily together in Milan, and as we took into consideration all that concerned the security of the public welfare, we believed ourselves obliged, before all things else, first to arrange what concerned the worship of the Divinity, so that we gave to the Christians the same freedom as to all others, to follow that religion which they considered best suited to their views and happiness; in order that, whoever is the Divinity in Heaven, that He may be gracious to us and to all our subjects. All former proclamations contrary to this are to be null and void. For it is clear and compatible with the peace of our time, that each one should have the choice to worship whatever divinity he will, and that hereby no sort of religious worship is to be excluded.

"In addition to this, whatever concerns the Christians in particular, we have found it good to determine, that their former houses of assembly, and the estates they formerly possessed, which, according to certain edicts, fell into the hands of the law or otherwise, shall be returned gratuitously, and if the present possessors ask for compensation, they must apply for it to the imperial governor."

Strangers admire to the present day the ruins of the triumphal arch which the Senate erected to the "Liberator of the City;" and who can behold Constantine's arch without being moved at the remembrance of that day!

But now there shall be a new contemplation of things, a lasting reconciliation made between religion and temporal power. The arm of the Church henceforward shall be free, equal to that of the State; both arms shall

S

have one and the same pulsation—the spirit of the Redeemer. The two highest institutions of the earth, a Christian Church, and a Christian State—these two arms belong to one and the same body, Jesus Christ. For the Messias Himself will rule the world for the future, with one hand, through the Church, in distributing the gifts of the spirit; with the other, through the state, caring for the temporal interests of the people. So will He, as Master of the world, guide His children to the home where He has prepared mansions for them. The period of that torturing conflict, in which Church and State seemed to bleed to death, was symbolically expressed in the figure of the crucified one. His two hands, intended to bestow blessings, were pierced, and the blood flowed down from the cross for three hours: He who wished to embrace all lovingly was crucified. The Church too, which was intended to raise man, and lead him towards his high destination, was galled by the State for a period of three hundred years.

After the Resurrection, our Lord appeared to His disciples, raised His hands, showed them His wounds, and said, *Pax Vobis;* and after the Church and State had celebrated their long hoped-for resurrection, they had also no words more beautiful to proclaim to the world, than the same peaceful salutation, *"Pax Vobis."*

Peace to the people, by the right that had its origin in the Divine will; and peace to each individual through religion, which with right took root in one and the same soil—the heart of Jesus.

This new ordination of all religious and civil events was first through the merits of the Son of God; to Him therefore the first thanks arc due. But after Him, these intrepid combatants claim our next thanks,—those who shrank not from any sacrifice to call forth the new state of things. How many tears, how many sighs, and how much blood were necessary to obtain this greatest of all good gifts! What did it not cause to save this precious inheritance from the shipwreck of the states, from the pestilential breath of heresy, and from the torrents of so many revolutions! This inheritance has passed on to the present century, and we are the possessors of it. Thoughtless is he who has never taken into consideration at what price it has been purchased, and the deepest contempt falls to his lot who sullies the treasure of faith with the rancor of mockery. But we have inherited this treasure unscathed, to deliver it over to our descendants. The light of our eyes will be soon extinguished, but when our graves will have disappeared, and our very names will have faded from the memory,—yes, when the temples erected, and palaces of our royal cities, fall to ruins, then will the later generations still reflect on the champions of the first century, and their hearts will beat stronger at the soul-stirring thought, "We are the descendants of Holy Martyrs!"

www.ingramcontent.com/pod-product-compliance
Lightning Source LLC
Chambersburg PA
CBHW030635030726
47497CB00006B/1799